Relatively inSane

in ^a

by

Phoebe Richards

ISBN-13:
978-1986735766

ISBN-10:
1986735761

Bolyn-Codhi Publishing
phoeberichardsbooks.com

DEDICATION

To my sisters, because you love me. You *know* me, but you love me. And to my family for the same reason.

Phoebe Richards

Acknowledgements

I cannot, in good conscience, publish this book without recognizing the contributions of some very special people. A big thanks to my critique group. We have grown together under the leadership of our mentor, author James R. Nelson, without whom, I would never have crossed the elusive bridge to fiction. He and the group have been a constant source of support, encouragement and sage advice.

This print version would not exist without friends, Karen and Ellen, who not only slogged through early drafts, but offered helpful suggestions couched in love and praise. To AC, your feedback and tech support have been invaluable. I thank my entire family, of course, for listening to me yammer on about the story, for giving me the time to work on it, and for making spot-on improvements to the text.

June 20th

The taste of bile was his first conscious sensation, the pounding in his left temple the second. Forcing one eye open, he realized he lay on a concrete floor in a pool of befoulment so ripe, vomit again rose in the back of his throat. Despite the pain and vertigo, he pushed himself up on one elbow to lean against the steel post beside him. He could barely make out his surroundings in the black night. Adjusting to the dark, he remembered where he was.

What had happened? Someone... That's right. Someone hit him; knocked him out. The effort to remember made his head throb so hard his eyes bulged. Oh yeah. That bitch. That goddamned bitch had clubbed him. He'd kill her for this.

What was that? Footsteps? Yes, behind him. By the swamp. It had to be her.

Lifting his chin from his chest, he turned his head toward the noise.

Chapter 1
Saturday, June 8, morning

Pls, don't bother coming down. I'll be okay. Dr. said I'd only be in a cast about 3 months. Lute found me a scooter thing at the pawn shop. Sorry if I sounded desperate in the ER, but I'm okay. Really.

Maggie Lennon reread her sister's text from the night before as a man climbed over her to reach the middle seat. "Sorry," he said, hoisting his huge, mud-caked shoe over her knees. "These seats ain't half the size they used to be."

He wedged himself between the armrests. "You goin' to Florida for vacation?"

"I wish. I'm going to help my sister. She broke her leg."

"Aw, that's too bad. Them casts is a pain in the butt. Broke my ankle once when I jumped off the back of my daddy's pickup. I dragged that cast around half a my senior year."

She pulled out her book and pretended to read. When Rhoda called from the ER, she didn't say how she broke her leg. Well, she did, but as usual, Maggie didn't believe her. She had that airy tone she used when she was lying. "Oh, you know my stupid giant toe. I had on flip flops and caught it on the edge of the threshold just as I stepped out. Threw me right down on the sidewalk."

Maggie suspected another argument with Lute. Before the accident, Rhoda said he was "collaborating" with a guy for his new business venture. Lute usually conducted his so-called business at the pawn shop or The Broken Cleat Bait and Bar down by the river. Maggie's bet was on the bar. Most of Lute's get-rich-quick schemes hatched after a few bottles of Ron Rico.

She also suspected he wouldn't be much help to Rhoda. He'd prop her up in that sweat-slick, broken down recliner with the remote control and a big glass of RC before he headed out.

"I finally got that cast off just after baseball started, sos I missed the tryouts."

Maggie had forgotten about Big Foot. "Mmm. That's too bad," she mumbled.

"Ladies and Gentlemen, we are beginning our final descent into Tallahassee. Make sure your seat belts are fastened and all seat backs and tray tables are in their upright position."

She stuffed a bag of chips and the book in her carry-on. Rhoda would be surprised, but hopefully, pleased she came down. It was the beginning of summer, so Maggie had eleven weeks before the new school year started. Surely, Rhoda's cast would be off by then.

After talking all the way from the gate about how good he would have been in baseball, Big Foot was kind enough to pull Maggie's bags off the carousel. She dragged them into the nearest bathroom to freshen up before her other sister, Cheryl, came to get her. The trip was so last minute, Maggie didn't have time to put herself together before she left. Her ash brown hair had already started to frizz. By the time she stepped outside, its volume would double. Her short bob with blunt bangs that was so pretty and sleek in the salon now looked like a character in a Dilbert cartoon.

She leaned in toward the mirror; definitely should have bothered with makeup. Her skin showed signs of aging – a few brown spots, worry lines, and blue-black circles under her eyes. She didn't even look in the full-length mirror. There was no doubt she would not only outweigh her middle sister, her Walmart shorts and Greenville Devildogs polo would look dowdy next to whatever designer Cheryl was wearing today. Screw it. She didn't care about all that stuff. But her shoulders slumped as she grabbed her bags and rolled them outside.

"Yoo-hoo, MAGGIE," sang her sister from the loading zone. "Over here."

She spotted Cheryl a few cars down; her glossy, golden hair had grown to her shoulders, accenting her emerald eyes. Damn. She looked thinner than the last time Maggie had seen her. No matter how hard Maggie tried (which was never very hard) she could not lose that last ten (fifteen?) pounds.

"Hey, Cheryl." Maggie hugged her. "Thanks so much for picking me up and taking me to Rhoda's. How far is it from here?"

"Oh, it's a ways, but I love to drive. I want to help you with Rhoda at least for the weekend. Plus, I don't want to miss anything. I took Monday morning off, so I'll drive back then. Thank God you're here. Maybe we can figure out what happened."

Cheryl also doubted Rhoda's story. "I figure she was either so hopped up on pills she just fell down, or she and Lute had a fight. But I really don't think he'd hurt her."

"The hell he wouldn't," Maggie said.

"Oh, now, Maggie, he's not that bad."

Rather than challenge Cheryl's rosy viewpoint, she changed the subject. "Where's Chief?" Maggie couldn't believe Cheryl was traveling without her beloved teacup poodle, Chief Osceola. The dog had all the necessary gear - Gucci carrier, jeweled FSU leash and collar, canopied dog bed, and Royal Albert dishes.

"With such short notice, I hated to cancel his spa appointment, so my dog-walker, Pete, is staying with him for the weekend."

"I wish I were Chief Osceola," said Maggie.

Cheryl continued, "Are we staying with them?"

"I guess we'll have to. There's no hotel for miles, and that one B and B is way out of my price range. Plus, we won't be much help if we stay over in Starke."

Cheryl sighed. "I guess you're right. Their house kind of gives me the creeps - I mean there's not much room, and, well, you know."

Yes, Maggie knew. Neither Rhoda nor Lute cared about housecleaning. She shivered. "I don't know. We'll see how it looks. I think that sleeping porch has twin beds, but who can tell? Does Lute still have all those huge cans of pork and beans stacked to the ceiling in there?"

"Oh, I think it's worse now. He talks more and more about the revolution. God knows what all he has stockpiled," said Cheryl. "Last I heard, he was burying stuff in the yard."

Maggie shook her head. "How did Rhoda end up like this? Why does she stay with him?"

"Come on; you know why. Rhoda always was a rebel. Nobody was surprised when she ran off with Lute after just two dates. Plus, let's face it. He is incredibly charismatic."

"Says you. But he did seem like a real catch," said Maggie. "Back then, he looked like Hugh Grant, plus he had a solid business. Things seemed so promising. Who would have thought he'd go bankrupt in engine and fiberglass repair? In Florida, no less. Everybody has a boat, and boats always break down."

"He just can't seem to get along with anybody for more than a day or two. I don't know why she stays with him. They have some sick bond they can't break. As Dad used to say, 'I'm just glad they found each other, instead of ruining two more peoples' lives.'"

Maggie sighed. "I guess. Remember that time she tried to leave him? He followed her all over the state until she gave in and came back. So, here they are stuck in a swamp in the armpit of Florida."

"I know. At least she has her own money now since she went on disability."

This was news to Maggie. "She's on disability? What for? Why haven't I heard about this?"

"Oh, you know Rhoda. She didn't want 'the baby' to worry about her. The only reason she told me was because I know some attorneys through work," said Cheryl. "She claimed that fibromyalgia and depression made it impossible for her to do her job."

"Does she have those conditions?" Maggie was astounded she'd never heard any of this.

"Who knows? But she got it, so she must have had a pretty convincing case."

"So, how does it help her to be home all the time? Won't he still take her money when she cashes the check?"

"No. For once, she listened to me. I told her to have it direct-deposited into her personal account, so he can't get to it. The doctors she used to work for paid her in cash, and Lute always managed to get his hands on most of her money. Even better, though, being on disability, she actually has health care."

"God, what a life. It's so depressing. Let's change the subject or turn on the radio."

"There aren't really any stations out here in God's country, but, did I tell you about the Golden Chiefs reception I went to? It was just after the spring game…"

Cheryl talked the rest of the way. Maggie couldn't remember exactly what she said. Cheryl's lilting chatter and the monotonous landscape of northern Florida's scrub pines lulled her into a twilight sleep. Maggie heard something about the society events Cheryl attended and how many times she managed to get on the FSU JumboTron during football season. After a while, Cheryl just sang which was a pleasant break.

Three hours later (Cheryl always drove just below the speed limit), they arrived southeast of Starke in the small town of Eugenia. Rhoda and Lute lived in a fish camp by the Oolehatchee Swamp. Their home was a rusty double-wide. Actually, it was a single-wide attached to a camper with a wooden sleeping porch built on. This place did have running water and indoor toilets, though, so it beat their last one.

Maggie tried not to judge. She lived in a simple tract house, but at least she kept it clean and the yard mowed. No need to worry about mowing grass here, though. The canopy of live oaks prevented much lawn, and the black sandy soil stayed hidden under fallen leaves.

"YOO-HOO – Rhoda, guess who?" trilled Cheryl as they scrambled up the steps and burst in the door. "SURPRISE!"

From her recliner, Rhoda looked up to see her sisters. They ran toward her, arms spread wide. Rhoda's heart surged; no matter where it was, no matter what the reason, being together made everything better.

"Don't get up," Maggie said, as they stooped over the walker for a group hug.

"What are you guys doing here? I told you not to come," Rhoda asked, eyes glittering with relief.

"What, are you kidding?" said Cheryl. "Of course we're here. You're hurt; you need help - the 'Lemon Sisters' to the rescue."

Rhoda laughed. "The Lemon Sisters? I haven't heard that name in forever. I hated when Mom called us that. We were just trying to sing."

"Oh, Rhoda, she was just joking," said Cheryl, defending their mother.

"Go ahead and say it," said Maggie. "I was the one who couldn't carry a tune." She had been told that often by their music-teacher mother.

Cheryl, always ready to show off her singing, started in:

> *It takes a worried man to sing a worried song...*

Maggie and Rhoda helped her finish -

> *...Well, I might be worried now, but I won't be worried long*

Maggie laughed. "I told you I'm the lemon." She was glad for the ice breaker. She had been startled by Rhoda's appearance when they walked in. Despite a refrigerator build, Rhoda looked fragile and ashen. Her stick-straight salt and pepper hair, always poorly cut, hung to her chin in greasy strings. Her once smooth skin was now etched with lines and her big, bedroom eyes were puffy and dark. It broke Maggie's heart to see the statuesque, doe-eyed sister she grew up with in such a state of decline. "Okay. Enough chit chat," said Maggie. "Tell me what really happened."

"I already told you; I stubbed my toe and tripped." Rhoda looked down.

"Bullshit. Your toe looks fine." Maggie was determined to get to the truth.

Cheryl started humming to cover the tension between her sisters. Having survived a miserable marriage and bitter divorce, Cheryl was phobic about conflict.

"Come on, Sis. What happened?" pressed Maggie.

Rhoda glanced toward the door and the driveway.

"Lute wasn't out there when we pulled up. Go ahead; spill it."

Rhoda collapsed against the back of the recliner. "Well, I'd been at the doctor's. My back's been acting up. It was after lunch, and Lute was out in the carport when I pulled up. He'd been drinking."

Rhoda's hand shook as she sucked on the straw of her Big Gulp cup. "He started yelling at me for no reason, asking where I'd been, who I'd been with. You know how he gets."

"Focus, Rhoda. What happened to the leg?" Maggie demanded.

Cheryl simultaneously broke into hives and a chorus of "Nearer my God to Thee."

"It was all my fault, really. I told him I'd been at the quilting club at church. He hates Dr. Stout, so I don't tell him when I go there. Anyway, he said I was lying and shoved me, which, I don't have to tell you, pissed me off. So I charged at him. He stepped aside and tripped me, and I fell over that goddamn prop stick/boom thingy from his stupid crab boat. I landed on a pile of concrete blocks and heard it snap."

Maggie's eyes widened. "What did Lute do?"

"He said I deserved it and went in the house. Luckily, I still had my keys, so I dragged myself to the car and drove to the emergency room."

Maggie and Cheryl stood dumbstruck.

"No one ever deserves that." Cheryl's voice quavered with anger and sympathy. She had spent many hours in therapy to reach that essential truth.

Silence stretched on until they all became uncomfortable.

"Well, you know Lute," Rhoda finally said. "He gets in a mood. He's frustrated now with this new business."

"What is it this time?" Maggie asked.

"Crabbing." They all rolled their eyes.

"He says this is the big one," said Rhoda. "He got a great deal on an old crabber. It just needs a little engine work and some patching, and it'll be ready to go. In fact, that's probably where he is. He said he was going to try and hire a crew today down by the docks."

Dinner time, same day

"Hey, Sis? Where's your pizza pan?" Maggie called from the kitchen. After walking out of her shoes on the sticky floor and assessing layers of grime on the counters and stove, she decided frozen pizza was their best bet. Cheryl wanted something healthy, but the healthiest thing at the Eugenia Fill Up n Eat was a cello-wrapped onion burger.

"We don't have one anymore," shouted Rhoda from her nest. "Lute used it to patch the roof of the shed. Just put it right on the rack."

After scraping the rack with a spatula, Maggie set the oven to a sterilizing temp.

Cheryl told Rhoda they planned to stay on the sleeping porch for the weekend, if that was okay.

"Oh, I don't know...you know Lute," stammered Rhoda.

The screen door slammed open. "Just exactly what do you know about Lute?" a man shouted.

Maggie came out of the kitchen to see someone swaying in the doorway. The sun behind him shadowed his face and body, but those dirty bare feet were his trademark. Definitely Lute. His features came into focus as he stepped in and closed the door. Maggie had forgotten how handsome Lute was, or had been – tall and lanky, with sparkling blue eyes, perfect white teeth, and a full head of blonde wavy hair. Only his sun-weathered face betrayed his age.

"Maggie? Cheryl? Did I know you were coming?" he asked, glaring at Rhoda.

She cast her eyes to the floor. "Um, no. They decided to surprise me - to come and help."

The scent of rum rolled off him. They all tensed anticipating his reaction.

"Well, welcome. This is quite a surprise." He stumbled toward Maggie, arms outstretched, grabbing her in a bear hug. She wasn't fast enough to turn her head as he planted his big, boozy lips on hers and rammed his tongue down her throat. She wriggled away and made for the kitchen.

Cheryl was quicker and missed the kiss, but he did manage to goose her as she backed away. "Maggie has the summer off, so she decided to see if she could help Rhoda get back on her feet. I picked her up at the airport, but I'm headed home Monday morning. Some of us have to work for a living." Cheryl's nervous titter was more shrill than usual.

Rhoda, enjoying the lack of attention, slipped a pill out of her bra and popped it in her mouth.

After dinner, Lute finally agreed to let them stay for the weekend, "We'll see how it works out. Just keep it down. I have to preach tomorrow," he said as he headed to bed.

The sisters moved out to the sleeping porch, closing the door to keep from waking Lute.

"So," Maggie asked, "Lute's still preaching? Did he ever get ordained?"

Rhoda laughed. "No, unless you count self-ordination."

"On the internet?" Cheryl asked.

"No. Right out there in living room. He read a few Bible verses, poured a little oil on his head, said a prayer, and claimed himself ordained."

Maggie was incredulous. "And they pay him for that?"

"Not much. It depends on the collection totals each month."

"Well, it's a nice little church. They'd probably have to close it down if they had to pay a real minister," said Cheryl. "Hey, Maggie, get over here and help me make these beds." She began to sing as they worked. Cheryl frowned at Maggie's sloppy sheet-tucking skills. "Never mind. I'll finish up if you take a video of me on your phone. I'm in pretty good form tonight. I might need it for an audition tape.'"

Maggie and Rhoda exchanged a quick eye roll. Rhoda doodled crab logos on a paper towel while Maggie recorded the performance.

Chapter 2
Earlier that afternoon

Lute parked his truck at the Broken Cleat Bait and Bar on the edge of the Oolehatchee River. Tucked away in a copse of live oaks, pines and cedars, the tiny plywood building leaned to one side. A gravel walkway led around to the pier and marina. The Cleat was Lute's preferred watering hole because only locals came here.

He remembered how busy the place was when he was a kid. The docks had bustled with fishing and crabbing boats. Back then, the river provided access to lakes and wetlands through waterways and canals. The marina and town had flourished. Over the last few decades, the connecting waterways were filled in to make way for roads, housing and farming. Now the marina and the Cleat sagged from neglect. Black, splintered pilings poked up from the water – headstones of their former piers. Only two functional docks remained, their tilting walkways and weathered decking challenging boaters. He liked it this way; more private. No strangers to get all up in his business.

Lute walked across the warped deck to the service window, ordered a bottle of Ron Rico and two glasses.

"Double fistin' it today, Lute?" asked Pops, bar tender, cook and proprietor of the Broken Cleat.

"Got a business meeting. Interviewing a possible crew member for my crabber."

"Anybody I know?"

"I don't even know him. I put a sign on your bulletin board out there. Just gonna wait here until somebody reads it."

"Is your boat here?" asked Pops.

Lute pointed to a twenty-six-foot, slime-covered MAKO in dry dock. "There she is. She's a real peach, ain't she?"

"So, you're the one who bought Shivey's old crabber," said Pops. "Didn't realize you had that kind of green."

"I got some resources hidden here and there," said Lute. "Plus, I practically stole it from him. He even threw in the traps and trot lines."

"I thought it had a hole in the hull."

"Oh, I can patch that. Engine needs a little tweaking, but I can handle that too."

Sitting at a cracked plastic table under a sparsely thatched umbrella, Lute downed a shot and waited. An hour and half a bottle later, a man ambled up to the bulletin board. In a dirty Florida Gators shirt, cargo shorts and Chucks, he looked a little rough, but then most of the guys here were. He seemed healthy and strong. Just another twenty-something without a job.

Lute shouted over to him, "Lookin' for work?"

The young man turned and came over to the table, "Yep. You got any?"

"Depends. You got any experience on a boat?"

"Been on one a couple a times."

"Lute Mason," Lute half stood and extended his hand.

"Delmont. Delmont Crapps. What's the job?"

"Sit down and have a drink with me; I'll tell you all about it. I just bought that crabber over there. Pretty sure I can get it in shape before trap season starts next week. I could use a hand with repairs – lines, nets, traps, that kind of stuff."

Delmont looked at him vacantly. "-kay."

"I'll pay twenty-five bucks a day until we get it running, and then I'll pay you a percent of the catch. There's some great crabbing over on the St. Johns. We might even get lucky on some of the other rivers and marshes around here. We could make a fortune."

"-kay."

As the bottle emptied and the sun lowered, the two shook hands and agreed to meet in a few days.

Delmont said he could bring help. "My brother's due in town today or tomorrow. He'd be good. He's real strong and quick."

Lute watched him walk off. "Perfect. Dumber than a stump."

Phoebe Richards
Monday, June 10, morning

Lute tiptoed into the kitchen, hoping no one was up. He crept over to the table where three purses sat. He looked around before rummaging through Rhoda's and pocketing some money. He jammed his hand in the next, a faded canvas satchel monogramed with Maggie's initials.

"Can I help you find something?" Maggie asked from the doorway, eyebrow cocked.

"Oh, morning, Maggie. Do you know which one of these is Rhoda's?"

"Don't you?"

"Naw, they all look the same to me. Never paid attention to women's stuff. I'm looking for Rhoda's cigarettes. I know she started smoking again. I can smell it. Damn her. I told her those things are gonna kill her. Every time I find 'em, I throw 'em out."

"Well, that's my purse you're looking in." Maggie snatched it away from him.

"Good morning, everyone," sang Cheryl as she entered the room.

Maggie shook her head. Cheryl was already dressed (matching outfit), made up, perfumed and hair-styled. She had always been too damned chipper in the morning.

"I'm off to work. Church was nice yesterday, Lute. You did a good job on the prayer."

17

Maggie noticed she didn't mention the sermon, which bordered on bizarre.

"Thanks, Cheryl. We hate to see you go. Coffee?" Lute held up the pot.

"No, thanks. I'll just find a Starbucks on the road."

"Well, give me a proper goodbye then. I'm off to find the rest of my crew," he said. He threw his arms around Cheryl's neck for a hug, ground his pelvis against her, and deftly unhooked her diamond necklace.

Flustered but giggling, Cheryl pushed at him.

Lute, undeterred, prolonged the goodbye as he ran his hand across her neck and palmed the necklace. "See you later," he said as he hurried outside.

"God, he gives me the creeps," said Maggie.

"Oh, he's all right," said Cheryl. "He means well."

"Wow. Everybody's already up? It's only 6:30," said Rhoda, skating in on her scooter/walker. "Where's Lute?"

"He just left for the docks."

"Whew," she sighed, easing into a chair and propping up her foot.

"How's the leg this morning?" asked Cheryl.

"Rough night. I woke up and had to take a couple of pain pills. I hate to take those things."

Maggie rolled her eyes. "Cheryl's leaving, but I'm going to stay a while. I can drive you wherever you need to go."

"I can drive. My right leg's fine. Hell, I drove myself to the hospital," protested Rhoda.

"Just for a few days," said Maggie, "at least until the swelling goes down. And when you do need the car, there's a bike out there I can use."

Rhoda looked trapped. She knew Lute wouldn't like this plan. He hated when her sisters were around. He hated whenever anybody else around.

Rhoda squirmed. "We'll see how it goes. Are you going to try and make it to work, Cher?"

"Yes. If I leave now, I think I can get half a day in."

"It's been great having you guys here," said Rhoda, "especially at church yesterday. I can hardly sit through his sermons any more. The trustees told him to lay off the conspiracy stuff, but he can't stop himself."

"The bit about the 'Mark of the Beast' was out of nowhere," said Maggie. "What's that even mean?"

"Oh, Lute got in with this group of survivalists, the Brotherhood, who believe the antichrist is gathering forces to overthrow the world. Those forces, whoever they are, supposedly bear the Mark of the Beast on their foreheads."

Maggie was slack-jawed. "Huh."

"Well, the music was nice," said Cheryl, or Pollyanna, as they often called her. "Okay, I really have to get going," she said as she stooped down to hug Rhoda.

Maggie waved goodbye from the front door. She had to get busy: she needed to find out why Lute had been rooting in their purses, what he was burying, and how many drugs Rhoda was actually taking.

But first things first. She needed to get some heavy-duty rubber gloves, scrub brushes and bleach to make this place livable.

Chapter 3

Three days earlier

Rhoda stared at the sign on the door. Eugenia Medical Clinic – Dr. Ben Stout, Orthopedic Surgeon and Dr. Lisa Pascal, Pain Management Specialist. She lucked out when she found this place six years ago. Rhoda had known Lisa since high school, but didn't meet Ben until she started working here. Rhoda remembered being startled by his good looks the first time she saw him. He was tall and lanky back then. He'd had a strong square jaw with a permanent five-o'clock shadow. And that slightly crooked nose suggested a man who was not afraid to stand up for himself. His eyes were so dark they were almost black, but still they reflected a kind heart. Back then, his black hair was full and curly. Working here would spell nothing but trouble for her. She took the job on the spot.

She searched the parking lot and road. Empty. She liked to visit Ben during lunch when Lisa and the receptionist were gone. She let herself in the back door, slipped into Ben's office, and stripped off her clothes.

A half hour later, she sat up on the extra wide ("guaranteed to safely accommodate patients up to 800 lbs.") exam table and put on her bra and underwear. "That was an extremely thorough exam, Ben," smiled Rhoda.

"You, dear Rhoda, are an animal. Not bad for a disabled person. I don't know where you get the energy," said Ben as he, too, got dressed.

21

"I never would have gotten disability if it hadn't been for you," she said as she looked in his eyes. Rhoda still saw the Ben she first met, though now, his thick hair was more of a comb-over and his tall frame bulged around the middle. His sharp jaw had softened, as well. Of course, her own transformation had been a sea change. Once considered tall and well-proportioned, she had let things slide since she quit working. But Ben didn't seem to notice. He still enjoyed her keen wit and her clever mind, not to mention her sexual appetite.

"I was glad to help, though if you'll remember, you did most of the paperwork. Too bad you can't work here anymore, though. I miss seeing you every day."

"I know. We made a heck of a team."

"I have yet to find another medical coder who can get a hundred percent from the insurance companies. My revenues are way down since you left."

Ben had suggested Rhoda apply for disability after he realized Lute made off with most of her money. "How are things, now that you're home most of the time?" he asked. Lute worried him. He had seen bruises and knots on Rhoda that were well hidden by her clothes.

"He has his good days and bad. He's on the manic side right now; all revved up to start a new business."

"Going to get rich this time," winked Ben.

"You got it," said Rhoda. "Of course, I'll never see a penny. I don't know what he does with whatever money he makes. He says he's putting it away for me - so we'll be safe after the 'revolution'."

"Jesus, he's crazy. Just who does he think is going to revolt?"

"THEM. At least that's all he tells me. He says they're going to come storming into our house and take everything we have. Good God. Like we have squat. Probably the most valuable thing in that place is my grandmother's engagement ring, and I don't even know where it is anymore. Who in their right mind is going to search a broken down double-wide in a swamp to finance a world revolution?" she laughed.

"Well," said Ben, "be careful. We all know what follows the mania. When he tanks, he tanks hard. You really ought to get away from him and come live with me."

"He'd hunt us down and kill us both. I tried leaving him before. He chased me all the way to Everglades City, ran off my friends, the guy I was dating, and everyone else. It's just easier to stay with him."

Ben shook his head. "I wish he'd croak. But he'll probably live to be a hundred. Too mean to die."

"I know. I keep thinking I could kill him off with bad chicken. It wouldn't take too long if I just kept serving it to him. He'll never go to a doctor again."

"Not bad, Rhoda," smiled Ben.

"But then I'd end up doing time. He's not worth jail."

Finally, dressed and composed, they both left the exam room. Ben called his next patient. Rhoda made sure he was occupied before heading to the back of the office. Having worked here for years, she knew where the sample medications were. Thank God she had hung on to her key to the storage room. After stuffing her purse with opiates and antidepressants, Rhoda peeked out the door, ensured safe passage and left.

Chapter 4

Saturday, June 8, outside Florida State Prison

Buddy Crapps, Department of Corrections number P75003, stepped through the chain link gate onto the tarmac outside. He wore the clothes he was arrested in almost three years ago for aggravated battery with a deadly weapon against his father.

Outside. He never thought this day would come, but here it was, day number eight hundred twenty-one. Even the blazing Florida sun was cooler than inside those walls. There was no breeze. There was never a breeze in the barrens surrounding the prison.

He looked across the parking lot and up and down the road. No one waited for him. Not that he was expecting anyone. He told his brother the time of his release, but Delmont couldn't drive.

Walking south on Rt. 16 toward Starke, Buddy hitched a ride with a trucker who dropped him off downtown. With forty-five dollars from his prison savings account, he stopped at a diner and grabbed lunch. "Best meal I've had in years," he told the waitress. She nodded. No doubt there'd been lots of ex-cons in here; he probably looked just like the rest of them with his standard prison haircut. His old jeans were too loose and the tee-shirt too tight, evidence of the many hours he'd spent working out in the prison gym. He lingered a while in the air-conditioning trying to catch the waitress's eye, with no luck. Finally, he decided to get on the road.

He was headed to his brother's, who lived further south in a rundown trailer in an even more rundown trailer park. "If you ever want to disappear off the face of the earth," his bastard father once told him, "move into an old trailer park."

That kind of anonymity sounded good right now. He'd prefer not to see even Del, but his kid brother was the only person he could trust. And Delmont would go along with whatever he said. What Buddy needed was to reinvent himself. He hadn't been a bad guy before jail – but he hadn't been especially good. A little larceny never hurt anybody; he was just trying to provide for him and Del. He used his sly smile and deep dimples to get away with petty crimes and bent rules. (His mom used to say, "The girls better watch out for you, Bud. You're going to be a real heartbreaker.") If he could just stay under the radar long enough to get some money together and get a real job, he might be able to turn things around. Prison actually helped him; he gained some skills in the machine shop, and with the classes, he finally passed his GED.

On the sidewalk outside the diner, Buddy scanned the road. Empty. With the confidence of an owner, he walked over to an unlocked bicycle, kicked up the stand, and headed south on Rt. 100. Finally, at dusk, he pulled into the Gone Fishin' Mobile Home Resort.

"Bud," nodded Delmont when the door opened.

"Del," he nodded back. Del tossed Buddy a beer from the cooler/coffee table. Popping the tops in unison, the brothers sat on the couch, watching *Florida's Hidden Treasures* in silence.

Monday, June 10, en route from Eugenia to Tallahassee

This train is bound for Glory, well, this train

This train is bound for Glory, well, this train ...

Cheryl belted out the old folk song they had sung the night before when the Lemon sisters had again tried to perfect their harmony. About halfway through her trip home, though, the tune turned into an earworm. Cheryl had no choice but to sing along. Only the ding of the fuel alarm interrupted her.

Darn. She had hoped she'd make it without stopping. She was already late for work, but she pulled into a gas station, started the pump and went inside. After using the facilities, she grabbed a drink and a snack and went to the counter.

"I've got gas on pump seven - oh, that sounded kind of funny," she chuckled to the fifteen-year-old Goth clerk, "plus this stuff."

"Twenty-seven eighty-five," said the clerk without looking up from under her blue bangs.

"Oh, I think I have enough cash in here somewhere." Cheryl dug through her Tom Ford snakeskin bag. "I know I had plenty of cash. What did I do with it?" Panic crept into her voice.

Goth-girl shrugged. Cheryl emptied the contents of her purse on the counter, while a line formed behind her.

"Sorry," she said to the crowd. "I know I had plenty of cash."

"Whatever. Twenty-seven eighty-five, lady."

"Here, use this," she handed her a debit card and shoved tissues, brushes, lipsticks and gum back in her purse. She nervously typed in her PIN guarding the machine so no one could see. Cheryl's faith in humanity had its limits.

Back in the car, she again dumped out her purse and sifted through it. No money. Well, two dollars and three cents in change.

She called Maggie before she left the station. "Maggie? Hey. Um, can't talk long, but I'm kind of in a panic here. I know I took over a hundred dollars in cash to Rhoda's, but I only have about two bucks left. Did I spend that much on groceries? Doesn't seem possible. I only went to the store once. Oh my God, I bet I put a fifty in the collection plate at church thinking it was a five. Not that I don't want the church to have the money. Surely, I could tell a fifty from a five, wouldn't you think? But I was so distracted by Lute's sermon, I guess I could have."

Maggie didn't try to interrupt. When Cheryl got wound up, there was no stopping her.

"I mean, when he went off on the left-wing fascists planning to take all our earthly goods and rape all of us women, I heard people around me whispering that they wanted to fire him. They wouldn't do that, would they? They all adore Rhoda. I'd hate to see her lose her church family…."

Cheryl began to lose focus and steam, so Maggie jumped in. "Take a deep, cleansing breath." She waited until she heard Cheryl exhale.

"I was going to call you after work just to give you an update, but I have an idea what happened. When I got up this morning, I found Lute rummaging through Rhoda's purse and then stick his hand down in mine. I caught him before he took anything out of it, though. I don't know if he looked through yours or not."

"What? What did he say when you caught him?"

"Oh, he gave me some crap about not being able to tell whose was whose. He said he was looking for Rhoda's cigarettes so she'll stop smoking. Asshole. Acting all concerned about her health, after tripping her and making her drive herself to the hospital. Dickwad."

"Now, Maggie, watch your mouth. Surely he wouldn't steal from us." Cheryl always believed the best in people no matter how often they proved her wrong. Maggie, on the other hand, had a pretty cynical view of people in general and her brother-in-law in particular.

Cheryl continued, "I'm sure it'll turn up, unless I gave it to the church, which is okay. What's going on there?"

"Lute supposedly went to the docks to work on that broken-down crabber he bought. Rhoda and I watched some old movies on TV, and then she took a pain pill and passed out. I took the car to the Walmart in Starke and bought a few gallons of bleach, a mop, sponges and other stuff to scour this place."

"Good idea. I'll try to come back next weekend. Oh, just pulled into the parking lot at work. Gotta go."

Chapter 5

Monday, June 10, Rhoda's house

After waking from her nap, Rhoda had gotten a ride to her women's circle at church. Maggie was relieved. She would be able to clean without offending anyone. Ripping open the heavy-duty rubber gloves, she filled a bucket with hot water and bleach and grabbed a scrub brush. She checked her chore list. An obsessive list maker, she often wrote one post-task just so she could cross things off.

- Clear path through sleeping porch.
- Mop path through sleeping porch.
- Strip beds on sleeping porch.
- Clear path through carport to washer.
- Clean off top of washer.
- Sterilize washer.
- Run load of laundry.
- Weed whack under clothes line.
- Shore up clothes line.
- Clean clothes line.
- Hang out clothes.
- Sweep kitchen floor.
- Sterilize counters and floor.

Maggie put down the list. Time to quit procrastinating and get those damned survival supplies out of the way. She shoved towers of rusted, commercial-sized cans of pork and beans from the center of the room into the closet. God he was crazy. Even if he turned out to be right and there was a revolution, they'd bloat to death with all these beans. Plus, the expiration date was five years ago. But maybe he was smarter than she thought. They could probably power this place with all the methane they'd produce. She shook her head at the absurdity of the whole situation.

A few hours later, Maggie finally cleared the path through the carport. She started stacking rusty coffee cans filled with junk on the shelves above the washing machine. Stretching just beyond her limit, one of the cans slipped through her hands. Up-ended, the can's brittle plastic lid cracked and greasy bolts and screws fell, scattering across the floor, into the laundry basket and into her shoe. She grabbed a broom, and while she swept them into a pile, a dark blue glint caught her eye.

Hunh. What could that be? She bent to pick it up, sweat dripping in her eyes, and grabbed it. Their grandmother's sapphire engagement ring.

"Whaddaya think you're doing?" yelled Lute from the edge of the carport. "Why are you snooping around out here? You and your damned sister. Fucking busy bodies, always trying to get Rhoda all stirred up." His mouth formed a straight line from the tight clenching of his jaw.

Before standing up, Maggie managed to slip the ring inside the rubber glove. She rose to meet his gaze.

"Hey Lute," she said as breezily as she could. "I'm just trying to help Rhoda out by doing some laundry. Thought I'd save you the trouble. But this can fell off the shelf and spilled. I was just sweeping it up. I'm sure you'll need these bolts and stuff for your new crabber."

His jaw relaxed a little. "Oh, well. You don't need to do that."

"Oh, I don't mind, really. Just trying to earn my keep. By the way, do you all have a dryer?"

"Naw, used too much electric."

Maggie remembered he was in charge of the electric bill. Rhoda paid everything else.

"Oh, then, I'll just use the clothesline. Bet they dry in no time down here. It's okay if I clear out under the clothesline, right?"

Lute furrowed his brow. "I guess. Just don't go messin' with the yard. That's my job. I got all kinds of rare plants and stuff. Don't want you to mistake them for weeds."

"No need to worry about that," Maggie said. "I hate yard work. Thanks."

"Well, you get your laundry done. I'm gonna talk to Rhoda about exactly why we need you here. We get along just fine by ourselves."

Sure, Lute. What's a broken limb here and there?

Tuesday, June 11, Tallahassee

"Oh my God, Rhoda; you wouldn't believe what I found today at work," Cheryl called, breathless. "I was checking Facebook, and WEBT Channel 6 posted a link to send in your very own audition video to *Florida's Hidden Treasures*. You've seen that show, right? It comes on after the lottery game on Saturday nights? It's like *America's Got*

Talent. I think I have a better shot starting locally, don't you? I mean Larry, our worship band sax player, says I could definitely make it big time."

Rhoda laughed. "Well, yeah, I do think you have a good shot, but let's remember, Cheryl, Larry just wants to get in your pants."

"Ick. That would never happen - unless he was a Hollywood talent scout," Cheryl laughed. "Kidding, of course. Kinda. Anyway, I'm going to try to record one tonight. Choir practice was cancelled so I have some time. I'll send you a copy when I get it done. SOOOOOO EXCITED!"

Cheryl rang off without waiting for a reply. She made a quick mental assessment. She'd just stay in her work clothes – so much more sophisticated than those tatted-up, hip-hop wannabes that try out all the time. She searched through the closet for her best selfie stick, grabbed her pitch pipe, her tambourine and her music, and headed for the bathroom. The new red satin shower curtain was perfect; it looked just like a stage.

Unplugging the house phone and putting Chief Osceola in his carrier with a treat, Cheryl propped the selfie stick in a tissue box holder and pressed record.

Oh, when the saints

Go marching in...

Cheryl remembered her stage training from her lead role in the high school musical. She smiled at the camera until she was transported by the song. Then she threw her head back and lifted her arms toward heaven.

   ... Oh, when the fire begins to blaze

   ... When the saints go marching in.

On the last note, she shook the tambourine with a flourish then smacked it against her hip. Satisfied, she hit the stop button. "This is going to be great. I can't wait to see what Rhoda and Maggie think," she said to the star in the mirror.

Chapter 6

Tuesday, June 11, Broken Cleat Bait and Bar

"Yep, Pops, we're ready to get started. Got me a crew that's strong and stupid. Ought to be pretty easy to lead them around," Lute leaned back in the cracked resin chair and threw down a shot.

"Is that them?" asked Pops, watching two young men walking up from the docks. "Who are they?"

"Well, the skinny one sporting the mullet is that kid I met with the other day, Delmont Crapps - what a name. I guess the other one is his brother. I haven't met him yet, but the kid was right - he does look strong and quick."

Pops and Lute laughed as Delmont tripped over a rotting deck board.

"I don't know how much help that one's gonna be. But the big guy – he might be good. Kinda got a scowl on his face, though," said Pops. "Hope he's not trouble."

"Naw. Probably too slow to be trouble," murmured Lute as Buddy and Delmont approached the table. "Howdy, Delmont. Glad you could make it." Lute extended his hand for a shake. "And who are you?"

"Buddy. Buddy Crapps. Delmont's older brother." Buddy kept his arms folded across his chest. A faded Metallica tee shirt stretched across his bulging muscles. "Delmont says you got work?" He looked down at Lute.

"Sure do. Sit down and have a drink, and I'll tell you all about it."

Buddy stood. "What's the pay?"

Lute tried to get a bead on him, but couldn't see through the stranger's mirrored sunglasses. The guy was tall, probably six-three or four. And strong. His scarred and calloused hands showed he was no stranger to hard work.

"I told your brother here I'd pay twenty-five a day while we fix 'er up. After that, I'll give you a percent of the catch. From what I hear, those blues are really hittin' this year, so we ought to all get rich."

Lute's toothy smile reflected from Buddy's glasses.

"What percent?"

"Well, uh, I'm not sure yet. I gotta spend a little time figuring my costs - you know, the boat, fuel, licenses, repairs, but it'll be fair, I can guarantee you that."

"What percent?"

"How about this? I'll pay you the twenty-five a day while we fix 'er up, and I'll know by then what my overhead's gonna be."

The mirrors bore into Lute for what seemed like an hour. "We'll help. If I ain't happy with the percent you come up with, we walk. And whatever it is, you pay us in cash. No reporting, no taxes, no contracts."

"You are speaking my language, Buddy," said Lute. "I haven't paid taxes for decades. Don't want those slimy bastards in Washington using my money to finance their unholy revolution."

"Where's the boat?" Finally, the sunglasses turned toward the docks.

"Right this way, boys. And grab that bottle," Lute said as he threw his arm around Buddy. This was going to work out just fine.

Buddy shrugged him off and followed him down the sagging dock to the boat.

"Here she is - the *Eula Mae.*" Lute swept his arm like Vanna White toward the filthy crabber. "Just needs a little fiberglass patching and some engine work. Either of you ever worked on engines?"

Buddy flashed back to sweating over farm equipment and metal fabrication in prison. "Yeah."

"Perfect," said Lute. "The good Lord must have brought us together."

Buddy shook his head. All the good lord ever did was give him a daddy that beat the shit out of him and his brother, killed his mother and ran out on both boys before they were teenagers.

"Let's toast our new venture," said Lute, filling the glasses. Buddy poured the rot-gut Ron Rico in the water while Lute upended his.

They began by scrubbing the hull and preparing the hole for a patch. Buddy tossed out old beer cans, broken Styrofoam, and dry-rotted life jackets. The boat had obviously been neglected for a while. Delmont and Buddy did most of the work, while Lute continued to down rum and ramble about some bizarre conspiracy.

Recognizing a real tool bag when he met one, Buddy slipped into defense mode. In prison, he learned to keep his head down and his ears open. Eventually, he found out, you would hear something you could use to your advantage.

"They're coming to get us, you know. All of us. The only people left standing will be those with the Mark of the Beast." Lute stabbed a finger toward the center of his forehead. The Ron Rico, however, directed the finger to his eye. "But I'm ready for those bastards."

"How's that?" asked Delmont.

"I been savin' up. I got food to last me for months, guns to fight 'em off with and enough stash to survive anything."

Buddy's silence rewarded, he kept working. At sundown, he signaled to Delmont. "Let's go, bro."

Lute started to step off the boat when Buddy crowded in front of him. "You owe us fifty dollars."

"Oh, well, yeah. But I mean, we didn't really work a whole day."

"We worked plenty."

"Right. Um, here," Lute searched through his pockets taking out Rhoda's cash. "Here's thirty bucks. I'll give you the rest tomorrow, if you show up."

"Oh, we'll be here. Bring the rest of today's pay and tomorrow's. Then we'll decide if we work."

Buddy and Delmont walked away, pocketing their cash.

"Dumb shits," muttered Lute.

"Dumb ass," said Buddy.

Chapter 7

Tuesday, June 11, at Rhoda's

"Do we tell her?" snorted Maggie, wiping tears from her eyes as she stopped Cheryl's video.

"Oh, it's not bad," Rhoda said, struggling not to laugh. "I mean, really, her singing is good. But that shower curtain - you can see her bra and panties hanging from the towel rack on the edge of the shot. I guess we just let her send it in. She'll be devastated if we say anything. She's so sensitive."

Maggie agreed. "It is better than most of the ones that actually make it on the show. Maybe the undies in the background will be just the kitsch the producers are looking for. They can nickname her 'The Underwear Alto'."

"Oh, stop," Rhoda laughed, slapping the arm of her recliner.

While they tried to reign in their hysterics, their phones kept dinging - Cheryl begging for feedback.

"You call her," Maggie gasped between giggles. "I don't think I can keep it together."

"No way, chicken," said Rhoda, "This is one time the Baby isn't going to get her way. You call her."

"Better yet, I'll text her - tell her we're on our way out and will call her later." Maggie started typing. "How's this?" Fantastic. You sound like an angel. LOVE the tambourine. All you need is a mike, and you are on TV! Great job - will call later; taking Sis to choir practice. LU

"Perfect. And we're not lying," said Rhoda. "I do have choir practice. Could you drive me? I would, but my foot's a little sore. I'd rather sit in the back with it propped up. I can put it on a chair when I play the piano."

"Sure. That's why I'm here. Let me go get cleaned up." Maggie hummed Cheryl's song as she headed for the outside shower which she had bleached white, cleared of spider webs, and put a new bath mat on the pallet floor.

Tuesday, June 11, evening

Maggie pulled in the handicap space by the door. Rhoda and Lute's church was one in a succession of storefront churches in the town. The previous business's name had almost been painted over, as were the large display windows. These homegrown houses of worship always made Maggie wonder. What went on in there that they had to paint the windows? And why were there so many of them in small towns? She ascribed to the "Amoeba Theory"; any congregation will eventually grow too large to contain the conflicting opinions and tenets of those who belong, and one or more of the worshippers will split off and start a new church. Lute had been one of the splitters.

"Are you coming, Mags? Kind of lost you there for a minute," Rhoda said as she stood waiting.

"Oh, sorry." She opened the door and followed Rhoda in. Until she came here, Maggie hadn't been in a church for some time. This one didn't do much to inspire her. Both glaring and flickering fluorescent bulbs hung from water-stained ceiling tiles. Gray folding chairs served as pews and a six-foot plastic table acted as the altar. A large wooden cross, handmade from railroad ties, stood on a plywood dais next to the lectern.

A bespectacled, middle-aged man rushed toward them. "Rhoda, we didn't expect to see you here. That leg must be feeling better."

"A little. I think I can play piano though; I only use my right foot on the pedals. Arnie, this is my youngest sister, Maggie. She's come down from South Carolina just to help me out. Maggie, this is Arnold Chance, our choir director."

"God bless you, dear," said Arnold, shaking Maggie's hand. "When Rhoda plays piano, it's like the angels in heaven are at the keyboard. Her musical gifts are some of our greatest assets here at the Eugenia Healing and Helping in the Name of Jesus Tabernacle. Do you sing?"

"Nice to meet you. And, no, I do not sing. All the musical talent in our family stayed at the top of the gene pool. I play a mean kazoo, though."

"Now, now; remember, the Lord doesn't require that we be great singers; only that we make a joyful noise." Arnold winked. "We're glad to have you among us. Make yourself comfortable."

Maggie made a list while the choir practiced -

- find library and get a book
- get creamer, chips, frozen pizza, Advil

She paused to listen. She had to agree with Arnold. Rhoda did play piano like an angel from heaven, if there was a heaven, and if they had piano playing angels. Finally, Rhoda stopped, and the choir sat in the first pew. Arnold addressed the group.

"That was terrific, ladies and gentlemen. Your music will be the highlight of Sunday's service." Maggie noticed the entire choir, including Rhoda, nodded, no doubt because Lute's sermons were only endured to hear the music and have coffee and donuts afterward.

"I have great news for you. One of our parishioners' uncle is an executive producer for the popular program, *Choir Wars,* and he has agreed to come work with us and decide if we can enter the competition. He's coming this weekend for rehearsals Sunday at 4:00 p.m. and Monday at 7:00. Let's pray for a heavenly performance that'll put Eugenia Healing and Helping in the Name of Jesus Tabernacle on the map."

The group whooped and clapped. "Wow," said the soprano. "That's so exciting. But what'll we do for an alto? Birdie Jean was the only one we had and she run off with that golf pro over to Green Cove Springs."

Maggie and Rhoda locked eyes. "Arnie?" said Rhoda. "Our other sister is a pretty strong alto. If I can get her over here, could she give it a shot?"

"Rhoda, you know all are welcome here at Healing and Helping - especially a good, strong alto." The choir laughed in unison.

44

Mary Chance, the choir director's wife, suggested the women's circle provide a nice covered dish dinner beforehand. "We want to make sure this big shot from Hollywood knows how kind and generous we God fearing, humble people can be. Who wants to bring a dessert?" Three hands shot up. "Okay, how about a few vegetables or salads?" More hands rose. "Wonderful. God Bless you all. Instead of our usual cream of mushroom and chicken casserole, I'll bring my famous Meatloaf Surprise," she clapped her hands. "I make the best meatloaf, isn't that right Arnie?"

Arnie nodded.

"I mix up all the meats with lots of ketchup and breadcrumbs, but then," she dropped into a loud whisper, "I form the loaf around two hardboiled eggs. When you cut into it, why, there's the surprise. Looks like big eyeballs starin' at ya'!"

Mm-mmms rippled through the pews.

Maggie cringed. The whole Healing and Helping experience was a bit more than she could take.

Chapter 8

Tuesday, June 11, evening

"Gosh, Buddy," said Delmont on their walk home from work. "Do you really think we'll make a lot of money with this crabber guy?"

Buddy looked at his kid brother. Poor guy had always been a bubble off plumb. No wonder. Their dad seemed to connect with Delmont's head more often than not when he was a kid. Buddy had been quick enough to duck and dodge.

"Oh, we're gonna make money all right. Not sure how much of it's comin' from the crabbing business, but we're gonna make plenty of money."

"Yeah? Cool," Delmont smiled for a minute. "How? You got another job lined up?"

"Not exactly. Weren't you listening to that jerk on the boat?"

"No," said Delmont. "I was just tryin' to work hard so the guy would pay us. Plus, my left ear don't hear too good."

Buddy remembered the night that happened. He was fourteen and Del was five. The neighbors called 911, and the ambulance took Del and their mom to the hospital. Mom never made it home. It was also the last time they saw their dad, until Buddy found him four years ago.

"Lute said he's got some kind of money and guns stockpiled. I thought we'd find out where he lives, then go over there sometime. Look around for the goods, you know?"

"I don't know about that, Buddy. That'd be stealin'. I don't want to get in no trouble. Ramona wouldn't like it if I got in trouble."

"You got yourself a girlfriend, Del?"

Delmont blushed. "Yeah, kinda."

"You gettin' plenty a pussy, Delmont?" teased Buddy.

Del thought about that for a minute. "Huh?"

Buddy shook his head. "I meant are you getting laid, Del."

"Oh, no. I wouldn't do that to Ramona, at least not till we're married. She's a good girl. She lives in a real house and goes to church and everything. Her dad's the choir director."

Buddy watched his brother beam. "Well, good, Del. Good for you. I hope it works out."

"You shouldn't steal either, Buddy. They might send you back to jail. I don't want you to go back to jail."

"Believe me, bro. I don't want that either. Don't you worry about me. I'll be just fine. We'll stick with this crabber until we get a little cash. It'll all work out. And, Del?"

"Yeah?"

"Don't mention the jail stuff to anybody. It's nobody's business what I did. I served my time. That's over."

"Okay, Buddy."

Chapter 9

Wednesday, June 12, early morning

Rhoda, I'm taking the bike to run a few errands. Let me know if you need anything while I'm out. Should be back in a bit, but you never know. I'm pretty out of shape. LU

Rhoda sighed after reading the note. At last, some peace and quiet. Hopefully, Lute would be gone for the day, and Maggie, God bless her, had hovered like a moth on a light bulb. She settled down by the TV and watched the rest of *Fiddler on the Roof*, one of her favorites.

Finally, she pushed herself out of the chair and scooted into the bedroom, singing, "If I Were a Rich Man". After changing into a caftan, she pulled a baggie filled with colorful pills out from under her side of the mattress and headed to the kitchen.

Enjoying the solitude, she turned up the TV, fixed herself a big RC, grabbed some cold pizza, and sat down to business.

Same morning, 10:30 a.m.

Maggie glided up on the bike. From the driveway, she could hear the TV blaring. She carried the groceries toward the kitchen where she spotted Rhoda, broken leg propped on a garbage can, reading glasses on the end of her nose, concentrating on two medicine bottles on the table.

"Whatcha doin' there, Sis?" asked Maggie.

"AHHH! You scared the hell out of me. Don't sneak up on me like that." Guilt radiated out of Rhoda's big eyes.

"I didn't sneak up. You have the TV so loud I could hear it from the street. Again, what's up here?" Maggie indicated the pills on the table.

Rhoda looked out the window. "Did you see Lute anywhere?"

"No. He said he was going to the church to practice his sermon, and then he was going to work on the boat."

"Oh, good. That ought to keep him busy most of the day."

"Again, Sis. What in the world are you doing?"

"Promise you won't say anything?"

"Depends," said Maggie.

"All right. Well, you know how moody Lute can get, right?"

"You mean crazy?"

"Whatever. Anyway, I've started putting Prozac in these herbal supplement capsules. He hasn't figured it out yet, and it seems to keep him a little calmer. Unless he starts drinking."

"Where did you get Prozac?"

"I have my sources."

"How did you get him to start taking an herbal supplement? He thinks all that stuff is hogwash."

"I tell him it's get-hard medicine - see?" Rhoda held up a brown bottle labeled "Smiling Dick's Erectite."

Maggie snorted. "Are you kidding? Why would he take that? He's the king horn dog, isn't he? I mean, he tries to bang every woman he meets, including Cheryl and me."

Rhoda looked around again. "Well," she whispered, "I guess I can tell you. But you have to swear not to tell a soul. If he ever found out someone else knew, he'd kill us all."

"WHAT? I'm dyin' here."

"Late last year, he started having some, um, trouble. You know, um, getting it up."

"Stop - I think I changed my mind," said Maggie. "I'm not sure I want to know."

"Too late - in for a penny…. anyway, you know he doesn't have any health insurance. We've never had any. And he can't use my disability, though he's tried."

"And?"

"So, he got worried about his manhood, and he went to this 'doctor' in a strip mall over in Lake City. The guy said it was very common in men his age and recommended a new implant to help move things along. And the whole procedure would only cost three hundred dollars."

"Stop, please," Maggie covered her ears.

"No, you gotta hear this. So, he makes an appointment to have the thing put in. I had to take him because the localized anesthesia would make it hard for him to drive, no pun intended."

"How does that relate to these pills?"

"I'm getting there. We go and the guy hands us a pamphlet of the different models of penile implants. I had no idea what an industry that was." Rhoda was clearly enjoying telling this. "Lute looks them all over and finally decides on the 'King Cobra' model."

"The what?"

"You heard me. The King Cobra. The picture shows a penis about a foot long standing ramrod straight with the end blown up like a cobra hood. The picture showed it casting a shadow like the snake."

Maggie honked with laughter, which got Rhoda going. They fed off each other until Maggie screamed, "I think I just wet myself." Maggie crossed her legs and tried to regain some control.

Maggie's incontinence only made Rhoda laugh harder. She took a deep breath, blotted the tears from her eyes and tossed Maggie a dish towel. "Sit on this while I finish the story."

Maggie did as she was told and refocused. "Okay. So, back to the need for what he thinks are get-hard pills."

Rhoda resumed dumping the contents out of the herbal capsules and refilling them with Prozac. "Turns out the doctor wasn't really a doctor, big surprise. The thing hasn't worked right since. Sometimes it won't inflate, or it'll go off without warning, sometimes it oozes and needs bandaged, and sometimes - I can't even think about it - you have to use a little finger-operated pump."

Maggie's jaw dropped. "I would so lose that pump."

"That's another reason for the Prozac - it seems to inhibit the libido, as it were."

"Only you, Rhoda. Only you," Maggie shook her head. "I'd say you're lying, but even you couldn't make that up."

Chapter 10

Wednesday, June 12

Hey, Cheryl. It's Rhoda and Maggie. Call or Skype when you get off work. We have big news!

"That's gonna drive her crazy," said Maggie.

"I know. I love it." Rhoda gave Maggie a high-five.

As they thought, Cheryl didn't wait until she was off. Skype began to ring within minutes.

"Hey, Cheryl. Cheryl? We can hardly see you. Why's it so dark?"

"Shhh. I'm right in the middle of an interview with a client. I just ducked in a closet to call. What's the good news?"

Rhoda lowered her voice, "Maggie took me to choir practice last night and at the end of it Arnie - you've met Arnie, the choir director, right?"

"Yes - hurry up - what's the news?"

"Arnie said an uncle of someone in the church is an executive producer of - get this - *Choir Wars*."

"Oh My Gawd," said Cheryl.

"Exactly, and he wants to come hear our choir and see if we have what it takes to enter."

54

"Too bad I'm not in the choir."

Maggie jumped in, "Ahhh, but you are, my dear, thanks to your brilliant sisters who confirmed what a great alto you are. Can you take any time off? The rehearsals with the guy are Sunday and Monday."

"For this? You bet I can. I have plenty of leave coming. Kind of short notice, but I'll put in my request right now. Oh, I'm so excited. A real executive producer of a national show? OH, MY GAWD!"

Over the phone, Rhoda and Maggie could hear muffled voices.

"Gotta go," Cheryl whispered and hung up.

A few minutes later, Skype rang again.

"Hey, it's me. Real quick - did I leave my diamond necklace on the sleeping porch or in the bathroom?" asked Cheryl.

"I haven't seen it," said Maggie. "And I've cleaned up pretty well out there." Understatement of the year.

"I don't know what I did with it, but I miss it. It's the only tangible thing I have left of Mom's." Cheryl's voice broke as she mentioned their mother.

"Oh, that's terrible," said Rhoda. "That thing is worth a lot of money. Surely it'll turn up."

"I hope so. I mean, it could have fallen off in the car, or maybe it's somewhere in my suitcase, though I looked once. Anyway, keep an eye out for it. I'd hate to lose it."

"I'll do a real thorough search, Sis. Don't worry. We'll find it," said Maggie.

"Thanks - gotta go. Love you."

Maggie had plenty of ideas about what happened to the necklace, and none of them included the sleeping porch or Cheryl's suitcase.

◆◆◆

Buddy rode his bike into Eugenia. Surely somebody around here would know a blowhard like Lute Mason. He parked in the center of the typical hick town. The recently paved county road ran one way and the narrower, pock-marked village street crossed it at a four way stop. On one corner sat the Fill Up n Eat, Eugenia's only grocery, such as it was. Directly across from it was Vern's Pawn and Payday Loan, a standard fixture in the small towns Buddy had been through. On the other two corners were a store-front church and an abandoned pharmacy. Yep, this looked like a nice nowhere place to lay low for a while.

Buddy parked his bike and crossed the street. The church had hand-painted lettering across the display window - The Eugenia Healing and Helping in the Name of Jesus Tabernacle, and just below the scrawling letters - Luther Mason, Minister.

Pay dirt.

Buddy tried the door, but no one answered. It looked dark inside, so he decided to check the pawn shop. He knew some pawn shops were run by shady people with little regard for privacy. Hell, his old man ran a pawn shop once.

A bell jingled as he entered. "Be with ya in a sec," a voice shouted from the back. Buddy looked around at the typical junk - guitars, power tools, TVs, computers, metal detectors. A metal detector might come in handy. The locked glass counter held the good stuff - knives, jewelry, cell phones, laptops and the like. A sign on the counter said, WE HAVE GUNS AND AMMO – ASK MANAGER. Good to know.

"What kin I do ya for?" asked a bull of a man, emerging from the back.

"Afternoon," said Buddy. "I got a couple of questions. I just started working down at the docks for a guy named Lute Mason. He ended up leaving some of his tools on the boat we were fixing, so I grabbed 'em and took 'em home. I was wonderin' if he lived around here."

"Who'd you say you was?"

"Sorry, Buddy Crapps." Buddy extended his hand.

The man gripped it like a vise. "Vernon Burwinkle. You Delmont's brother?"

"Yessir. I just got in town, and Del and me hooked up with this Lute guy the other day."

"Why don't you just give it to him at work?"

"He didn't show up today, so I thought I'd try to find him."

"Well, sir, I do know Lute. We do a lot of business together. Comes in here all the time. If you hang around long enough, he'll prob'ly come by. Or you could leave the stuff with me."

"I'm afraid if I left it here, he'd think I stole it and tried to pawn it. I'd rather give it to him myself."

Vernon nodded. "I can't give out addresses. You might try that church across the road. He's the parson there. You said you had two questions."

"Right. Just wonderin' what kind a guns you got?"

"'Bout anything you might want. Whatcha lookin' for?'

"Just a handgun; something to keep me and Delmont safe. Delmont don't pay much attention to people around him."

"Yeah. Nice kid. But I know what you mean."

Buddy shook his head. He had to warm this guy up some, see if he could pry more information out of him. "He had a bad accident when he was a kid. He ain't been right since. But he's a hard worker."

"Like I said, nice boy. Not a mean bone in his body."

Buddy walked over to a pile of junk and grabbed a metal detector. "How much for one of these? Del loves this kind of stuff."

Vern puffed up his chest. "Normally, you'd pay close to a hundred and fifty for one, but I'll let you have that for twenty-five since the handle's cracked."

Buddy dug some cash out of his pocket. "I got twenty. How about it?"

Vern looked him up and down. "Sure. If it'll make the kid happy. Twenty bucks. You seem like a pretty good guy yourself."

"Well, I try to watch out for him when I'm around. That's why I took this job with Lute. Delmont was workin' with him, and I just want to make sure he gets treated right."

Tell you what," said Vernon, looking around out across the street. "Lute's a little moody at times, but bein' a man of God and all, I think you can trust him."

"Good to know. I been looking for a church since I got to town," lied Buddy. "Like I said, I just wanted to get these tools to him before he wastes his money on more."

"Well, you didn't hear it from me, but if you take a ride out by the swamp, you might run into him."

"Thanks. And yeah - we never met," Buddy winked at him.

Chapter 11
Wednesday, June 12, afternoon

- Get Rhoda fed and settled
- Do laundry
- Necklace?
- Gas station and market
- Get room ready for Cheryl

Maggie got Rhoda propped and pilled up in front of the TV with her big gulp of sweet tea, a bag of Doritos, her cell phone and the remote control. *The Long Hot Summer* was on so Maggie figured she had at least ninety minutes to search for the necklace. Lute had an appointment in Lake City (going after the man who implanted the King Cobra, perhaps?), so he would be gone at least two to three hours.

"Rhoda? I'm going out to take down the dry clothes and hang up some more. Text if you need me," she said, donning the rubber gloves. Hoping to score another find in a can of bolts, she looked through them. Nothing. She shook out all the empty plant pots stacked along the wall. Nothing.

She had been avoiding the wood-rotted dinghy overturned next to the carport. God knew what lived under there. But, of course, that made it a good hiding place. She whacked on it with a stick, and sure enough, a feral cat shrieked and streaked off over the fence. She screamed.

Her phone dinged. Was that u? U okay?

Yep. Sorry. A cat just scared the bejeesus out of me. OK here. Thx.

She used the same stick to flip the dinghy. Besides dead rodent skeletons, chicken bones and other feral cat debris, there did not appear to be a necklace.

Maggie turned the dinghy back over and sat on the hull. Where the hell would he have put that thing? She scanned the yard for clues and noticed a shovel leaning against the back of the house. Walking over to it, she thought she saw freshly turned earth, though it was hard to tell, the yard being such a leafy mess. On closer inspection, she decided the sandy grit here did look darker and heaved. It was worth a shot.

Seeing no one coming, she grabbed the shovel and began to dig. About two scoops down, she hit metal. Huh. Sneaky bastard. Maybe he was burying stuff out here. She got down on her knees and started to brush off the metal container. It was much bigger than she expected - and rusty and pitted. She grabbed the shovel again and tried to clear off more sand, but punctured the fragile metal instead.

Oh my God. What was that smell? She gagged as fumes permeated the still air. With the neck of her tee shirt pulled up over her nose, she covered the mystery object with dirt and leaves, put the shovel back as she found it, and ran in the house.

"What in the name of heaven do you have out in that back yard? It smells worse than an outhouse out there," she asked through the tee shirt.

"What?" Rhoda's eyes were glazed as she stared at Paul Newman sweating over a trench.

"I was out in the yard and an awful smell just about knocked me over."

"What'd it smell like? Swamp?"

"No. Crap. Poop. Raw sewage." She gagged again just talking about it.

"Ohhhh. Yeah. That's the septic tank."

"Why would it stink like that? Aren't they deep underground and made of concrete?"

"I don't know about most of them. Ours is an old oil barrel Lute found. This place didn't have any septic when we got here, so he made one himself."

"Of course, he did."

"He's handy. What can I say?" Rhoda rolled her eyes.

Chapter 12

Thursday, June 13, pre-dawn

"Okay, boys. You ready to take this virgin for a spin?" Lute smiled as he stepped on the *Eula Mae*.

"I thought we was gonna go catch some crabs," said Delmont.

"We are, Del. He's just jokin' around," Buddy told him.

"Oh," Delmont frowned. "How's a boat a virgin?"

"That just means she hasn't been in the water yet," said Lute. "We're gonna see how good a job we did patching her and try to haul in some crabs."

The men made short work of loading the trotlines, traps, nets, gaffs and the bushel baskets. It took forty-five minutes, though, to load the unwieldy boat onto a trailer that looked too small. Finally, with lots of bungee cords and straps holding the *Eula Mae* in place, they jumped in the F150 Lute had borrowed from his old friend at the retirement center, Burt. Burt was too addled anymore to drive, but he would not give up his beloved truck.

After grinding a few gears, Lute pulled out onto the road. Buddy let Delmont ride in the cab while he sat in the bed watching the boat and trailer. What a cracker-rig. It'd be a miracle if it floated.

Up front, Delmont asked Lute where the St. Johns was.

Lute explained it was about forty minutes away and ran north and south along most of northern Florida. "It's a good place for crabbing, plus there're lots of brackish savannahs and marshes feeding it."

Delmont just nodded, then looked out the window until they reached the docks.

After a few unsuccessful attempts, they finally got the boat in the water. "She ought to turn right over. I tuned her up real good last night," said Lute as he pushed the starter. The boat sputtered a few times before roaring to life. "Thank you, Holy Father. Let's go make some money, boys."

Lute put it in gear, and they headed out. They dropped twenty traps, and then moved downstream to set the trotlines. Lines were more labor intensive but promised a bigger yield, so Lute was determined to give it a try.

"For Chrissakes, Delmont. You gotta attach the line anchor to the buoy. That was an expensive anchor, you idiot," screamed Lute.

Mirror-eyed Buddy got in Lute's face. "Easy there, boss. He's a kid." Buddy clenched his jaw and fists.

"Damn kid just cost me money. That's comin' out of his pay," said Lute, backing away. "Grab that old brake drum there in the corner and use that to anchor the lines in place. And tie it to the buoy BEFORE you throw it in."

Buddy turned and walked to the other side of the boat and showed Delmont what to do.

With a total yield of ten regulation blues on the lines, they moved back to check the traps. On the first check, they had four or five per trap. This cycle repeated for several more hours, each check yielding less than the one before. When the afternoon sun baked the boat and everyone in it, they pulled up the lines and traps, covered the one full bushel of crabs and headed to the marina to measure their catch. Since there was no need for all three men to line up and toss several baskets holding their catch, Lute grabbed the one and set it on the dock.

"I'd say you got close to forty-five pounds, sir," said the man at the weigh station. "That'd be seventy-two bucks. You got your license and a ticket?"

Lute rummaged around for the documents. "You know what? I must've left those in my other truck. We'll just keep these for personal use. Thanks."

Buddy glared at him.

"Okay, boys, let's load her back up and hit the road. We'll try again tomorrow."

"Why didn't you sell them? You owe us a cut."

"Don't you worry about that," said Lute. "I got a guy back home who won't require licenses or permits. He pays as good as those guys."

By the time they returned to Eugenia, Lute's "guy" was nowhere to be found. "I'll keep 'em alive till morning and bring you your cut then."

Chapter 13

Thursday, June 13, evening, Tallahassee

Every outfit she had was piled on the bed. "This black and silver Michael Kors is always nice – very chic and trendy. But the royal blue Ralph Lauren, so American, highlights my eyes," said Cheryl holding up possibilities in front of the mirror. "What do you think, Chief? Michael or Ralph?"

"Yip!" Chief Osceola wriggled at the Kors.

"Good choice," Cheryl agreed staring at the two outfits. "Oh, the heck with it. I'll take them both. Now I just need to get us all packed, then off we go to fame and fortune. Oh, shoot. I forgot to ask Rhoda if I could bring you along."

I forgot. Is it ok if I bring Chief Osceola? Pete can't watch him this weekend. He'll be good, though. You'll never know he's there. He loves being in his carrier. He can stay on the sleeping porch. And I promise to clean up after him.

Reading Cheryl's text, Rhoda groaned. The dog, who craved attention and loved everyone, hated Lute for some reason. The minute Lute pulled in the driveway, the little sissy started growling and barking. Lute didn't care much for frou-frou little dogs, either. But, she knew Cheryl wouldn't ask if she had any other choice. She needed to be clear in her response. I guess. Just be sure to keep him in his carrier or with you. Lute should be crabbing, but you never know. When r u coming?

Cheryl could almost hear Rhoda groaning through the text. Thanks. I know it's a pain for you. But it's the only way I can come. B there Sat night so I can hear the choir at Sun service and meet this guy before evening rehearsal. I'll leave after the audition on Mon night.

OK. See you soon. Be careful driving over here. LU

Thursday, June 13, midnight

Maggie raised her head off the pillow. Did she dream that? She lay still and listened to see if the sound that woke her was real or imagined.

There it was again. Something crunching? She sat up. She knew that sound, but was still too sleep-fogged to remember it.

Again, kind of a muted scrape - it sounded just like when she dug into that old septic tank.

Bingo - clarity and consciousness merged.

She stood up and padded barefoot across the room. Grateful she had cleaned up, she managed to reach the door without tripping over anything. Standing between the window and the door, she peeked out.

A man in dark clothing, shovel in hand, was digging near the back fence, or what used to be a fence. A bag of some sort sat on the ground behind him. Laying down the shovel, he grabbed the bag and shoved it in the ground. He looked around, so she flattened up against the wall until she heard digging again. Sure enough, whoever it was filled in the hole.

Tiptoe-running, she eased back into bed, pulled up the covers and threw a pillow over her head. Despite the pillow, she heard the front door creak. Frantic it might be an intruder, she armed herself with the can of Raid she kept on the nightstand for palmetto bugs. Her senses buzzing, she heard the telltale creak of Rhoda and Lute's bed as someone settled in.

Silence descended on the house.

She knew it. Lute was burying stuff in the yard. That necklace had to be out there somewhere. She would find it. But not tonight. It was late. Unclenching her fists and dropping her shoulders, the adrenaline drained from her system and left her practically comatose.

Friday, June 14, a few hours later

She half-woke to the same sound. This must be a dream. Maggie uncovered one eye. From outside, a light flashed and a cat screeched.

Raid in hand, she propped herself up and got her bearings. The light flashed from near the clothesline.

Why wouldn't Lute bury everything at once? He was an idiot, but he wasn't stupid. As Rhoda often said, he had more degrees than a rectal thermometer. He wouldn't go out there twice in one night.

The door to the carport was one of those 1950's styles, with the three little rectangular windows diagonally across the top. She slithered off the bed and crawled over to the door. With her back against the wall, she rose to the little windows and peeked out.

A large, dark figure hunched by the pile of pavers against the fence. She couldn't make it out exactly, but it was much bigger than Lute. The light seemed to come from its face. She'd seen people on CSI put a little flashlight between their front teeth when searching in the dark. The light jerked in her direction, so she collapsed onto the floor. Afraid of being spotted, she inch-wormed backwards toward the closet. If she could just get behind the sheet that acted as a door, she'd be hidden.

Finally curled in the crowded space, she lay still. When a light again shone through the window, her leg jerked, toppling the stacks of bloated, expired cans of food Lute was saving for the revolution. The explosion rivaled an atomic blast.

The deafening percussion sent Buddy running from the yard. He didn't bother turning around to check for flames. He hopped on his bike and took off for Del's. He'd try again when nobody was home.

The detonation also woke Lute. All the lights came on. Clad only in a jock strap, he stormed into the sleeping porch waving a sawed-off shotgun. "Come on out, you son of a bitch, before I blow your nuts off."

The irony of the comment would have made Maggie laugh, seeing that his jock strap was packed with wads of gauze, but the gun was pointed at her.

"Lute, stop; it's just me," she screamed.

He looked around the room. There was Maggie, lying on the floor in the closet, covered in pork and beans, as was the rest of the room.

"What the hell is going on?" he demanded, still holding the gun.

"I don't know. I heard something outside and got up to look."

"What was out there?"

"I couldn't tell - it was big, whatever it was. And I could see light coming from it. It was hunched over by the clothesline. I got scared, so I crawled in here to hide, and, well…"

"Was it human?"

"I think so, but I don't know for sure."

Rhoda rolled up on her scooter, dazed and confused. "What's going on?"

"Your goddamned sister thought she saw something and made a big fucking mess," shouted Lute. "I want her out of here tomorrow."

"What'd you see, Maggie?"

"I don't know. I heard some noise in the yard, so I looked out and saw a big figure hunched over by the clothesline. Then I saw a light shine in my direction so I hit the floor."

"Was it a yellow light?"

"Maybe."

"It was probably just a gator. They come in out of the swamp looking for cats and raccoons. Their eyes glow yellow in the moonlight," said Rhoda.

Maggie doubted gator eyes would cast light in windows, but decided to keep quiet. She was still at the wrong end of a gun.

Lute slid through the beans toward the door to the carport. He threw the wall switch, bathing the backyard in light.

He scanned the area and saw nothing amiss. Lowering the gun, he turned back toward Maggie. His face was crimson. "Stupid city girl. Look at this mess. I want all this food replaced. These are our survival supplies."

Maggie finally sat up. She couldn't tell if she'd messed her pants or if she was sitting in a pool of beans. Not that it mattered. She was well and truly shaken.

"I'm sorry. I'll clean it up, I promise," she sniveled. "And I'll pay for the beans. I just got really scared. Whatever it was, it was big and it was headed this way." She convulsed into sobs.

Rhoda hobbled down the steps and stooped to comfort her. "It's okay. As long as you're safe."

The tears and the promise of money hit a soft spot in Lute. "Yeah, it's okay. I'm sorry - had me a little scared too when those beans blew up. Thought THEY were here at last," he pointed to the middle of his forehead. "Lucky nobody got hurt."

Rhoda sighed. "The revolution probably won't start with pork and beans, Lute." She rose and hobbled back up the steps. "You gonna be all right, Mags?"

Maggie shook her head yes.

"Come on, Lute. It's late."

Long after Rhoda and Lute went back to bed, Maggie sat in the mess, staring into the darkness. Her mind raced. Who was out there? What was he looking for? Was she in danger? Was Lute going to kick her out or worse yet, kill her?

Finally, she stood up, threw a sheet over the bean pool till morning and changed clothes. How-did-I-get-here again looped through her mind for what seemed like hours.

Chapter 14

Friday, June 14, 9:00 a.m.

Maggie could hear Rhoda's TV blaring when she woke. She tried to open her eyes, but they were crusted shut. Finally, she unstuck her hair from the pillow case, wiped the dried mess off her eyes and surveyed the damage.

Stepping carefully across the floor, she joined Rhoda in the kitchen.

"Holy cow," laughed Rhoda. "Stay right there - I gotta get a picture. You are a sight."

Maggie glared toward the phone.

"I'm sorry," Rhoda dissolved. "You should see what you look like."

"I have a pretty good idea." Humor was nonexistent.

"Sorry. Sorry. Want something to eat?" Rhoda's lips quivered. "Beans?" An eruption of giggles forced coffee out her nose.

"Forget it," said Maggie, tears welling in her eyes.

"Oh, Maggie, I am so sorry. That could have been a real tragedy. Let's just praise Jesus that you're okay."

"Right. Praise Jesus."

Rhoda could see she was not going to break through Maggie's funk. "Listen, do you need the car today? I have to meet my reading group this morning."

"No. I'm going to be busy cleaning up that HAZMAT zone out there. You go ahead." Maggie went back to the sleeping porch. She started to clean and decided a long, hot shower was the first order of business. She would no doubt need another one, but she couldn't exist like this another second.

When Rhoda heard the shower going, she hobbled down the steps and headed for Ben's. She needed a break from Maggie's omnipresence and the aura of tension that surrounded Lute.

Friday, June 14, 10:30 a.m.

Ben and Rhoda lay facing each other on the exam table.

"You're lying," Ben laughed.

"No, I swear. I am not making this up."

"So, you woke up to an explosion, went out to the sleeping porch and found Lute in his jock with a shot gun leveled at your sister?"

"You left out the beans dripping off her chin." Rhoda could not erase the scene from her mind.

"That does it. You are getting the hell out of there. And I'd make sure you sister does too."

"I don't think she'll need much convincing. She was pretty upset this morning. If she doesn't leave today, Lute

74

will probably run her off by tomorrow." She propped herself up on her elbows. "Help me up. I can't wait to get this damned cast off."

Ben helped her get dressed and opened the door for her. "Be careful, Rhoda. You're living with a ticking time bomb."

"I'll be fine," she said as she followed him into his office. He gave her one last kiss and a good rub down, then went to the waiting room and called his next patient.

♦♦♦

On his way to the docks, Lute spotted Rhoda's car behind that damn Dr. Stout's office. He was sure something was going on between them. He never had trusted that guy or Rhoda for that matter. Fuming, he punched the gas pedal. She was going to pay for this.

Chapter 15

Saturday, June 15, afternoon

"Jeez, Cheryl, what took you so long?" Maggie asked as she helped Cheryl unload her car.

"I got a late start. I forgot I had to work the Ladies Auxiliary booth at the festival this morning. It's the annual Flying High Circus event; lots of performances, classes, art shows and games. They also have the Taste of Tallahassee. Anyway, everybody who's anybody goes. Then I had to go home to get Chief and my bags."

"Traffic must have been terrible."

"I was going against the flow, so I just zipped right out of town. Enough of that. What's going on around here?"

Maggie had already caught her up on the bean explosion. She was still pretty shaken about the whole thing. "It's more that somebody or something is digging around in that yard at night. And I'm alone in that sleeping porch, which is basically all jalousie windows and a flimsy door with no locks."

"You said you thought one of the guys was Lute though, right?" asked Cheryl.

"Yeah, but that other guy - I don't buy their gator story; gator eyes don't shine in windows - he creeped me out. He was a big dude."

"Now you've got me scared. I hope we're okay out here tonight. Did you get all the beans cleaned up?" Cheryl scanned the room as she set down her bags.

"Yes. I washed all the sheets and curtains; wiped down the windows, walls and furniture and mopped the floors, again. I even dragged all the shit out of the closet and cleaned it. I've been at it for two days. I never want to see another bean in my life."

"Well, it looks better than when we got here last week. How much is the bean replacement going to cost you?"

"I gave the bastard fifty bucks. Only about three cans blew up, but he was so pissed, I was afraid he'd kick me out."

"That must have placated him," Cheryl said. "Why do you want to stay? I'd be scared here by myself."

"I know I should go, but I'm worried about Rhoda. Every time I turn around, it seems like she's popping some kind of pill in her mouth which sends her into the ozone," said Maggie.

Cheryl nodded. "I wondered what was going on. Sometimes when I talk to her she's real perky and hyper. Most of the time, though, she kind of slurs and gets distracted in the middle of the conversation. It's almost like she's falling asleep while I'm talking to her."

"Exactly. I think she's been messing around with pills since she went on disability. Heck, I'd probably do the same if I had to sit around this place all day with Lute. He makes me a nervous wreck the way he sneaks around stealing things and burying things and God knows what else. Plus, his mood swings are crazy; he'll be real nice one minute and vein-bulging furious the next. I'm afraid he'll kill her someday."

"He might kill you too." Cheryl's eyes watered at the thought.

Maggie waved off the idea. "I don't know what he's up to, but I fully intend to find out. Surely to God I can outsmart that idiot. I just need to be better prepared, though. I'm going to arm myself with a baseball bat instead of that can of Raid."

"You couldn't hit anything with a bat if you tried," laughed Cheryl. "Remember high school P.E.? What did you do the arm hang for - two seconds?"

"Yeah - still a school record," Maggie smiled.

"And what happened in softball?"

"Okay, okay. Just because I hit myself with the bat and took a ball to the back, doesn't mean I can't stand my ground."

Cheryl was glad she got Maggie laughing. When she called this morning, Maggie had sounded so scared. "Okay, we'll keep an eye on things until I have to leave on Monday. But if it gets worse around here, you and Rhoda should both come with me, unless, of course, we're on our way to Hollywood."

Maggie nodded. "Okay - that's a plan. By the way - where's Chief?"

"Oh my God, I've been so worried about you and excited about the audition, I left him in the car. I hope he's not too hot." They ran out to the car and found the dog perfectly content, sound asleep. "Rhoda said I have to keep him in his carrier except to walk him. She's afraid Lute will be mad."

"What else is new?"

"Where is Rhoda?"

"I'm not sure. She said she was going to the library in Starke, but who knows? She seemed okay to drive, so I let her go alone. I'm kind of glad she's gone, though. I wanted to show you what I found."

Maggie reached under her mattress and pulled out the sapphire ring.

"Grandma's ring. Rhoda thought she lost it. Where was it?"

"In a can of old bolts in the carport. I'm sure she didn't put it there. And Lute walked up just when the can upended and I was sweeping it up. He seemed really pissed that I was messing with his things."

"Did he see it?"

"No, I hid it before he could get close enough. But he warned me to stay out of his stuff and the yard."

"What did Rhoda say?"

"I haven't told her. I'm going to hang on to it for a while. She'll just leave it out or tell him she found it."

"You really think he'd steal from us?" Cheryl said. "Surely not. I mean, we're family."

"I'm telling you," said Maggie. "He's up to something. I have a very strong feeling he stole your necklace."

"Oh no. I had it on the whole time I was here. How would he have gotten it?"

"He's a sneaky bastard, I tell you."

"He's a preacher," Cheryl protested.

"He's a psycho," Maggie replied.

Rhoda pulled into the drive, so Maggie stashed the ring. "Don't say anything to her about this, Cheryl."

"I won't. Hey, Rhoda," Cheryl called from the sleeping porch.

Rhoda scooted in through the carport. "Hey, when did you get here?"

"About a half hour ago. How was the library?"

Rhoda's eyes grew wide. "Library? Uh, it was great. Just a little book group I sit in on sometimes. Gets me out of the house." She leaned down to pet Chief O. "Hey, little buddy. How are you?"

C.O. wagged until he fell over.

"So what time is rehearsal tomorrow?" asked Cheryl.

"I think it's at 4:00 with a carry-in dinner first and then the practice. Church is at 10:30, as usual, so we'll have time to go over the music in between."

"Sounds good. I'm so excited; we're going to be famous," squealed Cheryl.

"Maybe you and Rhoda," Maggie said. "I thought I'd make a video of the practice, so we can see what needs improvement before Monday."

"Good idea," said Rhoda. "Has Lute been home?"

"I haven't seen him all day," said Maggie. "And I haven't left the house."

Chapter 16

Saturday, June 15, late afternoon

"Whaddaya think, Vern?" Lute leaned both elbows on the counter, watching Vernon Burwinkle inspect the diamond with a loupe.

"Not bad. Not bad at all. Good cut - kind of old fashioned, but it's got enough facets to be a sparkler. The color's pretty good too. Just a few little specks in there, nothing to devalue it much."

"So?"

"Well, I'll have to weigh it, though I'd say it's at least a carat, maybe more."

"What about the gold chain?"

"Looks like it's twenty-four carat. That's a pretty big setting, too. You sellin' or pawnin'?" Vern looked up.

"Selling. And I need it paid out in gold - either bars or coins," said Lute. "How much am I up to with the stuff I've brought in this month?"

"Let me pull your card." Vern looked in his file. "Okay, you've brought in two iPhones, sterling candlesticks, and a diamond tennis bracelet."

Lute had told the Board of Trustees that flames were a fire hazard so near the wooden cross and promised to store the candlesticks in a safe place. "About those sterling 'sticks

– I don't want Rhoda to see them. We got them as a wedding present. She's never used the stupid things, but she'd be pissed if she found out I sold them."

"I hear you, man. Women are funny about stuff like that. Don't worry, though. I can sell them straight to my precious metals guy. They'll never see the light of day here." Vern was used to clients trying to protect their privacy. "Anyway, with the candlesticks, I'd say you have enough to buy at least a half ounce - close to $800 in today's market. It'd be a lot more if you add in this necklace."

"Great. Add it to the list. I'll try to come up with more stuff this weekend. I'd like to get at least a few more bars."

Vern's eyes darted around the room as he lowered his voice, "Revolution, right?"

"Damned straight," said Lute. Both men stabbed a finger to their foreheads and said in unison, "Beware the Mark of the Beast."

Sunday, June 16, morning

With his stained tee shirt hidden by a clergy robe, Lute looked like a Hollywood version of the benevolent country preacher. The corners of his eyes crinkled as he beamed his perfect smile at the congregation. He nodded affably to the crowd, then cleared his throat and began the service. **"The grace of the Lord Jesus Christ be with you."**

"And also with you," the flock replied.

"The risen Christ is with us," he said as he raised his arms.

"Praise the Lord," came the response. He waited patiently until the rustle of church clothes and the creak of metal folding chairs stopped, and the group was seated.

"Welcome, brother and sisters to our 'umble church. We are gathered here today to celebrate Jesus who died for us to save us from our sins."

Amens and halleluiahs peppered the room.

"The Bible tells us Jesus rose again to promise us eternal life."

Several praised the lord.

"And though we are promised forgiveness for our sins if we repent, Jesus also showed us through example how not to behave. Matthew 21:12-19 tells us

> *And making a whip of cords, he drove them all out of the temple, with the sheep and oxen. And he poured out the coins of the money-changers and overturned their tables. And he told those who sold the pigeons, Take these things away; do not make my Father's house a house of trade.*

> *And Jesus went into the temple of God, and cast out all them that sold and bought in the temple, and overthrew the tables of the moneychangers, and the seats of them that sold doves, And said unto them, It is written, My house shall be called the house of prayer; but ye have made it a den of thieves.*

Some in the congregation clapped for Jesus's fight against evil.

"Yet today we shirk our Christian duty as we sit idly by and let our government take over health care, our values, our very way of life. As we speak today, they are taking over our banks, so even our money is not ours. THEY have control of all the money; THEY make all the decisions. I warn you now, the revolution is upon us. So sayeth the Lord. "

Rhoda shifted uncomfortably on the piano bench, then reached down and palmed something out of her purse.

Maggie's phone vibrated in her pocket. She looked at Rhoda's text.

UH OH

WTF? Maggie replied.

"The Good Book also tells us not to engage in sodomy," Lute paused for the expected praise until silence deafened, "but in our military today, young women and men are forced to sleep next to homosexuals who only have to promise they will not engage in sodomy." Lute closed his eyes and stretched his arms toward the dropped ceiling panels. A full minute passed.

Seeing Cheryl's jaw drop and her face turn crimson, Maggie suppressed the urge to laugh out loud. She texted Rhoda. This is hysterical! Does he do this all the time?

Cheryl grabbed the phone and read the conversation. She looked at Maggie, and they were immediately consumed by the church giggles. The harder they tried to control themselves, the worse it got until they were hunched over, shaking uncontrollably, tears streaming.

Rhoda, looking to them for help, saw their convulsions and started in herself. When Maggie finally snorted, Cheryl replied to Rhoda. Start playing!

Rhoda put down her phone and turned to the doxology. She struck the first notes and gave a nod to the choir director, who signaled the choir to stand and begin.

Praise God from Whom all blessings flow…

During the song, Lute emerged from his trance. He looked down at his notes, scrambling to find his place.

"Call for the collection," Rhoda hissed from the piano.

While the ushers passed through the church, someone came in the front door. Cheryl turned at the sound and saw a tall, handsome gentleman walking down the aisle. Wearing what had to be an Armani suit, this man obviously did not hail from Eugenia. "Who's that?" she said to Maggie.

Maggie, still fighting the giggles, said, "Probably Jesus," without looking up.

"Maggie, have some respect," Cheryl scolded. "Now look back. Who is that Adonis?"

"Wow," whispered Maggie. He looked like a GQ model. "I don't know, but if that's Jesus, sign me up."

Cheryl slapped Maggie's arm. "Behave. I bet it's that producer."

As soon as Lute blessed the gifts and the givers, Rhoda played again to prevent him from continuing the sermon. The choir sang until an alarm sounded from the clock on the wall which the Board of Trustees had installed soon after Lute took over as minister.

His peaceful visage returned, the Parson Mason bowed his head, raised his hand and delivered the benediction. The church emptied in seconds.

Sunday, June 16, after church, Rhoda's kitchen

"That sure is some good fried chicken, Maggie," said Lute, reaching for another piece. "Rhoda always says you're one great cook. You can tell that by lookin' at ya," he laughed as he smacked her behind.

Maggie held her tongue. After the sawed-off shotgun incident and his insane rant in church, she decided to employ their mother's advice, "If you can't say anything nice…"

"So, what are you girls up to this afternoon?"

"Getting ready for the choir rehearsal with the producer, of course," Cheryl burst with enthusiasm. "We have to leave here about three-thirty. Don't want to be late. Are you coming with us?"

"I think I'll come a little later. I feel like I spend half my life there anyway, for all the thanks I get."

Chief Osceola let out a growl from the sleeping porch at the sound of Lute's voice.

"Are you taking that dog with you?" he asked.

"No, he'll be fine here. I'll walk him before we leave."

Lute rose from the table and went out in the carport to tinker on boat parts. Cheryl cleaned up the dishes and then herded Maggie and Rhoda to the sleeping porch. "Should I wear my hair up," she swooped it up, "or just leave it down? Which is sexier?"

"It's a choir competition, Cher. You sure you want to go sexy?" asked Rhoda.

"You bet I do. Did you see that producer in church? HOT, HOT, HOT," Cheryl fanned herself and giggled.

Rhoda and Maggie oohed and ahhhed at everything she tried on, agreed with her choice, watched her peel off her Insta-Brite whitening strips, apply makeup and fasten jewelry. At 3:00, Cheryl hoisted her girls into a new UberBoob pushup, dressed, and drowned herself in perfume.

"Let's go. This is SO EXCITING," Cheryl said as she headed out the door.

Maggie and Rhoda trailed far enough behind to allow the scent to dissipate.

Sunday, June 16, afternoon

Lute sat outside the Gardens of Babylon Nursing and Rehabilitation Center near Starke. Burt Cosgrove, an old friend of his dad's, had been there for years. Burt was always good to Lute, treated him like more of a son than his own father had. Without fail, Lute went to see him on weekends. He could tell his old friend anything, and all he got back was love and admiration. Not that Burt understood or remembered what Lute told him, but he listened and never judged. The old man would ruffle his hair like he did when Lute was a kid. Usually, Lute wheeled him down to dinner and fed him.

Years ago, before Burt's mind started going, he told Lute he would always be there for him. If Lute needed money or anything, Burt promised to help. "What's mine is yours, son. I mean that." Burt wasn't a millionaire or anything, though he might have been before he moved in here and signed over most of his assets. Not that he'd had any choice. When Burt started failing and had trouble taking care of himself, did his no-good, pasty-faced son, Weldon, lift a finger to help? No. Even now, the ingrate never came to visit. Only Lute.

So, Lute didn't feel guilty about taking the old man up on his offer. Having the only key to Burt's house and all the contents in it, he had removed and pawned things over the years. He had to be careful, though. He didn't want anyone seeing the old man's things lined up in the Vern's Pawn Shop window. Too many in town had been in Burt's house before his decline. They would know his stuff if they saw it, and they would know who pawned it. Most of the time,

Lute drove to a shop down in Gainesville. They paid better anyway.

As he entered the nursing home, Lute promised himself this would be the last time he'd impose on Burt's generosity, but for now, he needed to tap the old man again. Then he'd have enough gold bars to stay afloat for a long time. In fact, he'd have enough to get himself and Rhoda out of this godless country, away from her nosy-ass sisters and that SOB Ben Stout. Then she'd be happy with him. Filled with a renewed sense of purpose, he continued down the hall to find his friend.

"Hey, Burt. It's me, your old buddy, Lute."

Burt raised his chin off his chest and smiled, "Hey, son. Good to see you." He patted the chair beside him, "Come sit with me."

Sometimes Lute thought Burt recognized him, but he could never be sure.

"How you doin'? How's that pretty wife of yours?" Burt seemed unusually alert today.

"Rhoda? Rhoda, she's fine. She asks about you all the time," Lute lied.

"You be good to that woman. A good man always takes care of his woman," Burt said. "I don't ever want to hear about you doin' wrong by her, ya hear me?"

"Yes sir. I promise," Lute felt a slight twinge of guilt as he bent down to hug his friend who would not remember the promise or any of this conversation. "Come on, Old

Man," he said grabbing the handles of the wheelchair. "It's time for lunch."

Burt looked up and smiled. He patted Lute's hand all the way to the dining room.

Chapter 17

Sunday, June 16, 4:45 p.m.

Arnold was still dressed in his three-piece suit from church. In fact, the entire choir was dressed in Sunday finery, but no one from Eugenia had on a Michael Kors ensemble with Ferragamo slides. Cheryl blinded like the June Florida sun. Maggie tried to suppress her jealousy, sitting there in her Walmart yoga pants and a Gamecocks tee shirt. But, she wasn't on stage and had no desire to be. One of her many mottos - I prefer to remain anonymous - was especially true at church or any organization where getting noticed equaled volunteering for something.

Rhoda scooted over to the piano and got out the music they had practiced.

"Welcome, brothers and sisters," Arnold said, sounding more like a game show host than a choir director. "I'd like to introduce you to our esteemed guest, the executive producer of TV's *Choir Wars,* Mr. Edward Bowling."

Applause and Welcome-Brother's erupted.

Mr. Bowling flashed a beatific, iridescent smile. "First, I'd like to thank you all for that delicious, home-cooked meal. I haven't had meatloaf in years. What a special treat." Mary Chance beamed at the praise for her contribution. "But now, down to business. Ladies and gentlemen, it is an honor to come to my niece's humble church," he nodded toward the young mezzo-soprano. "She tells me all the time what a wonderful group of people you are, and what

Phoebe Richards

tremendous talent you have hidden here in rural Florida.
This is exactly the kind of group we like to see on *Choir
Wars* - David vs Goliath, if you will," he winked.

Maggie was tempted to put on her shades when he
smiled again. Cheryl, though, sat in perfect portrait pose,
her sparkling eyes focused on the producer.

"Now, I understand we're missing an alto. Is that
correct, Arnold?"

"Unfortunately, yes," said Arnold. "However, the
talented sister of our piano player came all the way from
Tallahassee to audition for the part tonight. Everyone, meet
Cheryl Lennon."

Cheryl stood with the grace of a Miss America
contestant, her eyes still locked on Mr. Bowling. "Thank
you, Arnold. And thank everyone for giving me this
opportunity." She lowered her eyes to show her humility.
Maggie noticed she had added fake lashes to her makeup
regimen.

"Welcome, Sister Cheryl," parroted the crowd.

"Well, then," said the blazing smile. "How about we
start there? Ms. Lennon? Are you ready to start your path to
glory? Do you have a selection you'd like to use for your
audition?"

Cheryl, still entranced, nodded her head slightly toward
Rhoda to ready her music. Only Maggie noticed her taking
a calming yoga breath before speaking.

"Thank you, Mr. Bowling. I have chosen what we consider an American classic, which was actually written and sung first in England in the late 1700's - *Amazing Grace*," Cheryl tried to impress the producer with her musical knowledge. "This simple hymn best expresses my own relationship with Our Heavenly Father." The false eyelashes again emphasized her humility as she stepped in front of the altar, faced the group, and gave the most moving rendition of the song Maggie had ever heard.

Maggie and Rhoda wept as she sang, remembering singing it together at the deathbeds of their mother and father. Cheryl, transcended, channeled any grief into the powerful performance.

All sound and movement ceased as Cheryl bowed her head at the end. Maggie, trying to hold the video steady as she filmed, scanned the crowd for their reaction. Several also bowed their heads in reverence. She sensed that, after to listening to Lute's rambling diatribes on Sundays, they were reminded of why they attended church in the first place.

Slowly, the reverie abated, and everyone began to clap, including Mr. Bowling. "My word, Ms. Lennon. You are definitely star material." Maggie zoomed in on him, so Cheryl could relive that moment indefinitely. "Consider yourself the new alto in the Eugenia Healing and Helping in the Name of Jesus Tabernacle Choir."

Cheryl blushed and threw her arms around Mr. Bowling's neck. "Oh, thank you so much, Mr. Bowling. It will be such an honor to work with you," she heard Rhoda clear her throat, "and with this incredible choir." Not breaking eye contact with Ed, Cheryl gave a head-toss of acknowledgement to the group. Mr. Bowling did not discourage Cheryl's expression of affection.

"All right, ladies and gentlemen - let's get ready to slay some giants." Ed walked to his briefcase and handed a file to Arnold. "There are some forms and papers you'll need to complete, so I can enter you in the competition."

Arnold looked surprised, "I thought we had to rehearse for you a few times before getting selected."

Mr. Bowling smiled. "Oh, you will. I just have a good feeling about this group," he said, his eyes staring straight at Cheryl's cleavage. "I think good things are going to happen here."

Amens and Hallelujahs echoed in the room.

Chapter 18
Sunday, June 16, dusk

Buddy stood at the counter of the filling station when he noticed Lute's truck pulling into the church parking lot. In fact, the lot was filled.

"They have evening services on Sundays?" he asked the clerk.

"Not usually, but tonight's a big night. My wife's in the choir, and they got a big audition for a Hollywood producer. I bet near ever-body'll be there."

"Wow," Buddy feigned interest. "Wouldn't mind seeing that myself. Did it just start?"

"No sir, I think it started a while ago, but my wife texted me and said they were probly gonna be there late. Told me to get my own dinner."

"Great. I have some errands to run, but I'd love to catch some of that," said Buddy. "Love listenin' to a good choir."

"I know what you mean. Brings peace to your soul."

Buddy bought a stick of gator jerky and headed out. "Thanks."

"See ya around."

Elated at his good fortune, Buddy jumped on his bike and pedaled toward the swamp.

After a longer ride than he remembered from his first visit, Buddy spotted the mailbox with "Mason" scrawled on the side. He stopped, stashed his bike in high weeds, and surveyed the property. It had been dark when he was here the other night. Ole' Lute had himself a bigger shithole than Delmont's. Buddy unhooked the pawn-shop metal detector from the handlebars and moved toward the fence line, such as it was. Practically falling down, it was supported by stacks of empty cans, cinder blocks and rusted mowers. Once he was hidden by the clothes on the line, Buddy looked toward the trailer. The lights were out. There were no cars around. Except for swamp sounds, the place was quiet. Deciding it was safe, he dashed across the yard to the house, peeking in windows.

Empty. Perfect.

Grabbing a shovel under the window, he walked the perimeter, scanning as he went. On the first hit, he found an empty coffee can. At the next signal, he found a coin purse with a few gold coins. Things were lookin' up.

Energized, Buddy continued his search. Back by the clothesline, he had to turn off the detector, it beeped so loud. Digging deeper this time, he hit an old cookie tin. What kinda goodies you hidin', Lute? Popping off the lid, he gasped. Nothin' better than a Glock. He looked around, pocketed the gun and returned the tin to the hole where he found it. The yard was such a mess, he didn't see much need to cover his tracks, so he just kicked some leaves around. He put the shovel back, jumped on his bike and smiled all the way home.

Sunday, June 16, two hours later at the church

Maggie's phone died after the first hour recording the rehearsal. She had read hymnals, Bibles, and religious tracts until she could no longer focus. Feeling like a six-year-old in church with Mom and Dad, she grabbed the little golf pencil that was velcroed to the back of the chair in front of her and began another list.

- Get Rhoda and Cheryl home
- Charge phone
- Call neighbor to check on house
- Keep looking for Cheryl's necklace
- Make grocery list for tomorrow

She glanced at the clock in the back of the church. Nine-thirty. Good god. They'd been there almost six hours. Even Rhoda was starting to fade, though Maggie suspected the pill she saw her take between songs had something to do with that.

Cheryl, though, not only maintained her energy and enthusiasm, she had become more animated as the night wore on. Maggie noticed she had sidled her way to the end of the group closest to Edward ("Please, Ms. Lennon, call me Ed") and managed to consult with him after every song. Maggie was shocked those eyelashes hadn't taken flight, Cheryl batted her eyes so much. And the UberBoob kept her girls high and mighty.

Maggie considered getting one to offset her pear-shaped figure, though she hated to wear a bra at all unless she was teaching. Plus, she thought, who would I wear one for? Ever since her boyfriend, Robert, left, she had sworn

98

off men. It was all too painful - he had demanded she terminate the surprise pregnancy, which she refused to do, so he left.

Then she lost the baby. She would never put herself through that again. If it hadn't been for Rhoda and Cheryl coming to stay with her until she recovered, she might have given up all together. But stay they did, until, finally, she found herself laughing and singing with them once again.

But the scars ran deep. Her mistrust of men had grown steadily ever since. Lute and Rhoda's relationship certainly didn't cause her to reconsider. Nor had Cheryl's marriage, which ended abruptly when Cheryl found her husband in their bed with two barely legal coeds. Despite the acrimonious split, though, Cheryl managed to move on, thanks to her amazing capacity for forgiveness. Maggie did not share that ability with her sister.

As depression started to cloud Maggie's brain, Ed finally signaled the choir to stop. "Ladies and Gentlemen, while this has been an exhilarating rehearsal, I fear jet-lag is starting to catch up with me. Why don't we all go home and meet again tomorrow. Don't forget to review and practice your parts, and I'll make sure we get a good quality recording of your dress rehearsal. Wear your fanciest choir robes - everything counts in these auditions - song selection, spirit, overall cinematic impact of the group, and most importantly, the quality of the singing. I feel very, very good about this."

After the excitement of the group died down and people dispersed, Ed approached Cheryl, who had busied herself long enough for everyone to leave except Maggie, Rhoda and Ed. "Ms. Lennon?"

"Call me Cheryl, please."

"All right, Cheryl Please," he chuckled, flashing his perfect dental work. "I must tell you," he looked around the room, "you completely outshine the rest of the group. But, you manage to do so without overwhelming the total effect of the choir."

"Oh," lashes fluttered, "thank you. I just love to sing and am so thrilled to be a part of this."

"In fact," he said, "I have a few ideas I'd like to discuss with you privately - maybe over a drink or some dinner?"

"Ooooh, that sounds nice," Cheryl purred. "But I don't think there are too many places open this late around here."

"Then how about lunch tomorrow? Over in Starke?"

Feeling like a third wheel, Maggie headed to the piano to help Rhoda gather music and get moving.

"You ready to go?" she asked.

"Lord, yes. I'm exhausted," said Rhoda as she hoisted her casted leg off the folding chair. "Let me wake this foot up, and I'll be ready to roll."

Maggie groaned at the pun and turned toward Ed and Cheryl, who from the looks on their faces, were ready to peel down to their altogether and have at in front of the altar. The Rapture, indeed. "Uh, Cheryl? I hate to interrupt, but are you ready to go? My phone's dead. I need to charge it and call home before it gets too late to check in with my neighbor."

Cheryl looked at Ed.

"You go ahead, Cheryl. We'll pick this up tomorrow like we planned."

Shooting Maggie the closest thing to an evil glance Cheryl could muster, she said, "Okay, then. If you're sure?"

Ed nodded.

Still standing close to him, Cheryl called over her shoulder. "All right, Mags. Get Rhoda and let's go. I have a lot of rehearsing to do. Plus, I want to watch your video. See what needs work."

Getting Cheryl away from Mr. Hollywood was like disengaging two electromagnets, but Maggie and Rhoda finally managed. Back in the car, and far enough out of earshot, Cheryl screamed, "OH MY GOD. DID YOU HEAR THAT? HE THINKS I'M FABULOUS AND HE WANTS TO TAKE ME TO LUNCH TOMORROW. EEEEEEEE!"

Chapter 19

Sunday, June 16, evening

Delmont waited till Buddy left to shower and change. He didn't want to get all fixed up nice in front of him; he knew Buddy would make fun. He got out his good collared shirt, khaki pants and his newest sneakers. The shirt wasn't too dirty, but he sprayed it down with AXE Gold before getting dressed. Clean, combed, and shaved, he headed out to Ramona's.

He usually went to see her on Tuesday nights since her parents were always at choir practice. Ramona couldn't sing a note, so her dad didn't encourage her to join. Tonight she said there was something special going on with the choir, so Delmont could come over.

He still had twenty of the thirty dollars he'd made last week, so he went by the market and got them both a Red Bull and some roller dogs. "Thought we could have kind of a special dinner together," he'd told the clerk.

Ramona, too, had gussied up. She put her church dress back on and brushed her teeth again. She hadn't ever really had a boyfriend before. Her mom and dad were so strict, plus she had a shrill, squeaky voice that kids at school had mocked. She'd learned to keep her mouth shut, so she didn't have any friends to speak of.

But then Delmont came along. She met him at the big graduation party they had at the high school two years ago. They'd been in the same grade, but Ramona had never talked to him before. At the bonfire though, they both kind of hung in the background and before she knew it, they were talking away like long, lost friends. He didn't seem to notice her voice. And he was real polite. He even walked her home to make sure she got there safe. They'd been seeing each other ever since, though they didn't go out on real dates. Delmont couldn't drive and Ramona didn't like to.

But she didn't mind. They both liked sitting at her house watching TV or playing Jenga together. By now, everybody considered them a couple.

"You here, Mona?" shouted Del.

"Come on in," she said, hurrying to the door.

"I brought us a celebration dinner." He held up the plastic sack.

"Wow, Red Bull and roller dogs. You know them's my favorites. What're we celebratin'?"

"Got me a job," Delmont blushed.

"Really? Doin' what?"

"'Member I told you about that crabber guy? Well, he hired me and Buddy to work on his boat. He's been payin' us by the day, but pretty soon, he says we're gonna come into the big bucks."

"Wow," she squeaked. Then she frowned. "Is it legal? This job, is it legal?"

"Oh yeah. We're crabbin'. And Parson Lute, he's my boss, says this is just the beginnin' of high season, so we could make tons of money. He's gonna give Bud and me a cut of everything we haul in."

Ramona threw her arms around his neck and gave him a big kiss. "That's great. Mmmmm, you sure smell good," she said as she hugged him tight.

Delmont dropped the bag of food, and they necked right there in the doorway for a while.

"I'm tellin' ya, Mona. This could be it. I might just make enough money sos we could get married."

Ramona's eyes widened. "Married? Really?"

"Yeah, I mean, that is, you know, if you wanna marry me." Delmont suddenly got worried. Why would such a nice girl want to marry a loser like him?

She thought for a minute. Her parents liked him well enough. He always said yes, ma'am and yes, sir when he talked to them. And he treated her nice. He even helped her daddy out in the yard a lot.

"Well, maybe not right away, but I wouldn't mind tellin' people we're engaged."

Delmont let out such a whoop that the sound-activated light went on by the couch. "Yippee!" He spun her around until he got dizzy and had to sit down. Ramona dug out the Red Bulls and handed him one.

"Let's toast," she said, tears welling in her eyes. Red Bull spewed out the top of the shaken cans. "Just like champagne," Ramona laughed, as they tapped the dripping cans together.

After eating their engagement dinner and mopping up the mess, Delmont told her more about the job.

"So, we load up the boat and go over to the St. Johns about three days a week. The other days we fix whatever needs fixed."

"You been all the way to the river three times already?"

"Well, we only made it once last week. Lute said he had to get some more supplies together before we go back out. Plus, he had to practice his sermon for this morning. Buddy said he's screwing us over, but I tole him, I said, 'Buddy, Parson Lute wouldn't do us wrong. We just gotta give him time to get this goin'.'"

"What'd Buddy say?" Ramona hadn't met Buddy yet, but Del said he was a good brother.

"Bud don't like Lute too much; says he's a schmoozer, whatever that is. Buddy says, though, that we are definitely going to make some money and to let him do all the worryin'."

"That's good, idn't it?" Ramona looked at him like she already depended on him.

"Yeah. It's all good. I tole him not to do nothin' that'll get him in trouble, and he promised he wouldn't."

"Do you believe him?"

"Yeah, I guess. Like I said, he's always took care a me."

Chapter 20

Sunday, June 16, after choir practice

"Lordy, lordy," Cheryl fanned herself. "What a hunk. Did you see how gorgeous he is? That chiseled face and those big broad shoulders. Be still my heart."

Maggie laughed. She hadn't seen Cheryl this wound up over a man in a long time. "Simmer down, there sister. You're going to have a heart attack."

"More like she's going to overheat," Rhoda teased. "He is a looker. I'll bet he'll have you singing like Madeline Kahn in *Young Frankenstein* after your lunch tomorrow."

"Rhoda, stop. You know I'm not that kind of girl. Well, maybe just this once," Cheryl flushed again. "But you're right. I need to calm down. I didn't act silly around him, did I? I felt like a teenager in heat up there. At first, I was so nervous about singing, but when he told me I was star material - hoo-baby, that really flipped my switch."

Maggie shook her head. "The UberBoobs didn't hurt. I don't think he looked at any one or anything else the entire night."

"Really? I wanted to wear my diamond necklace - it hits right in the middle of my décolletage," Cheryl added with a French accent. "But I still can't find it."

Rhoda looked surprised. "You haven't found Mom's necklace yet?"

Maggie shot Cheryl a warning glance. She had not discussed her theory of Lute's stealing with Rhoda.

Cheryl nodded at Maggie. "I've misplaced it somewhere. It'll turn up."

"Trust me, Cheryl," Maggie steered the conversation, "you did not need an additional spotlight on those hooters tonight. Poor man would have drowned in his own drool."

"That man can drool on me anytime, anywhere," said Cheryl, shimmying her buoyant breasts. Maggie snorted, launching them into hoots and giggles the rest of the way home.

Sunday, June 16, 9:00 p.m., Gone Fishin' Mobile Home Resort

When Buddy arrived back at Del's, he was relieved to find the place empty. Seeing the can of AXE deodorant and strangling on the pungent scent, he guessed Del had gone to see his girl. Perfect. He could hide the few coins and gun he'd unearthed. He was still practically vibrating from the thrill of finding stuff in Lute's yard. There could be a real mother lode out there. Why had he left in such a hurry?

He grabbed a six-pack of lukewarm malt liquors out of the cooler/coffee table and shot-gunned them. He tapped his fingers on the cooler top as minutes crawled by. Why had he come home so fast? He could still be out there mining for gold. Energized and reckless, he decided to chance it and go back. The metal detector was still strapped to the bike, so he grabbed the Glock, saddled up and took off. If someone was home, he'd just ride on by.

By the time he reached the swamp, he was beginning to second guess his decision. Chances were good that someone would be home by now. He slowed and pulled close to the marsh as he approached the property. Taking great care not to make noise, he stashed his bike in a tangle of brush on the edge of the yard. The place still looked dark.

Unstrapping the metal detector, he started toward the fence when headlights lit up the night. "Shit," he whispered, dropping the detector as he dove into the overgrown jasmine bush and trained the gun on the carport door.

◆◆◆

"I'm starved," said Cheryl as she helped Rhoda out of the car.

"We can tell, Hot Pants," said Rhoda.

"OK, enough about my raging hormones," said Cheryl. "I hope there's still chicken left from lunch."

The three made their way into the trailer, relieved Lute wasn't there. "I wonder if he's still at church. I noticed he never came out of the office. I saw one of the trustees go in while Cheryl was singing," said Rhoda.

"Is that bad?" asked Maggie.

"Usually. They're always on him about his sermons."

"Why do they keep him, beside the fact that he works for pennies?"

"He does a good job with the outreach program. He always visits the elderly and the sick. He just can't control himself in the pulpit. I've read his sermons, and they're not usually too bad on paper. But then he gets lost when he's giving it and ends up screaming about some wild conspiracy theory."

Cheryl set the leftovers on the counter and piled half of them on her plate. "I'll have to wear my Spanx tomorrow night."

Just as Maggie and Rhoda fixed plates and the three sat down to eat, the front door slammed open. Forks stopped midair.

Rhoda jumped up and rolled into the living room. "Hey, honey. Want something to eat?"

Lute stormed past her and headed for the bedroom. "No. I do not want anything to eat, especially not with that brood of hens in there. I'm going to bed."

Rhoda, wide-eyed, rolled into the kitchen and grabbed the pseudo-Erectite pills. "I think he's gonna' need a couple of these tonight, which means I am also headed to bed. Pray for me."

Cheryl looked at Maggie. "Erectite? What is that all about?"

"You don't even want to know. Definitely a story for another day. Suffice it to say, I think Rhoda actually knows what she's doing," said Maggie. Seeing that Cheryl was ready to hear the whole story, she went for the re-direction. "So, let's talk about this producer, now that you've cooled off a little."

Her tactic worked.

"Oh, goody."

"What do you expect to happen here?" Maggie's cocked eyebrow warned Cheryl a lecture was coming.

"What I expect is to sing my heart out and get this choir, including me, on national TV. Period."

"Period, my ass. Have you forgotten your orgasmic fit in the car? You're going to sleep with that man, aren't you?"

It was Cheryl's turn to arch an eyebrow. "If you are suggesting that I will pimp myself out for a part, then you owe me an apology," tears glistened in her eyes. "I am a moral, God-fearing woman. I live a good, clean life. But I am a woman, a divorced one at that, so if and when I decide to sleep with someone, not only is it NOT your business, it is because I have determined that the relationship is ready for that step."

"Right."

"You listen to me, baby-sister," Cheryl emphasized baby. "You have crossed a line. Just because you had the bad judgment to let that low-life SOB move in, knock you up, and then leave you does not give you the right to deem all men bastards."

Maggie was stunned. And hurt. Normally, Cheryl "wouldn't say shit if she had a mouthful," as their mother used to say. Several tense seconds passed before Maggie could bring herself to speak. She straightened her spine and took a deep breath. "I apologize if my moral turpitude has clouded my view of the world. I only want to protect you. Watching you suffer after your divorce and being around this dysfunctional train wreck of a marriage, I admit I have become cynical." Maggie pushed away from the table, walked out the screen door and down the street.

Cheryl shoved her plate out of the way and dropped her head on her folded arms. They would fix this. They had to. They were sisters, after all, closer than any other sisters she knew. She would give Maggie time to cool off and then talk to her.

She went in the bathroom and washed off the layers of make-up she had applied. She carefully put the eyelashes back in their container and peeled herself out of the spandex and foam-padded undergarments. Finally, dressed in her rattiest but most comfortable robe, she put on shoes to go look for Maggie.

As she stepped toward the door, Rhoda hobbled in. "What's up?"

"Maggie and I had a fight and she stormed out, so I'm going to look for her."

"What about?"

"Oh, she went *Judge Judy* on me about that producer, and I fired back. Basically, we were mud-wrestling. Then she got all haughty and took off, like she always does."

"I don't think her self-esteem got any boosts tonight, with you looking like a movie-star and that producer slobbering all over you."

Cheryl's eyes filled with tears. "Oh, you're probably right. I was only thinking about me. I feel terrible. I have to go find her."

"Let me go. She's more likely to listen to me right now."

Cheryl grabbed Rhoda's scooter for her and held the door. "Tell her I'm sorry. I was out of line."

"Don't worry." Rhoda rolled out to the road. Letting her eyes adjust to the dark, she walked about a quarter mile where she found Maggie sitting on a guard rail.

"Watcha' doin' there, Mags?" Rhoda sat, enclosing her in hug. Behind them, deep in the swamp, a bull gator bellowed.

Maggie collapsed on her shoulder and sobbed. "I don't know what the hell I'm doing. I guess everything just got to me tonight. I mean, it has been a pretty crazy week. I haven't slept since the intruder/canned food explosion/gun wielding brother-in-law incident. Then she comes in all gorgeous and talented while I sit there smelling like pork and beans."

"Maggie, no one could smell the beans over Cheryl's choking perfume."

"Point." Despite her tears, Maggie smiled. "I just lost it. Sitting there with no talent, watching the two of you steal the show. Not to mention that you're married, Cheryl's snagged a rich Hollywood producer, and I am, once again, all alone."

Rhoda guffawed. "You're jealous of me being married? To a controlling, paranoid nut-bag? Baby-sister - trust me on this one - you, free to do as you please, are the luckiest woman on the planet."

Maggie looked at her, confused at first and then laughed. "You're right. I feel bad. I have to apologize to Cheryl."

Rhoda patted her on the back. "Come on. Let's get out of here before that gator has us for dinner. Now THAT would qualify as a bad week."

Cheryl intercepted them at the end of the drive. They hugged, sobbed, and I'm-sorry-please-forgive-me'd before heading inside.

The figure crouched behind the jasmine did not breathe until the screen door slammed, and the carport and inside lights went out. Even after all was quiet, he sat on the ground and waited.

Chapter 21

Monday, June 17 1:30 a.m.

Chief Osceola's low growl first woke Cheryl. Thinking Lute was probably up, she stroked CO on the head and pulled him tighter under the covers. Drifting back into the zone toward sleep, Cheryl heard a noise. Outside. Close.

She muzzled Chief with her hand. Afraid to move, she strained to see through the open wooden jalousies on the porch. Scanning the room, she noticed Maggie too was awake, still as a corpse, except for one raised finger signaling Cheryl.

Another thunk and slight beep sounded from the yard. More faint this time. Maggie slid from her bed to the floor and into Cheryl's. Cheryl had stuffed CO in his carrier - the little plush palace rendered him oblivious to the outside world.

Had the person in the yard been looking, he would have seen two foreheads and four eyes staring through the bottom slat of the window. They dropped back to the bed. "Who is that?" Cheryl whispered directly into Maggie's ear canal.

She pressed her lips against Cheryl's ear. "No idea. Same thing I saw the other night."

They popped their heads back up to the window in time to see the intruder grab a long, thin object off the ground, then walk behind the jasmine bush. Seconds later, he emerged on a bicycle and rode off. They waited a full ten minutes before speaking.

"I told you Lute was burying stuff in the yard," whispered Cheryl. "I wonder who that was."

"I have no idea, but I'm sure it's the same one from the night of the bean-bomb. Gator my ass. Knowing Lute, he's blabbed all over town about burying gold and guns. I'm surprised it doesn't look like an archeological dig out there every night."

"We have to check this out tomorrow," said Cheryl. "What if my necklace is out there?"

"I've thought of that. I looked one day, but dug into an old oil drum that serves as their septic system…"

"What?"

"Really? You're shocked? Rhoda says Lute put it in himself because he wasn't going to line the pockets of those crooked SOBs in county government buying permits with his hard-earned money."

"He earns money? Doing what?"

"Hell if I know. But he's getting some somewhere. I know he got some when his folks died, and he has that rich old guy at the nursing home he dotes on."

"Whatever," said Cheryl. "Hopefully, the diggers are gone for the rest of the night. I have to get my beauty sleep for the big performance tomorrow."

"You mean tonight," Maggie said, noticing the clock. 2:30 a.m. She would never get back to sleep now. She watched as Cheryl slipped on her sleep mask and willed herself unconscious.

Maggie checked her phone. 3:30 a.m. The house had been quiet for over an hour, so she felt safe snooping around. All but levitating off the bed, she tiptoed silently toward the carport door, praying it wouldn't creak. Prayer answered. Maybe all this church-going was doing some good after all.

Slipping on the flip flops she left outside, she stayed on the cleared path to the yard. This time the shovel lay under the clothesline, probably where mystery man dropped it when he left. A pile of leaves a few feet away got her attention. She dug there, moved a few feet, dug again, moved a few feet and dug.

After the several attempts, she saw another phone light in the carport. Just as the beam hit her, she raised hers toward it. They blinded each other.

"Who's there?" she whispered.

"Maggie? It's Rhoda."

Maggie waited while Rhoda limped over. Those big feet couldn't walk softly even without a cast, but no one seemed to stir inside. "What are you doing?"

"And you?"

Maggie held up the shovel. "Cher and I saw the digger again. I thought I'd try to find what's so interesting out here."

"Me, too. I heard a noise about an hour ago."

"Oh. Don't bother. I've dug up half the yard." Maggie shoved her phone in the bulging pocket of her pajamas.

"Find anything?"

"Nope. Nada. In fact, I'm done. Want the shovel?"

"Sure. At least I can use it as a cane. I'll be in in a minute. Gonna have a smoke while I'm out here."

Maggie reentered the house and climbed in bed.

Smoke curled over Rhoda's head as she stood in the airless night waiting for Maggie to fall asleep.

Chapter 22

Monday, June 17, 6:00 a.m.

"You know what, boys? I got a good feeling about today," Lute rubbed his hands together as Del climbed aboard. Buddy stood on the dock holding the rope.

"Let's go, Buddy. On board," yelled Lute over the engine.

Buddy, mirrored glasses again focused on Lute, stayed put. "We ain't goin' nowhere until we settle up our cut. Here's the deal - twenty bucks a day plus fifteen percent of the profit."

"I said we'll discuss the terms later," Lute shifted the boat into gear.

"We talk now or we're gone." Buddy pulled harder on the rope.

Lute pushed the throttle forward hoping to lose Buddy, but he underestimated the man's agility. Buddy leapt on the boat, grabbed the throttle and threw it into neutral, shoving Lute against the side of the boat.

"Get off me."

Buddy had Lute bent backward over the side. "Twenty dollars a day and fifteen percent."

"All right, all right. Jesus." Lute finally regained his composure and shoved Buddy out of the way. "Didn't know

I was dealing with a federal mediator. Don't worry. You'll get yours."

Buddy moved to the back to ready the equipment.

Even Buddy's shoulders started to ache after a while. They had repeatedly hauled in full trot lines and were even successful with the traps. By noon, with all the bushel baskets full, they headed to Eugenia.

Lute, elated by their success, met with his guy, sold the crabs and handed Buddy and Delmont their fair cut. "I told ya we were gonna make plenty of money. And here, I got you both a little something to make up for what I owe you from last time."

"It better be money," said Buddy.

"It's better'n money," Lute smiled as he handed them both a gold coin.

"Gee, Bud. Would ya look at that? That's real gold." Delmont held it up to the sun.

Buddy turned the coin over and over checking for any sign of a scam.

"It's real," said Lute. "You guys earned it."

"It better be," said Buddy.

Delmont, still mesmerized by his treasure, asked Lute, "When can we go out again?"

"I don't know. I've got some church business tomorrow." Lute looked at Del. The goofy kid seemed so excited. "Oh, what the hell? But we'll have to go early. Meet me back here before sunrise, and we'll get a few hours in. Then Wednesday, we'll go out all day."

Monday, June 17, 7:30 a.m.

Stripes of sunlight painted the sleeping porch. Of course, a missing jalousie brushed the widest stripe across Maggie's eyes. Cheryl and Chief O snored. The rest of the house was quiet. Desperate for sleep, Maggie threw the pillow back over her head, squeezed her eyes closed and tried to doze off. The longer she tried, the more tense she got. Ten minutes later, she unclenched her fists, lowered her shoulders from her ears and sat up. The hell with it. She headed for the bathroom.

She didn't know how Cheryl and Rhoda did it. Both of them could get up, have coffee, return to bed and sleep for hours. Not so Maggie. Once her eyes opened in the morning, she was awake, making lists in her head or fretting about possible doom. The school psych had called it catastrophizing. Getting up and active helped her fight it.

First, she wanted to see if there was evidence of last night's three-ringed circus in the yard. From the shade of the carport, she surveyed the scene. She had to admit, it was a great place to bury something. Between the weeds (rare plants, indeed), the ubiquitous oak leaves, sand, grit and white-trash debris, the yard stayed in a perpetual state of chaos. The shovel seemed her only clue. A trail of sand led from the edge of the carport to its new location by the door. Rhoda had used it as a cane. Odd that Maggie hadn't heard her come in. She must have smoked a whole pack of cigarettes out there. She did notice a few piles of black sand pocking the yard, but decided against investigating. The siren of a cool shower beckoned.

♦♦♦

"Rrrrrruff. Rrrruff-rrruff-rrruff."

Cheryl's eyes popped open. Chief Osceola whined and scratched at the door of his carrier.

"Oh, poor baby. I forgot to let you out." CO dashed across the floor and whined at the door.

"Shhhh. I'm coming. Shhh. Don't wake everybody. They'll kick us out," she whispered. She opened the door, foregoing the leash, and walked outside. CO bolted for the weeds and relieved himself, then started sniffing the ground. It wasn't until the sleep-fog lifted that Cheryl heard the outside shower running.

"You about done in there?"

"Just got in. It's gonna be a while. It's so refreshing."

"Take your time. I'm not going to shower until later. Looks like Lute's gone and Rhoda's still asleep." Cheryl couldn't imagine it being refreshing. The well water (at least that what she hoped it was) stunk like rotten eggs and left rust stains on the floor and walls. But it was the only working shower at the house. Apparently, about a month ago, Lute decided to remodel the bathroom. He got as far as taking out the old tub, but after pricing shower kits, he placed a plastic kiddie pool under the shower head, cut a hole over the drain, then sealed it with Gorilla Glue and duct tape.

Cheryl noticed Chief O had wandered a bit too close to the swamp, so she waded through weeds to get him. He had sniffed out something of interest and dug as deep as his short, little legs would allow. Cheryl grabbed him and brushed him off. "You're going to get all dirty, and I can't get you to the groomer's until next weekend." It was then that she noticed a glint where he dug. She started to dig, but didn't want to ruin her manicure. Returning CO to his carrier, she checked on Maggie.

"You all right in there?"

"Yep. Just feels good. I'll be out soon."

Cheryl's curiosity overwhelmed her. She grabbed the shovel and headed for the glint. It might be her necklace. A few scoops in, she realized it was bigger than a necklace. It glistened in the sun. She reached down and grabbed the baggie that was filled with what looked like shiny dominoes. She squinted to read the print on them. Suisse 100g Gold 999.9. Wow. He really was burying gold bars. Mercy; where did he get these?

Hearing the creak of the shower handle, she scurried back to the garage, replaced the shovel and went inside. She realized she still had the baggie, so she stashed it in her robe pocket until she could rebury it. Feigning calm, she took Chief to the kitchen to feed him.

"Z'at you, Mags?" called Rhoda from the bedroom.

"Nope. She's in the shower. Just me and Chief out here. Can I get you anything?"

"I'll love you forever if you start some coffee."

The smell of strong coffee pulled Rhoda and Maggie trance-like into the kitchen. Cheryl gave them both a steaming cup.

Rhoda stirred in five spoons of sugar, took a huge slurp and raised her eyes toward heaven. "Bless you, Cher. I needed this after last night."

Maggie, after swallowing her coffee, agreed. "No kidding. I only got a few hours of sleep. Here I thought I was coming to stay in the country, but your yard is busier than Times Square in the middle of the night. Does this happen all the time?"

"We get critters out there a lot. And sometimes I'll find Lute out there when he's particularly manic. But it hasn't ever been like this until lately. Until you got here, Maggie."

"Hey, I didn't do anything. I'm the one manning the front line. Cheryl saw somebody, too - and I was right next to her. How late were you out there, Rho? I didn't hear you come in."

"Just a few minutes after you. You were zonked out."

Cheryl slapped her hands on the table. "Let's talk about something more pleasant and exciting - the audition tonight."

"Oh, that reminds me," said Maggie, pulling her phone from her pocket. "Let's watch the video I took. My battery died before it was over, but it might be helpful."

They took their coffees into the living room and sat on the couch. Maggie pressed play.

"You sounded incredible, Cheryl."

"I did, didn't I? And I looked pretty good, too, don't ya think?"

Maggie and Rhoda nodded. They continued through the recording past Cheryl's solo. Then the picture showed the floor, the edge of the piano and the door to the church office.

"What happened to me?" Cheryl looked hurt.

"Oh, I think I was getting some gum out of my purse," said Maggie. "I must have moved the phone."

Rhoda leaned toward the screen. "Who is that in the office with Lute?"

"Can't tell. Whoever it is is facing the wrong way. Looks like a man, though. Gray hair, tall? Anybody you know?"

"I don't know. I can't tell."

They watched for several seconds. The gray-haired man leaned in and wagged his finger in Lute's face.

"Looks like he's telling Lute off, but I can't hear anything over the singing and piano. Oh look. Lute's shaking his fist …"

Cheryl and the rest of the choir were back on the screen.

"Great camera work, Mags," said Rhoda.

"Sorry," Maggie said. "Wonder what that was about?"

"Oh, Shhhh. Look," Cheryl clapped her hands. "This is when he tells me I'm star material. Show that again, Mags. Better yet, just send me the whole video."

Chapter 23
Monday, June 17, midday

Buddy sat close to the take-out window at the Broken Cleat relishing the cold Budweiser. So far, things were going better than he could have dreamed. He'd been reluctant to come to Del's after prison, but this area was so isolated he felt safe. Plus, these self-absorbed rednecks didn't get involved in anybody else's business. And what a gold mine, literally, that idiot Lute had turned out to be. So far, Buddy's nighttime sojourns to the swamp had been successful. A few more trips and he'd be able to get a fake license and maybe even a car. It'd be nice to have wheels again.

◆◆◆

Maggie had had it. She could not sit in this dump another minute listening to Cheryl practice hymns. She tried to join in, but Cheryl told her she was too off-key. Sometimes old Pollyanna could be a bitch.

"Rhoda, can I borrow the car? You can ride with Cheryl to the church, and I'll meet you guys there."

"Oh, um, sorry. I need to go to the doctor. What do you need it for?"

This was the first time Rhoda had mentioned a doctor's appointment. Maggie guessed listening to the command performance was weighing on Rhoda, too. "Oh," she said, "No big deal. I was just going to get out, you know, relax a little, maybe get a bite to eat. But, I can do that some other time. I'll take you to the doctor's."

Rhoda's eyes grew wide. "No, no. You've done enough. You deserve a break. I can drive myself. In fact, I'd love to drive myself. I've felt so helpless lately."

Maggie considered being a martyr and insisting on helping. Screw it. "Well, if you're sure. I can take the bike. It's a nice day for a ride, and I could sure use the exercise."

Rhoda looked relieved. "I'll be fine. And Cheryl's gotta get ready for her big lunch with Mr. Hollywood. Go - you go have fun. Take your time. Like you said, we'll just meet at the church later, maybe around 5:30? I'll leave my car here for you, and I'll ride with Hot Lips."

"Sounds good to me. Will you tell Cheryl?" Maggie asked.

"Yes. Quit worrying and trying to control everything. GO!"

Just pedaling away from the crazy-house, Maggie felt her shoulders relax. She wasn't sure where she was going. Just away. Maybe find normal somewhere.

She took the gravel road that wound around the swamp. The air felt cooler as she moved through it. And the swamp, so dark and creepy at night, was beautiful and quiet. Almost peaceful. For the first time in over a week she felt a sense of calm.

Up the road, a snowy egret stood like a sculpture. She stopped to watch until it finally stretched its sinuous neck, lifted its wings and disappeared into the dark morass. She rode on until a faded sign in the brush caught her eye. Broken Cleat Bait and Bar - next right.

Maggie had heard plenty about the place from Rhoda. It might not qualify as normal, given that Lute went there, but a cold beer sounded pretty good right now. She was afraid to bring any alcohol in the house between Rhoda's constant pill popping and Lute's penchant for booze.

She turned right. Through the tunnel of live oaks, she could see sun sparkling off the water. Just the balm she needed after this past week. She pulled into the parking lot and walked to the dock.

Buddy watched from behind the mirrored shades as she made her way to the window. Her hunched posture screamed self-consciousness. No wonder. She was a little plump. Not fat, but definitely not thin. Thirties? Forties? Not that it mattered; she was legal. He scanned her again. Big behind, small boobs, shapely legs. Her hair exploded out of a red kerchief tied around her head. Not bad looking, he decided - high cheekbones, upturned nose, smooth skin. Just plain enough to appreciate a little attention.

"I'll take a Bud Light, please," Maggie said to the bartender.

"Let me see if I got any. Don't get much call for the light stuff," he winked. "You new around here?" he asked as he pulled one out of the cooler.

"Just visiting my sister."

"I know 'bout everybody in these parts. Who's your sister?"

"Rhoda Mason."

"Oh, Lute's wife."

Buddy leaned forward.

"Yep. That's her. I'm helping out till her leg heals."

"I heard about that," a wet, calloused hand shot through the window. "I'm Pops. Nice to meet you."

"Maggie. Maggie Lennon. Nice to meet you, too," Maggie shook his hand. He seemed normal enough.

"That'll be two bucks," he said, as he opened it for her.

"I'll get that," came a voice from behind her.

Startled, Maggie let out a small gasp.

"Sorry, ma'am. Didn't mean to scare you."

She turned and saw her reflection in dark mirrored sunglasses about a foot above her face. The man behind the glasses was massive. And buff.

Buddy stepped back. "Again, sorry," he said as he handed Pops two dollars.

"You don't need to do that."

"Well, ma'am. I gotta tell you; we don't see too many women down here. Mostly there's just a bunch of smelly old salts around. Ain't that right, Pops?"

"Too true."

Though skeptical, Maggie wasn't going to get into the old "I'll get this; No, I'll get it" over two bucks. "Thanks. Thanks a lot." She grabbed the beer and turned to find a seat.

"Here, I got a table over in the shade. You can sit there. It's okay. I don't bite." A benign smile formed below the shades.

Seeing her reflection, Maggie realized she looked like a terrified spinster. Forcing herself to relax, she smiled back. "Sure. Why not."

Chapter 24

Monday, June 17

Cheryl wanted to save the Ralph Lauren for the dress rehearsal/audition. That only left a sun dress from J. Crew. But it was just lunch. She didn't want to appear too eager. With the right accessories, she'd be fine. Thank goodness Maggie had sanitized the place, so she could get ready without getting schmutz all over everything. Cheryl fluffed and preened until it was time to go. She insisted on meeting Mr. Gorgeous, so he wouldn't have to pick her up at the trailer.

They agreed on the Lakeside Bistro, the highest rated restaurant in Starke. Pulling into the parking lot, Cheryl worried she had the wrong place. There was no sign of a lake unless you counted the stagnant retention pond by the parking lot. But it had four stars on YELP and was one of the few eateries in town without a drive-through window.

Ed was waiting for her at the table when she arrived. He stood, grabbed both her hands and leaned in for a continental kiss. "You look even more beautiful than last night, if that's possible," he said as he pulled out her chair.

The fact that he pulled out a cracked vinyl-padded chair at a chipped Formica table escaped Cheryl. Staring into his eyes, she could have been at a sidewalk café on the Riviera.

"Well, thank you. I'm so glad to have the chance to get to know you and hear more about what you do. What an exciting life you must lead."

"It can be tough being on the road so much, but it helps having the opportunity to meet so many wonderful folks across the country. The true excitement comes in discovering a rare talent like you."

Maggie had warned Cheryl to be careful of slick come-ons, but he seemed sincere. She casually checked for a wedding ring when he summoned the waitress. No ring; no tan line. "I don't know about that," she demurred, "but I do love to sing. It just takes me to a different place and fills my heart with pure joy."

"It shows," he said. "I have to tell you, I was dreading this trip. Since I took the job as E.P. with *Choir Wars*, my niece has driven me crazy with emails and texts begging me to come listen to this wonderful choir. She's a sweet girl and all, but I never considered her a talent scout," he winked. "However, my sister would never forgive me if I hurt her baby's feelings. Who knew she was right?"

Cheryl nodded, "They do have a wonderful choir. It's a long drive from where I live, but the music makes it worth the trip. I'm so fortunate they needed an alto this week."

"I wondered about that. You live in Tallahassee, and you drive all the way here to sing on Sundays?"

"Oh, no. My sister, Rhoda, the pianist, called and asked me to come this weekend to help with the audition."

"So, if the choir makes it to the next level of competition, will you be able to stay on?" Ed looked worried. She was the best voice in the group. Without her, they didn't have a chance.

132

"Oh yes. I've already talked to my boss about it. I have plenty of annual leave, and I'm pretty senior there, so I shouldn't have any problem."

"What is it you do?"

Cheryl briefly explained her job as a cognitive neuroscientist. "But I'm not in a lab all day. I do a lot of field research with patients."

Ed looked impressed. "Talent, beauty, and brains too. You really are the whole package."

The compliment had the desired effect as Cheryl blushed, then leaned forward. "Aren't you sweet? You know, it's just a job, but I love it. Almost as much as I love singing."

By now, knees touching under the table, eyes and hands locked above it, the current between them was practically visible.

"Hey, folks. Welcome to the Lakeside Bistro." The waitress, stuffed into her LB tank top and spandex mini skirt, broke the romantic spell. "What can I get you to drink?" she asked, handing them laminated menus.

Ed asked for a Belgian ale and a glass of white wine for "the lady."

"Oh, sorry, sir. We don't have a license to sell alcohol."

Cheryl, not wanting to drink before tonight anyway, piped in, "I'll just have San Pelligrino, then."

"Make that two," Ed added.

"Like I said, we don't sell alcohol."

Cheryl laughed. "No, San Pelligrino is an effervescent spring water."

"Water we got." The waitress snapped her gum as she wrote 2W on the order form. "I'll get those while you look over the menu. The specials today are the Gator Tail Caesar, and the Mullet Alfredo. That's my personal favorite."

Ed was slack-jawed as the waitress walked off. Giggling, Cheryl patted his hand. "I guess you're not used to backwoods Florida cuisine. It sounds downright 'Gor-may'."

Regaining his composure, he whispered, "Is it real gator tail? Wouldn't that be tough? And I thought mullet was a hairstyle."

"My suggestion would be to stick with regular salads or chicken," Cheryl said, "though that gator tail can be mighty tasty."

They both ordered regular Caesars and crab gumbo and washed it down with chlorine flavored tap water.

"I apologize," said Ed, as they left the restaurant. "Let me make this up to you. How about you come by my bed and breakfast tonight after we tape the audition. I can have the hosts fix up an al fresco meal for us, and we can eat on the patio out by the lake."

Tread carefully, Cheryl heard Maggie in her head. "Well…"

Ed held up his hands, "No, no. I didn't mean that to sound like a come on. Really. I just like your company, and I'm hoping we'll be making big plans for the choir's next step toward stardom."

Maggie's voice evaporated from Cheryl's head. "I'd love to. Sounds like fun."

She sang the "Hallelujah Chorus" all the way back to Rhoda's.

Chapter 25

Monday, June 17, Broken Cleat Bait and Bar,

2:30 p.m.

Maggie had a good buzz going. She hadn't had a drink since spring break - alcohol ate up too many Weight Watchers points unless it was a special occasion. And if surviving life around Rhoda's - scary things going bump in the night and a two-megaton bean bomb - wasn't a special occasion, she didn't know what was. Plus, she didn't mind hanging around. This guy was extremely well-built. His sun-bleached hair, tanned face, strong jaw and stubbled chin suggested an outdoorsy type, but she couldn't tell for sure. She wished he'd take off those damn sunglasses, so she could see his eyes. The sun was bright coming off the water, though. Maybe later. At least he hadn't tried to make a move or act like a horny teenager. He actually seemed pretty laid back.

He said his name was Warren. He was on a break from working on an oil rig in the Gulf, and he came here to take care of his disabled brother.

"What a coincidence that we're both here for the same reason. I'm here to take care of my sister. Her husband broke her leg," Maggie said.

Buddy didn't doubt that. He had witnessed Lute's volatile temper.

"He's an ass," Maggie said before finishing off her beer.

Obviously he and this woman had some things in common. "Wow. So what do you do when you're not here?"

"I'm a high school English teacher in Greenville, South Carolina." She regaled him with horror stories of teaching freshmen. "The boys are still drawing pictures of army battles or hobbits, and the girls are so made up they look like hookers. It's a pretty goofy mix, but I like it. They're good kids, and, as they say, the best part of the job is June, July and August."

"So, you're going to spend the whole summer down here? Your family at home must be upset you'll be gone so long."

"I don't really have any family there. Friends, yes, but they're all busy during the summer, too."

"Well, your sister must have some pretty comfortable digs." Buddy had been trying to move the conversation in that direction for a while.

"Um, no. Comfortable is not a word that comes to mind. Bat shit crazy, maybe, but not comfortable. But, she and I are very close, and she needs me. Plus, I have the time. I guess I could ask the same of you. Is your brother your only family?"

"Yeah. Kind of the same story. Not a great place to visit, but he and I get along, and I like to watch out for him when I can. He's real trusting; gets taken advantage of a lot. So - bat shit crazy, huh? What's that mean?"

"Well, it's a small town. I don't want to say too much. It's just my brother-in-law teeters on the edge of sanity most of the time. He's a conspiracy theorist, I guess. He's been packing in provisions for some revolution he thinks is coming."

Buddy couldn't figure out a way to ask about the provisions. Plus, he had a pretty good idea. "I know the type. There's a bunch of those on the rig. I just nod and mind my own business. What's your brother-in-law do?"

"Who the hell knows? He's always hopping from one money-making scheme to another. His only real job is as the preacher at a local church. Enough about that mess though. I really ought to get going."

"You sure? Pops has some darn good fried catfish and hushpuppies, and he said he was going to preview a band tonight. They have live music here sometimes. Sounds like you could use a break from crazy-town."

Why not? She really didn't think she could stand watching Cheryl in all her glory again. "Well, it probably would be a good idea for me to eat something. I'm not used to drinking very much. But I insist on buying. You've gotten the last two rounds."

The smile curved below the sunglasses. "That sounds like a plan."

Chapter 26

Monday, June 17, afternoon

Rhoda was pissed. She was "all dressed up and no place to go," as her mother used to say. She finally got everybody out of the house and even had a car, and Ben was unavailable. He had returned her call saying he was on his way to Gainesville to pick up new physical therapy equipment. "Maybe we can meet up later?" he suggested.

"I have that audition at church tonight. Plus, Lute will be there to meet with the Head Trustee."

"Oh, come on. Surely you can get away from him afterwards."

"I'll try." She hung up and threw down the phone, pulled the bag-o-pills from under the mattress and slammed back a few. Settled in the recliner, she turned on TMC and drifted off as Maria sang "I Feel Pretty" before the big rumble claimed its victims.

◆◆◆

Lute parked behind Burt's old house. He didn't want Burt's family or the neighbors to see him. Not that he was doing anything wrong. Burt had told him to help himself, but he knew the family members would raise a stink about it. Lute had easily figured out the gun safe combination – 1, 2, 3, 4. Just like Burt to make things so easy for him. Inside, there were some beautiful antique pistols, and finally, pay dirt. The gold coin collection. Years ago, Burt had been the one to tell Lute about the coming revolution. "It's the beginning of Armageddon, I tell you."

Lute had been inspired by Burt's dedication to "save REAL Americans from all these foreigners" that were buying up their land, their businesses and even their government. Burt had even shown Lute some articles on the internet as proof of impending doom. "You'll know them because they bear the Mark of the Beast. They have sold their souls to the antichrist. It's up to good folk like us, Lute, to save our women and children and our way of life. Take up arms. Stock up on supplies. They will stop at nothing, I tell you."

Rhoda had tried to tell Lute that Burt was just an addled old man, but Lute knew better. Burt wouldn't lie to him or steer him in the wrong direction. If Burt said it, it was true.

Lute figured he would use some of the stuff he got from Burt's to protect the old man, too. He grabbed a pillow case off the bed and loaded it with guns, ammo, jewelry, and gold coins. Except for grabbing a silver tea service off the buffet, Lute was careful to leave the place like he found it. Jubilant, he headed for home, hoping all those crazy women were gone, so he could hide his new stash.

From a beat-up panel truck parked a few houses away, Weldon Cosgrove watched the security cam app on his phone as Lute, carrying a bulky sack, locked the house, got in his car and left. Weldon's pudgy face and balding head turned crimson. He knew that phony minister had been stealing from his dad. Now he had the proof he needed to get rid of that SOB. He closed the app and dialed the number for his attorney.

♦♦♦

Rhoda, lost in an opiate miasma, became aware of the strains of "Bad to the Bone" being played over and over. She tried covering her head with an afghan, but the music continued. Finally, she realized it was her phone. "Hullo?"

"Rhoda? You okay?" asked Ben. "I've been calling off and on for a half hour. What's wrong?"

"Sorry," she slurred through dried lips and cotton mouth. "Been sleeping. Where are you?"

"I'm back at the office. Do you have time to come by before church?"

"Oh damn," Rhoda said, looking at the clock. 4:45. "I must have slept a long time. Cheryl ought to be here any minute, and then we need to head to the church. I'll try to text you when we're done. Sorry."

As predicted, Cheryl came whistling in the door a few minutes later. "Anybody home?"

♦♦♦

Lute could tell the girls had just left. Cheryl's perfume hung in the air like fog. Thank God. He went back to his car, grabbed the pillowcase and carried it inside. He raised his eyes toward the ceiling mumbling his gratitude to his Beloved Savior for the generous gifts. He had just enough time to dig a hole and stash it before he had to meet with that asshole board member and the choir director.

He headed through the sleeping porch to the side door whistling with joy at his good fortune. This stash from Burt was almost enough to give him the security he needed when THEY tried to take over.

"Grrrrrrrrrr," emanated from the dog carrier on the bed.

"Crap. I forgot about you, you worthless rat." Lute turned and saw a note pinned to the dog's carrier.

Lute, I was hoping you could do me a favor. Before you leave, could you put Chief on his leash and take him outside to tinkle? You don't have to walk him; just let him get in the grass and do his business. He'll go right back in his carrier, I promise. Thanks so much, Lute. I owe you one.

"Put him on his leash, my ass." Scowling, Lute opened the carrier, jerking his hand away as the dog nipped at him.

Chief scampered out into the yard while Lute grabbed the shovel, upended the dinghy and dug a hole big enough for his treasure. The dinghy would help cover it. He shoveled dirt and debris over top. Turning the boat back over, Lute went inside, grabbed a piece of chicken off the counter and headed out the door for church.

Chapter 27

Monday, June 17, 7:00 p.m.

"This band's not half bad," shouted Maggie. "Wanna dance?"

Warren/Buddy glared through the dark glasses.

"Come on." Maggie, only willing to dance when she was amply lubricated, grabbed his hand and pulled him up from the chair. "I don't think you need those dark glasses anymore. The sun's down far enough. I don't even know what you look like."

He balked but took the glasses off just as the band broke into a slow rendition of *Layla*. Eric Clapton they were not, but Buddy couldn't resist the chance to hold a woman in his arms, and this one seemed drunk enough to hold on good and tight.

Maggie, mesmerized by Warren's crystal grey eyes, swayed to the music. Having a man wrap his muscular arms around her and nuzzle her neck went a long way to soothe the hurt feelings Cheryl had stirred up the night before. She didn't resist when his lips found hers.

Monday, June 17, 7:00 p.m., Eugenia Church of Helping and Healing in the Name of Jesus Tabernacle

Rhoda had to admit, Cheryl, dressed in her Ralph Lauren, looked both wholesome and beguiling. This outfit tamed the UberBoob with a higher neckline; *Choir Wars* would never go for a sex-pot.

Ed stepped up and addressed the group. "I hope you don't mind, but I'll be directing this evening. Arnold said he'd join us later. Rhoda? Rhoda? Are you ready to begin?" He looked toward the piano.

Shaking her head, she realized she was still a little dazed from whatever pills she had slammed down earlier in the day. "Um, yeah, sorry. Which selection do you want?"

"Let's start with an old country hymn, say, "Down by the River to Pray". We'll sing it once through with accompaniment and then try it a cappella." Ed knew the song had a strong alto part so he could showcase his main talent. "All right, everyone. Let's run through this a few times, so everybody's comfortable with their part before I record. Everyone sings the first verse, and then, Cheryl, you take the first chorus that starts with *Oh, sisters*. After that, Bob, I want you to take the second chorus - *Oh brothers.* Then the bass and tenors sing the *Oh father*s chorus and the altos and sopranos sing *Oh mothers*. Everybody join in on the last verse. Cheryl, we'll have you solo the final chorus with everyone joining in on the Amen."

All eyes were on Ed, but Ed's were only on Cheryl. After a few false starts, the group finally got through the first verse and Cheryl stepped up to the mike.

O sisters, let's go down
Let's go down, come on down
O sisters, let's go down
Down in the river to pray

Monday, June 17, 7:30 p.m., Broken Cleat

The food and dancing helped some, but Maggie still felt a little unsteady. She didn't know if it was the beer or the kiss. Finally, the band took a break. "But don't worry, folks. We're gonna keep the music goin' with some tunes from one of our favorites, *O Brother Where Art Thou?"*

"Weird choice," whispered Buddy/Warren, who still had her in a strong embrace. Just as he started steering her off the dance floor toward a copse of trees, the music blasted through the speakers.

> *O sisters, let's go down,*
> *...Down in the river to pray*

"Oh shit," Maggie jumped back.

"What? Did I hurt you?"

"No. No. Shit. I'm supposed to be at the church right now for an audition."

"Do you sing?"

"Not a note. My sisters are both auditioning for that show *Choir Wars*. I gotta go. How do I get there from here?"

"I don't know. Not much for church going, myself." Buddy/Warren did not want to tip his hand that he knew anything about Lute.

"I'll ask Pops. Sorry." Maggie teetered off toward the bar window.

Though disappointed he wasn't going get any tail, Buddy realized this was a prime chance to hit Lute's house again. Obviously, everyone who lived or was staying there would be at the church, including his almost-had-it piece of ass.

Chapter 28

The longer Maggie pedaled, the more her head cleared. She was kind of relieved to leave Warren behind. She didn't need a man to complicate her life, though the guy was pretty ripped. Maybe she'd go back to the Broken Cleat next weekend.

Pops had told her to head south on the gravel lane about a mile and then west onto another one. Eventually she should reach a paved street, where she was to turn south. The paved road would take her to the church, he promised.

That mile seemed more like two or three, but Maggie decided it was probably because she was half drunk and didn't know where she was. The further she went, the darker it got. She stopped and pulled out her phone. 8:30. God, she was going to miss the whole thing. Cheryl would be so mad. Maggie looked around. That beautiful swamp was turning creepier and darker with each passing minute. She wasn't even sure she was going the right way. She never did get the whole North/South thing. Why didn't people just say right or left? And now the sun was gone, so she couldn't use it as a reference point. She decided to check the map on her phone. No signal. Of course not.

She sighed, wondering how she ended up here in a swamp surrounded by gators and rednecks. It would make for a hell of a "How I Spent My Summer Vacation" essay to share with her students come fall.

The night noises were so loud, she barely heard the truck come up behind her. She just had time to steer off the road as it sped by, spewing rocks and dust in its wake. The soft dirt on the shoulder stopped her forward progress, throwing her and the bike to the ground. She tried to make out the license plate but could only tell it was a beat up light-colored panel truck. "Asshole," she screamed as she threw the bike off her.

◆◆◆

Burt's son, Weldon, hadn't even seen the bike until he almost ran over it. But he didn't slow down to check. He wanted to find that SOB Lute and get his dad's things back. He drove by Lute's house, but no one was home. Weldon knew Lute worked at some church in Eugenia, so he headed for town.

Burt had been giving that jerk stuff for years. Now the old man didn't know anybody anymore, including his own name. But this Lute character continued to prey on him. Granted, Weldon and his dad never had a great relationship. Burt had disowned him when he refused to go into the family business. But now, as the only legal next of kin, Weldon felt sure he could have the old man declared incompetent and get power of attorney. Then, his father's fortune would be his – if Lute hadn't siphoned it all away.

Weldon sped up. It was payback time.

Chapter 29

Monday, June 17, 7:30 p.m.

Lute was still whistling when he opened the back door to the church office. So far, everything was going his way. His crabbing business was off to a good start, his preparations for the revolution almost complete, and his wife was so drug addled and housebound, he didn't have to worry about her getting into his business. In fact, his life was almost perfect. He just had to get rid of those pain in the ass sisters-in-law.

Closing the door to the sanctuary, Lute walked to his desk to prepare for his meeting with the trustees. God only knew what petty complaints they had this time. He didn't even care. He was always able to sweet talk them into letting him stay on. He spotted a letter on top of his desk. It had his name on the front but, obviously, had not come through the mail. While waiting for his meeting to start, he opened it.

TO: Luther Mason

FROM: Eugenia Helping and Healing in the Name of Jesus Tabernacle Board of Trustees

On behalf of the Board of Trustees, we find it our regrettable duty to inform you of your immediate and permanent termination as minister and member of the Eugenia Helping and Healing in the Name of Jesus Tabernacle.

After many discussions among the board and with you, we can no longer tolerate your total disregard for our numerous admonitions regarding the nature of your sermons. While we have valued the service you give to our church community, we find that you have offended many of our parishioners to the point that they are leaving the flock. Our membership has dropped over thirty percent since you began preaching your conspiracy theories and fringe political views. Our congregation wants to hear about the word of God as written in the Good Book, yet you continue to depart from the text.

It is the unanimous decision of the board that you immediately gather your belongings, leave the premises, and sever any and all contact with our church and its members.

Lute felt the blood rising through his neck and face. Those chicken shits weren't even going to give him a chance to defend himself. They had no intention of coming to this meeting. Cowards. Write a wimpy-ass letter and leave it on his desk. His teeth clenched and his heart raced. They were the problem. Them. They all bore the Mark of the Beast. How did he miss it for so long?

"Fuck," he screamed as he pushed the desk over.

Chapter 30

Monday, June 17, after dark, Oolehatchee

Swamp

After determining nothing was broken or gashed, she assessed her situation. Maggie took great pride in her stoicism; whether breaking up knife fights at school, surviving failed relationships or losing loved ones, she remained calm and collected. She was known by all as one tough cookie. This cookie was crumbling fast. Sitting on the side of the road, inches from the edge of the swamp, she dropped her head in her hands. Wracking sobs mimicked the gator honks. Tears dripped off her face onto the ground for what seemed like hours.

Spent, scared and slightly hung over, she wiped her face on her sleeve. Once the pounding in her head abated, she listened to the swamp – owls, gators, frogs, and god knew what else kept a steady chorus. Wait. What was that? A crunching, sliding sound. Definitely not animal. Car?

No. Not a car. Too quiet for a car. She tensed. Whatever it was, it was getting closer. She tried to scoot back into the brush, but hit water, soaking the back of her shorts.

Another bike rode past. She peeked out of the brush. "Warren?"

The man on the bike slowed just ahead of her. He looked around.

"Warren, is that you?"

Buddy, forgetting his alias, started to ride off.

"Warren? Help. It's me, Maggie." She stood up and stepped into the road.

Damn. Just his luck. "Uh, yeah. Maggie? What the hell are you doing over there? Aren't you supposed to be at church?"

"Obviously, I didn't make it. I got lost."

Buddy took in her scraped up arms and face. "What happened to you?"

"I think I missed a turn. Then a truck almost hit me, and I fell over." Tears formed in her eyes again. "What are you doing out here?"

"Uh, well, this is the way to my brother's." He was glad he hadn't mentioned where his brother lived. "Are you hurt?"

"I don't think so," Maggie said as she brushed herself off.

"So, you've just been sitting out here? You've been gone a couple of hours."

"I know. You wouldn't happen to know your way around, would you? I just want to go back to my sister's, but I don't know if I'm headed the right way."

Be careful, man. Do not let on you know exactly where her sister lives.

Buddy walked up to her. "Do you have an address or a street name? I don't know the place real well, but I've been around a little."

"It's over off County Road 7 on the edge of the swamp. It's in an old fish camp. The house number is 40a."

Buddy scratched his head and thought. Finally, he said, "I think I've seen where some County Road splits off this one."

"Can you find it?"

"I can try. Follow me." He did not want to drive up to the house and have a chance encounter with Lute. "I'm kind of in a hurry to get back to my brother's, but I'll help you look for the road at least."

Maggie let out a deep breath. "Thanks so much. If you can get me on the right road, I can find it."

Chapter 31

Monday, June 17, 8:00 p.m., Eugenia Church of Helping and Healing in the Name of Jesus Tabernacle

"That's it, ladies and gentlemen. I think we're ready to formally record the next contestants on *Choir Wars*."

Fist pumps and cheers rose in the room.

Ed continued. "Take a minute to make yourselves picture perfect and then line up. Sing it exactly the way you just did." Ed used the time to adjust the camera for the audition.

The women checked themselves in mirrors, patting down their lacquered once-a-week hair. Cheryl, already picturesque, took a small sip of water and a few yoga breaths, visualizing herself on television.

After getting the equipment ready, Ed herded everyone into position on the risers. He checked the view through the camera, signaled Rhoda to strike the opening note and counted down from five with his fingers. Silently, he pointed at the choir to begin.

Monday, June 17, evening, Ramona's house

Ramona gasped at the small wrapped box in Delmont's hand. "What have you gone and done, Del?"

Delmont blushed and looked at the floor. "What's it look like? I got you a present. Go ahead. Open it." He looked at her face.

"You didn't need to buy me nothing," she said as she grabbed the box, tore off the paper and opened it. She smiled up at Delmont. "What is this?"

"It's a promise ring. You said you wanted to say we were engaged. Well, the lady at Walmart tole me that a promise ring says we're gonna get engaged - we promise." Delmont was getting nervous. He thought Ramona would jump up and hug him when she opened it, but she just kept staring at the ring in the box. "Didn't you mean that?" A fine sweat broke out on his upper lip.

Finally, she looked up at him. There were tears in her eyes. "Oh Del. It's the most beautiful thing I've ever seen. Of course, I meant it. I'd love to be promised to you. Quick. Put it on me," she laughed through the tears.

"Wow, you scared me. I thought you was gonna say no." He took the ring and put it on her finger. "It's what they call sterling silver and that's a real diamond. The jewelry lady kept callin' it one thirtieth of a carrot, and I said I wanted a real diamond."

"Is it? Real, I mean?"

"She swore it was. I asked her what a carrot was, and she told me that's just a word they use for the size of it. She promised it's a genuine diamond."

"I've never seen anything like it, Del. The way it spells out LOVE and how the O is heart-shaped."

155

"I know. See that little sparkle in the O? That's the diamond."

"I guess we're the real thing, too, then Del. A real couple." Ramona smiled up at him so sweetly he felt weak in the knees.

◆◆◆

"Does this look like it?" asked Buddy/Warren, stopping at a Y in the road.

"Oh, you found it. Thanks so much. I know where I am now. I can get there from here," said Maggie.

"No problem. I'd take you on home, but I gotta get back to my brother's. I'm already late." Buddy/Warren got back on his bike. "See ya' later, I hope."

"Yeah, me too," Maggie waved. "And thanks again."

As she watched him pedal away, a flash of recognition sparked. She shook her head to clear it. Must be the hangover. She mounted her bike and rode on to Rhoda's.

Chapter 32

Monday, June 17, 8:00 p.m.

Arnold came in the front door of the church intending to go straight to his meeting with Lute and the trustees, but he realized Ed was recording, so he stood silently in place. Cheryl, singing her first solo, would have stopped him in his tracks anyway. Every note and word she sang pealed like heavenly bells. He felt goose bumps.

As the tenors and basses started their verse in perfect unison and pitch, the church office door banged open. Everyone turned toward the sound.

"FUCK YOU ALL!!!" shouted Lute from the doorway, shaking a piece of paper over his head.

Arnold, seeing Lute's crazed eyes and crimson face, quickly moved from the entryway toward him.

"You and the rest of your Nazi, cock-sucking, limp-dicked, white-bread trustees can have this viper pit of hell and damnation," Lute screamed at Arnold, waving the letter in his face. "You godless infidels will feel the wrath of the Lord Almighty!" At this, Lute spread his arms wide and raised his face toward the ceiling. "His judgment is swift and certain." Spittle flew from his foaming mouth as he swung a hard right fist into the choir director's face, dropping him to the floor. "I am the only instrument of thy God." With his foot on the unconscious man's chest, Lute ripped the letter into pieces letting them drift down on his face. "There it is for all to see," he growled as he looked down, "the Mark of the Beast." Lute stabbed a finger in the middle of Arnold's forehead.

The choir, frozen in place, mouths open from singing their last note, stared in terror. Ed stepped toward Lute. "Reverend, please …" A fist shot in his face before he could complete the sentence.

Cheryl screamed like King Kong was after her. Tears streamed down her face as she rushed to help Ed. "You maniac," she sobbed toward Lute. "What have you done?"

Lute came at her.

"Get the hell away from me," she cried just as Ed, regaining his composure, grabbed Lute by the back of his collar and shoved him toward the door.

Lute paused under the EXIT sign. "Rot in hell, all of you," he snarled as he stormed out of the building.

Slowly the choir came to life. Arnold's wife, Mary, rushed to his side just as he came to. Other women ran to their husbands. Everyone talked at once.

"What happened to him?"

"Are you all right?"

"Deliver us from evil."

As the hubbub ensued, Rhoda slipped a pill out of her pocket and into her mouth.

Cheryl tried to get control of the group when she noticed Ed dismantling the camera equipment. Frantically, she yelled above the chaos, "Come on everyone. Let's rise above this. Let's sing to the Glory of God and drive the evil out of this church for good." She looked toward Ed. "Let's finish our audition tape and prove that our faith can overcome any obstacle."

Ed shook his head. "Sorry, Cheryl. It's not going to happen." He looked down at Arnold. "Sorry, Arnold. Best of luck to you."

Ed's niece flew toward him and grabbed at his sleeve. "Oh, please, Uncle Eddie. Please."

He looked at her and then at his sister. "Sorry sweetheart. This is just too much. We tried, but I don't need this. I can put up with a lot of bullshit, and I do, but tonight was over the top. Sorry." Camera equipment in hand, he headed for the door.

◆◆◆

Weldon didn't realize the main street of downtown Eugenia was lined with store front churches. He parked down the block from the Fill Up n Eat and started walking, getting angrier with each step. He passed the Run for Your Life Ministries, The Deliverance Through Aggression Chapel and the Eugenia Healing and Helping in the Name of Jesus Tabernacle. He could see a light on in the last one though the windows were painted white. Then he saw it – Parson Luther Mason.

◆◆◆

"Wait, please, Uncle Eddie," pleaded his niece.

"Well, I don't know…" he said.

As Ed hesitated, the front door slammed open.

"Where the hell is Lute Mason?" As the disheveled man strode into the church, Ed sprinted around him and out the door.

Ignoring the stranger and the men who approached him, Cheryl sunk into a chair and sobbed. Everything had started out so perfectly. She was so close to finally making it. It was all Lute's fault. And she had been his only champion on so many occasions. Whenever Maggie or anyone else they knew bad-mouthed him, she gave him the benefit of the doubt. And now he had ruined her life. Everyone had been right all along. Well, she wasn't going to wait for any judgment day to come around. She would ruin Lute if it was the last thing she did on this earth.

Energized with a thirst for vengeance, she stood up, wiped her tears and walked over to Rhoda.

"You ready to get out of this madhouse?" Cheryl asked.

Rhoda looked up at her with glassy eyes. "Huh?"

"Are you all right?" asked Cheryl, noticing Rhoda's dilated pupils.

Rhoda took a deep breath as her shoulders sagged. "Yeah. Yeah, I guess. I mean, it's been a hell of a night."

Cheryl nodded. "Understatement. Listen, I'm getting out of here. I can't stand it anymore. I'm going back to your place to pack and head home. I can't spend another minute in the same town as that jack-ass husband of yours. Let's go."

Rhoda didn't even react.

"Rhoda? Are you coming with me?"

Rhoda sighed again. "No. Not yet. I'm going to hang around here for a while and see if Lute comes back."

"He's not coming back here; are you crazy? After that rampage? Come on, let's go."

"No. I'm not ready yet. You go ahead. If he doesn't show up, I'll find a ride." She noticed Cheryl's arched brow. "Really, I'll be fine. Somebody here will give me a ride if I need it. You go on. I don't blame you a bit for wanting to cut and run. I wish I could."

"You can. You and Maggie come home with me. Come on. Get away from this insanity," Cheryl begged.

"I said NO."

Cheryl, having never heard a harsh word out of Rhoda's mouth, stepped back. "Okay, okay. Sorry. I'll probably be gone by the time you get home, though. I am not hanging around that place any longer than I have to. Goodbye." She stomped off, gathered her things and looked back at Rhoda. "Just be careful. Please."

Monday, June 17, 9:00 p.m.

"That son-of-a-bitch is gonna pay for this one. He's gonna learn you don't mess with me, by God," Cheryl screamed at the windshield the entire way back to Rhoda's.

She didn't anger easily, but once she did, it consumed her. She didn't even care that mascara-tears were staining her beloved Ralph Lauren. Still spewing verbal venom, she pulled into Rhoda's driveway, got out of the car, and marched up the steps. "Damn HIM," she said as she threw open the front door.

Maggie, sitting in the dark living room, looked up. "Cheryl? Were you swearing? What's going on?"

"Damn you, too," sobbed Cheryl as she flipped on the light.

"What happened?" Maggie jumped up from the couch and pulled Cheryl into a hug.

"Oh my God, you wouldn't believe it. It was a nightmare," Cheryl sobbed onto her sister's shoulder, then looked up. "Where were you? Why weren't you at the church?"

"Long stupid-Maggie story, but it doesn't matter. Tell me what happened."

Cheryl started relating the night's events as she headed for the sleeping porch to pack. "Everything was going perfectly. The song we rehearsed sounded great, and Ed had just started recording the audition tape," she said as she yanked her clothes from the closet and threw them in the suitcase. "Then at the exact moment I started singing my solo, that crazy-ass, bastard brother-in-law of ours came storming out of his office. I mean, he was completely unhinged - literally foaming at the mouth."

"You're kidding." None of this took Maggie by surprise.

"No, I'm not kidding. He was flailing his arms over his head and practically speaking in tongues about some Nazi, limp-dick something or other."

Maggie started laughing.

"It's NOT FUNNY. He single-handedly ruined my chance at stardom."

"Sorry, just the Nazi limp-dick thing…" Maggie struggled to suppress a smile. "So, what happened then?"

"Lute punched that sweet little choir director in the face and knocked him out cold. Ed tried to reason with Lute, and the son-of-a bitch hit Ed."

"You are making this up," said Maggie.

"Would I be cussing and crying and wadding up my designer clothes if I was making this up? Lute left the church, and Ed said he quit. He wasn't going to do the audition with us."

"Oh, Cheryl," Maggie knew how heart-broken she must have been. "I'm so sorry. Couldn't you convince him to stay and try again?"

"I tried. His sister and his niece tried, but just when he looked like he might come back, some other lunatic came bursting through the door screaming for Lute."

"That did it, huh?"

"Ed ran like a scared rabbit. Never looked back," Cheryl put her face in her Michael Kors outfit and wept.

Chapter 33

Monday, June 17, 9:00 p.m.

Rhoda looked toward the window in Lute's office. The room was dark. After everyone left, she yelled for Lute. No answer. She rolled to the office then looked in the parking lot to make sure he was gone. She searched her phone for Ben's last text and hit reply.

Can you come get me at church? I'll wait out back, so no one will see you.

You alone?

Yes. Place is empty. It's safe.

Be there soon. Watch out for Lute. Let me know if he shows up.

Ben waited right behind the church office door for Rhoda. He had driven by once and flashed his lights to signal no one else was in the area. "What took you so long tonight?" Ben asked, as he held the door for her and put her knee walker in the backseat.

"You wouldn't believe it if you'd seen it. I can't even talk about it. I just want to get the hell away from here. What a night," Rhoda sighed.

"Wow. Okay. You sure we're not going to get caught together?" Ben swiveled his head checking every direction for Lute.

"Relax," she said. "Everybody's gone home, and Lute will definitely not be back here tonight. I'm sure he's down by the dock getting hammered. I honestly don't know when I'll see him again."

"How'd you get away from your sisters? I worried you'd gotten tied up with them all night."

"I don't know what happened to Maggie. She never showed up, and Cheryl was so upset about the Hollywood producer quitting, she stormed off in a huff."

"The producer quit?"

"Like I said, I can't get into it all right now. Too upsetting. Just get me out of here." Rhoda looked so forlorn, he didn't press for details.

"Do you want to go home or to my office?" he asked.

"Definitely not home. Office, I guess."

"Okay." They rode without conversation.

The street was quiet when they arrived. Ben helped her and the scooter to the sidewalk out front. "I'll drop you here and park in back. You think you'll be okay for a minute?"

Rhoda looked around. The surrounding houses were dark. "Yeah. I'll be okay. Just hurry."

While she waited for Ben, she checked her phone. Lute hadn't called or texted. Good. He was probably halfway through a bottle of rum by now.

Before Ben could come back around the building, a car flew down the road, headed straight for Rhoda. Headlights blinded her. Just as the car swerved in her direction, it screeched to a stop. Stunned, she stood rooted to the ground.

Not bothering to turn off the car, Lute threw open the door and lunged, shoving her to the curb. "YOU LYING WHORE. I KNEW YOU WERE SCREWING THIS SHAMAN." Lute's face was purple as he stood straddling her. She started to kick him with her good leg when his foot stomped on her bad one. "Don't even think about it, bitch."

Ben, hearing the ruckus before he rounded the building, ran toward them. "Leave her the hell alone, you bastard."

His foot still pinning Rhoda to the ground, Lute swung out his arm and caught Ben across the throat, dropping him to the sidewalk.

"You've hit her for the last time," threatened Ben, as he jumped up. Taking a step toward Lute, Ben felt a hand grab his ankle. He looked down at Rhoda, crying and bleeding on the sidewalk.

"Don't, Ben, please," Rhoda whispered between sobs. "I'm sorry, Lute. It's not what you think. So sorry…."

The distraction gave Lute just enough time to scramble for the car, throw it in gear and annihilate the scooter as he sped off.

Monday, June 17, 9:45 p.m.

Maggie rubbed Cheryl's back until she stopped crying. "Let me get you some water. Just sit down and rest for a minute."

"I don't want to stay here one second longer than I have to. I swear if that bastard shows up while I'm here, I'll kill him with my own bare hands," said Cheryl as the tears began again.

Maggie was determined to calm her down before she tried to drive anywhere. "Well, your night certainly beat mine."

"Yeah? Why didn't you come to the audition?" Cheryl looked up at Maggie for the first time since she came in the door. "Dear God, look at you. You're filthy. What in the world is in your hair?"

"Leaves and mud and god knows what all is in my hair, under my eyelids, on my clothes and all over my arms and face," said Maggie.

"What happened?"

"I went to the Broken Cleat this afternoon and thought I'd sit there, have a beer and look at the water. I just wanted a little peace after this crazy week."

"And?"

"I met this guy who bought me a few drinks, and we danced some, and then I realized I was late for the audition. So, I took off on my bike, in the dark, and started riding down those creepy gravel roads by the swamp. Just when I realized I was completely lost, some stupid panel truck came flying down the road and almost hit me."

Cheryl gasped. "Oh no! Are you hurt?"

"No, but he ran me off the road, where I proceeded to fly ass-over-teacup into the muck. Hence, the hairdo and slime covered outfit."

"A panel truck? There was an old beat up panel truck outside the church when I left," said Cheryl. "I think it belonged to the crazy guy who came looking for Lute."

"Well," said Maggie, "I hope he found him. Maybe he actually ran him over." Maggie paused. "Did you hear something?" She paused again.

Cheryl cocked her head to listen. "It's Chief barking. That shit-head Lute was supposed to put him back in his carrier."

They both ran out the door to the carport and scanned the yard.

"Chief? Come here, boy. Chief," Cheryl called.

Maggie switched on the light behind the house and screamed.

Cheryl followed Maggie's gaze. An undulating, scaly monster made its way across the yard to the swamp. "CHIEF!" shrieked Cheryl as she took off running.

"Cheryl, STOP. It'll knock you down and drag you off," Maggie cried.

Slowing her steps, Cheryl kept calling Chief. As she neared the gator, it turned its head toward her. A jeweled collar hung from a huge tooth.

Cheryl wailed, "Chieeeeefffff...." as Maggie grabbed her arm and dragged her back through the carport into the house.

Chapter 34

Buddy cursed his bad luck all the way back to the Gone Fishin' Mobile Home Resort. Now there was no chance of treasure hunting at Lute's tonight. He should have left the bar the minute he heard that woman was Lute's sister-in-law. You're slipping, Bud. You're getting soft hanging around this hick town.

By the time he reached Delmont's, he had it figured out. First, he would go to the pawn shop and get some ammunition for the Glock. Then he would head over to Lute's some night and grab everything he could. He'd cash in, buy a car, leave a little money for Del and get out of this place. Look up one of the other guys who'd been released and look for some kind of work. The lights were on when he got to Del's.

"Hey, Buddy." Delmont, dressed in clean, neat clothes, sat on the couch like he'd been expecting him.

"Hey. What're you grinning about? You drunk?"

"I guess you could say that," smiled Del. "Drunk on love."

Buddy resisted the urge to roll his eyes. "Love, huh? You talking about your main squeeze, the church girl?"

Delmont frowned and jumped off the couch toward Buddy. "Don't call her a main squeeze. She's a good woman, a real lady."

"Whoa, Del," Buddy backed up. "I was just kidding. Sorry. What's going on?"

Del relaxed and started grinning again. "Well, I took that gold coin Lute give me and pawned it in town. Then I took the bus over to the Walmart and got Ramona a genuine diamond ring. We're promised to be engaged."

"Married? Are you…" Buddy was about to say crazy, but stopped short when he saw Delmont's beaming face. Poor kid. He'd had a rough life. Buddy had been too busy trying to keep them both safe from their daddy to try and have fun with him.

Before Delmont was born, their mom had read stories and sung to Buddy when she could. But that second baby had set his daddy off. Buddy could still hear him screaming, "I don't want no other kids. Shit, woman, I didn't even want this one," he would point at Buddy. The beatings began before Delmont was born and never stopped. So, no, Delmont had never really had a chance to be happy.

"Well, I'll be damned, Del," Buddy reached out to shake his hand. "Imagine that. My kid brother went and fell in love. Congratulations."

"Gee, thanks, Bud. We don't got any plans to marry yet or anything. I gotta save me some money. We haven't even told her folks yet. But she said yes, so I guess it's gonna happen."

"Good for you, Del. You deserve a little happiness," said Buddy. The news only strengthened his desire to get as much out of Lute as possible, no matter what. He'd leave more than a little of it for Del. He was glad, too, to think that Del had a nice girl to look after him.

◆◆◆

"I'm gonna kill that fucking asshole. I can't believe he did this." Ben knelt on the sidewalk and examined Rhoda's leg. It was hard to tell with the cast if Lute had reinjured the break or caused any further damage. "Can you feel this?" he asked, scratching the bottom of her toes.

"Yes," sniffled Rhoda.

"Try wiggling them."

They wiggled.

"Did that hurt?"

"Everything hurts, for chrissakes," she snarled.

He looked over the cast and determined it wasn't cracked or broken anywhere, only scuffed and dirty. "It's probably okay, but let me take you to the ER for an x-ray."

"No. I do not want to go back to that hospital. Help me get up," Rhoda said.

He hoisted her upright, then had her try to put weight on the injured leg. "How's that? Any new pain?"

"Not in my leg or foot anyway. I've got sidewalk burns and my head is killing me, but no. The leg is no worse."

Ben started walking her toward his car. "You're going home with me. I do not want you back in that house with him."

Rhoda stopped. "No. I have to go home. I'll have Maggie or Cheryl come get me."

"What the hell is wrong with you?" Ben screamed. "The man breaks your leg, tries to run you down, completely neglects you, takes all your money, and you're going home to HIM?" His eyes were bulging with rage.

"I can't explain it. It's just…" Rhoda started crying.

Ben turned, got in his car and drove off.

Can you come pick me up? I'm hurt, but not bad. I'll be sitting on the steps of the office where I used to work.

Chapter 35

Monday, June 17, 10:30 p.m.

Maggie stood at the end of the driveway, mouth agape, as Cheryl's tail lights were swallowed up by the dust and dark. She had begged her not to go until she calmed down, but Cheryl refused. "If I'm here when Lute shows back up, I'll kill him; but I'm a Christian woman and I won't spend eternity in Hell for that piece of trash. I hate to leave my precious Chief, but..." Cheryl was still sobbing as she climbed in her car.

Maggie looked up at the black sky. "If you're up there, Lord, please help her get home safe." Her attempt at prayer was interrupted by the ding of her phone. What else could possibly happen tonight? She looked at the screen to see the message from Rhoda.

Maggie's fingers flew over the keys. What are you doing there? Are you alone? Where's Lute?

Just come now, pinged the reply.

Fortunately, Rhoda had left the keys in her car, so Maggie got in and headed for town. She had enough of a signal to use the GPS. As she drove, she realized where she had missed the turn and ended up so lost earlier. She arrived at the doctor's office within minutes to find Rhoda sitting on the steps, slumped against the railing. Maggie threw open the door and ran to her sister. "What are you doing here in the middle of the night?"

Rhoda raised her bovine eyes, shimmering with fear, and shook her head.

Maggie's heart ached. Whatever happened, it had vanquished the spark of humor always present in her oldest sister. Wordlessly, she helped Rhoda up and into the car. Maggie didn't ask about the scrapes and scratches down her sister's back or the road-kill knee walker.

Settled in the seat, Rhoda leaned her head against the window, her arms limp, her breathing shallow. They rode in silence to the trailer. When they arrived, Maggie walked around the car to help her out.

"Is anyone home?" Rhoda finally spoke.

"No one was here when I left. You want me to go check?" Maggie asked.

Rhoda nodded.

After searching the place, Maggie came back outside. Rhoda had managed to turn in the seat and put her feet on the ground. She looked up for an answer.

Again, those saucered eyes bored through Maggie's heart. "No one's here," Maggie reassured her. As kids, Rhoda had always been the one to take care of Maggie. When Maggie broke something or forgot to do a chore, Rhoda took the blame. When Maggie came home crying over some stupid teenage squabble, Rhoda reassured her, bolstered her self-confidence and had her laughing within minutes. Her heroic big sister had tested and pushed through the stringent boundaries set by their demanding mother. Though Rhoda paid dearly for her insubordination, Maggie and Cheryl enjoyed easier childhoods because of it. To see her lifelong pillar shattered like this was almost more than Maggie could bear.

"Come on. Let's go in." Maggie led her up the steps and into the kitchen where she washed the gravel and dirt off Rhoda's arms and back. "Where's that little bag-o-pills you keep stashed around here?"

Registering a reaction for the first time, Rhoda looked up. "What bag of pills?"

"Easy, girl. Let's dig that baby out and find something to calm us both down. Then we can sort through this night from hell."

"Under my side of the bed," Rhoda sighed.

♦♦♦

Interstate 10 was deserted, except for Cheryl's car. "God must be watching out for me," she said, once she had stopped crying. She looked down at the speedometer. Ninety. She mashed the accelerator, tightened her already white-knuckled grip on the wheel, and continued toward home. She wouldn't allow herself to think about the night's events, especially Chief, so she sang. *Nobody knows the trouble I've seen. Nobody knows but Jeeeeesus...*

Her throat was dry and scratchy by the time she pulled into the safety of her own garage. Dazed and exhausted, she stepped over dog toys, fell on the bed and slept.

Tuesday, June 18, pre-dawn

"That son of bitch," said Buddy when they arrived at the docks. The *Eula Mae* sat dark and unhitched. "He said we'd go out again today. Said the yields were the highest of the season this week. Where the hell is he?"

Delmont climbed up on the wheel of the trailer and peered down at the mess in the crabber. "Here he is." Lute was sprawled on the floor of the boat, dead asleep and snoring. Del reached down and shook him. No response. "He don't look like he's ready to go crabbin'. Stinks like puke."

"Worthless asshole. Probably tied one on. Well, he may not need the money, but I sure do," Buddy's rage simmered.

"You?" said Delmont, coming as close to angry as he got. "I got to save up to marry Ramona." Delmont's bottom lip stuck out as he climbed down. "I'm startin' to think I don't like this Lute guy very much."

"Me neither, Del. Me neither."

Tuesday, June 18, morning

When sunlight seared through the missing jalousie and onto Maggie's face, she bolted upright. "Who's there?" She looked around and listened. Nothing seemed to stir in the house. 10:30. She couldn't remember the last time she had slept so late. Of course, she hadn't gone to bed until well after midnight, nor had she ever taken a Xanax before. But Rhoda said they shut down your mind, so they both swallowed one and went to bed.

She tiptoed through the house, finding Rhoda still asleep and no sign of Lute. A shower would help clear her head and wash away the swamp crud still caked in her hair. After drying off and getting dressed, she looked over the carport and yard. This became her morning routine since the nocturnal pandemonium had begun. Her bike, a little scratched and bent, rested against the jasmine bush. The car was where she left it last night. In fact, for the first time in days the yard looked undisturbed.

She looked back at the bicycle. A memory stirred. What was it about a bike and that jasmine bush?

"Did you ever hear from Cheryl last night?" called Rhoda from the kitchen.

The bike memory evaporated as Maggie went back in the house. "When did you get up?"

"Just now," said Rhoda. "Have you heard from Cheryl? I didn't, but she's probably mad at me after last night."

Maggie checked her phone. Sure enough, she had missed a text during her drug-induced coma last night. "Here it is. It just says 'home.' It was sent at two-thirty this morning. Oh, that poor thing. I hope she was able to get some sleep. She was inconsolable about Chief."

"Chief?" Rhoda was expecting to hear how mad Cheryl was about Ed shit-canning the whole audition. "What happened to Chief?"

"Oh, Rhoda, it was horrible." Maggie proceeded to tell her about Cheryl's rant and then hearing the dog bark.

"A gator ate Chief?" Rhoda gasped.

"I guess so. I mean, all we ever saw was the bloody collar in the gator's mouth, but, well, it was pretty gruesome."

"Goddamn Lute. He started all this. I mean, first he left the dog out, then he went all postal at church and started cold-cocking people. Sometimes I hate that man," Rhoda said.

"Sometimes? My god, Rhoda, what's it going to take for you to get away from that abusive son of bitch? Are you just going to sit here and wait for him to kill you?" Maggie was incredulous. No matter what kind of bond held their marriage together, last night had to have been the final straw.

Rhoda straightened her shoulders. "No. I'm not. I'm not going to take it anymore. But you leave it to me. I have an idea how to get rid of him for good. No more stalking, no more stealing, no more hitting."

Maggie stared. She had never heard Rhoda stand up for herself. "What are you going to do? I know Cheryl has a great divorce attorney. Let me get the number from her."

"No. You and Cheryl stay out of it. I mean it. I made this mess, and I'm going to clean it up once and for all. By myself. In my own way." Rhoda stood up and hobbled over to the sink, using the chair back for support.

"If that's what you want, okay. But we're both here to help if you need us."

"I know, and I appreciate it. I will handle this. But I'm warning you. Do not interfere. And don't question my actions. Promise?"

"Okay, okay." Maggie didn't like where this conversation was headed. "What happened to the knee walker?' Rhoda had not related the events that left her on the steps of the medical office, bruised and bleeding, in the middle of the night.

"Let's just say it broke."

At least that was something positive Maggie could do. "I'll find you another one today. Have you heard from Lute?"

"No. And I hope I don't. But I'm sure he'll come back, tail between his legs, begging for forgiveness," said Rhoda.

"Well, don't let him in, for god's sake."

"You leave everything to me, baby sister. I can handle Lute Mason."

The incongruity of that remark, coming from a beat up, broken woman, defied all logic. But then, Rhoda had never been known for her common sense.

Chapter 36

Tuesday, June 18, morning

Lute woke under the blazing sun with an empty bottle of rum still in his hand. His head pounded, and his stomach churned. His eyes were so inflamed, he could barely see. Something sharp poked his back. Slowly he turned his head and realized he was on the deck of the Mako, lying on the anchor. "Thit," he muttered, his swollen, gauzy tongue stuck to the top of his mouth. He propped himself up on an elbow. Had he fallen on the anchor or did someone push him down? He couldn't recall anything after pulling up to the Cleat. "Thit," he muttered again, as the memory of the church and the scene with Rhoda flooded his aching brain.

"How's it goin' in there, Cap'n?" called Pops from the dock. He stepped up on the boat trailer and climbed in, then handed Lute a bottle of water.

Squinting into the sun surrounding Pops, Lute sat up, grabbed the bottle and drained it. He promptly vomited the entire contents of his stomach in his own lap.

"Tough night, pal?" Pops was not laughing. In fact, he looked pissed. "Really tied one on, you know. I think you owe me for more than a few tables and umbrellas."

Lute put his throbbing head in his hands. "What happened?"

"Well, you came tearing in here like a madman about 10:00 and ordered your first bottle, which you drained in record time. Then, and I take some responsibility for this, you ordered a second one, which I served you. After that, you swung at everything and everybody in sight, including the sound equipment for the band. Cleared the place out fast. What the hell got into you?"

Lute squinted up at Pops. "What about Rhoda? How's Rhoda?"

"How the hell do I know? She wasn't here."

"I gotta get back to Rhoda. I gotta apologize."

Pops leaned down and jabbed a finger in Lute's chest. "What you gotta do is get your shit together. I'm gonna total up these damages, and I want paid in full, like yesterday."

Lute dropped his head back into his hands as Pops climbed out of the boat and stomped off down the dock.

◆◆◆

Maggie planned to drive into Starke for a knee walker when she remembered that Lute bought the first one at a pawn shop. She had seen a pawn and pay-day loan near the church in town. It would certainly save her time to check there first.

A bell jingled as she walked through the door. She looked around at the amazing array of absolute junk for sale, most of it coated with dust and cobwebs. Obviously, the articles on display were not the high-ticket items. She looked for some semblance of organization, like maybe records in one place, computers in another and, hopefully, medical equipment somewhere else, without success. She was digging through a pile by the window when a man said, "Can I help you find somethin', ma'am?"

She jumped. "Oh, you startled me."

"Sorry, ma'am. Name's Burwinkle, Vernon Burwinkle. What kin I do for you?" He was an impressively big, unkempt man. "Don't think I've seen you around before. You new in town?"

"Yes. I'm just visiting my sister, Rhoda Mason? She broke her knee walker, and I wondered if you had any others I could get for her?"

"It broke? Well, shoot, that was the nicest one I had. But yeah, I got some more over here." Vernon squeezed around the counter and started dismantling a pile along the wall. Beneath a giant boom box, two Tandy computer terminals, and a befouled handicap commode seat, he unearthed a rusted knee walker. "How 'bout this one?" he said, as he jerked it out from under the pile. "The handle grip's a little cracked, but I think some duct tape would take care of that for you."

Maggie tried to contain a gag. "Is that the only one you have left?"

"Yep, I'm pretty sure. We get a lot a call for medical supplies here. Can hardly keep these toilet seats in stock. You need one of these, too?" He shoved it in her face.

She turned her head, so he wouldn't see her retch. Recovering quickly, she said, "Um no. Just the walker. How much is that one?"

Vernon looked for a tag. "I'm not sure, but I remember who pawned it. Let me look up the card and see. You take a look around and see if there's somethin' else you might like while I check," he said as he went in the back room.

Maggie had zero interest in anything here, so she stood at the glass display case. After waiting for what seemed an extraordinary amount of time, Maggie looked down. Lots of watches, cuff links, rings, necklaces - each the broken or abandoned dreams of some poor soul. Then she spotted it. Cheryl's diamond necklace, displayed on a silk scarf like the Hope Diamond.

"Here we go," grunted Vern as he reentered the room. He noticed the object of her attention. Vern may have looked stupid, but he could put two and two together. He'd just bought the diamond from Lute a few days ago. "I see you've noticed our star attraction." He leaned toward her, narrowed his eyes and said, "You lookin' for some jewelry?"

If he was trying to intimidate her, it worked. Maggie stuttered, "Uh. Wow. Ha. No. I mean no. I'm not really the jewelry type. That's a real beauty, though. Who would ever part with that, I wonder?"

Vern stared at her a long time. "Sad story really. Guy over in the next town, his wife of sixty years died. Didn't have no kids, and he couldn't stand to see it layin' around the house. Broke his heart every time, s'what he told me. So, he sold it. Thought maybe some other guy who loved his wife just as much would want it."

Maggie noticed this heart-rending story was delivered with no emotion. He had sensed her wariness? "Poor old man. That's just heart breaking. Now, what do I owe you for the scooter?" She said quickly as she dug out her wallet.

"Normally, I'd take thirty dollars for it, but bein' as it's for Lute's wife, you can have it for twenty."

"Well aren't you sweet," she said, slapping two tens on the counter, grabbing the scooter and making her way toward the door.

"Don't you want a receipt for that?"

"Oh, no thanks. I don't think we'll be bringing this back. Kind of handy to have around. Thanks again. Nice to meet you," she said as she stepped through the door and hurried to the car.

Chapter 37

Tuesday, June 18, morning

As soon as Maggie left, Rhoda grabbed three fossilized chickens out of the freezer. Hobbling out to the carport, she threw them in the washing machine. Turning on the hot water heavy-duty cycle, she pushed start. That ought to get some high-grade salmonella and e coli growing. Whistling the Beatles' "Run for Your Life", Rhoda limped inside.

Back in the kitchen, she chopped and sautéed onions, carrots, and garlic, then stirred in a can of curry powder, a can of cayenne and a can of tomatoes. She smiled as she worked, listening to the washer all but walk across the carport, chickens banging like bowling balls during the spin cycle. When it finally stopped, she stumbled back out, removed the chickens to an empty paint bucket and set it directly in the sun.

She was slicing the spoiled meat from the bone when Maggie pulled in the drive. Tossing the chicken into the redolent sauté mixture, she set it in the oven on warm.

"Oh God Bless your sweet heart," she said as Maggie wheeled in the scooter. "That's a real humdinger."

"Yeah, sorry about that. It was the only one Vernon Burwinkle had. Let me disinfect it and tape up the handles. It's better than nothing, I guess."

Rhoda smiled. "It's fine. Kind of goes with the ambience of the whole house, don't you think?"

Maggie looked surprised, "What do you mean?"

"Oh Maggie, I know I live in a shit box. You don't have to pretend. But I'm going to take care of all that. Trust me."

"What in the world are you cooking?"

"Chicken curry. But, it's too spicy for you. Don't try it. Really, it's a killer. But it's Lute's favorite."

Maggie's eyebrows arched. "Why are you cooking for that bastard?"

"No questions, remember? In fact, I don't think I'm up to eating it either. Would you mind going to Starke to pick up some groceries? Some more of those frozen pizzas would be good."

Tuesday, June 18, mid-morning

Why the radio silence? Are you upset with me, too? You need to call me. I have big news that directly involves you. LU

Cheryl turned off the phone after reading Maggie's message. She couldn't call. Not even Maggie, although none of this was her fault. It was too painful to think about the last couple of days. She felt like her whole reason for being had vanished. Work was her only refuge right now. On the other hand, Maggie had mentioned big news. She was afraid to hope that Maggie found Chief. Maybe Ed had decided to try again, or maybe someone else had taped the practice. Perhaps she'd call over her lunch break.

Chapter 38

Tuesday, June 18, early afternoon

Steeled with a heavy dose of Xanax and Prozac, Rhoda prepared for Lute's arrival. He'd come home begging forgiveness, expecting her to buckle under, as usual. Well, she wasn't the broken-down mental case he thought she was, poor sucker. He was bringing a knife to a gun fight.

She smiled as she hid the knee walker Maggie bought and hobbled back into the kitchen. She was spooning the spoiled curry mixture into old cottage cheese tubs, or as Cheryl called them, Redneck Tupperware, when she saw him pull in the drive. Earlier, she scratched at several of the scabs on her elbows and shoulders, so blood had trickled and dried effectively.

The screen door creaked, and Lute thudded toward the kitchen. He looked up at her.

She could barely suppress a laugh. Bloodshot eyes, swollen face, clothes soiled with vomit and god knew what else, Lute looked like a beaten man. Perfect. She put her plan in motion. "What the fuck are you doing here?" she asked as she turned her back to him.

He saw the dried blood. "Oh, Rhoda. I'm so sorry," he hung his head. "Are you hurt?"

"Yes, I'm hurt, you bastard. You practically killed me last night."

"I'm sorry. I lost my mind…"

"No shit, Sherlock. YOU TRIED TO KILLL ME." The tears she had worked up flowed freely. "I've had it. I want you out of here, NOW."

"Rhoda, Rhoda, please listen to me. Just listen. Come out in the living room, and let's sit down and talk this through." He looked around the kitchen. "Where's your scooter?"

"WHERE'S MY SCOOTER????? WHERE IS MY SCOOTER????" Despite the high level of downers flowing through her system, Rhoda's anger was building. "MY FUCKING SCOOTER IS ROAD JAM, THANKS TO YOU." Real tears were flowing now, as she recalled the horror of last night.

Lute grabbed her elbow to help her into the living room. "Come on. We can work this out. We always do," he pleaded.

"Don't touch me." Rhoda jerked her arm away. "And go get cleaned up. You reek of vomit and rum."

Lute dropped his head like a scolded puppy and headed for the shower. At least she wasn't screaming anymore.

♦♦♦

Weldon found his father in the atrium of the Gardens of Babylon nursing home. He hated this place. It wasn't that it smelled or looked like some home for the criminally insane; it was just the opposite. This place was like a resort - beautiful gardens, light-filled spaces, babbling fountains and cozy little nooks and conversation areas where visitors could spend time with their loved ones. The dining room was more like a five-star restaurant than a nursing home cafeteria. This place was draining his father's considerable wealth so fast, Weldon feared he'd never get his hands on it.

He approached his father with a tight smile plastered on his face. "Hey, Daddy. How's it going today?"

Burt looked straight ahead. Weldon pulled up a chair and sat directly in Burt's line of sight. "Hey, Daddy. It's me, Weldon. How've you been? I've missed you."

The old man's eyes seemed unfocused. Weldon waited for a response. Finally, he reached out and grabbed Burt's hand.

"Get your goddamned, greedy paws off me," said Burt, yanking his hand away.

"Dad? Do you know who I am?" Weldon was sure Burt had him confused with someone else.

"Hell yes, I know who you are, you ungrateful slob."

"Dad, it's me, Weldon, your son."

"I don't have a son named Weldon. He died to me a long time ago. The only son I have is Lute." Burt signaled to the attendant standing nearby, who promptly wheeled him back to his room.

Weldon looked around to make sure no one was watching, then pulled out his phone and turned off the voice recorder. He hoped that conversation would be enough to prove the old man was mentally incompetent, convincing the lawyers and judge that Burt really didn't recognize his own son. He might have to erase the "to me" part, but that should be easy enough. And while he was at it, he would use the video he had of Lute leaving the house with a sack of something to secure a restraining order.

Chapter 39
Tuesday, June 18, midday

"Come on, Cheryl, answer the damned phone." Maggie had the phone on the seat next to her. Rhoda's ancient Oldsmobile sported an eight-track tape player, but nothing so twenty-first century as a Bluetooth uplink.

"You've reached Cheryl Lennon. Please leave a message."

Maggie punched the off button. She'd already left six messages. Maybe she should just drive this jalopy to Tallahassee and wait at Cheryl's house. The longer she drove, the better the idea sounded. She pulled into a gas station on the edge of Starke and called Rhoda.

"Maggie? Everything okay?" Rhoda whispered.

"Yeah, fine. Why are you whispering?"

"Never mind. What is it? Make it quick."

"Well, I hope you don't mind, but I thought I might drive over to Cheryl's tonight to see how she is. She won't answer my calls. But I don't want to leave you stranded."

"Actually, that's perfect."

"Are you sure? Aren't you worried Lute will come home?"

193

Rhoda whispered again, "I told you, no questions. I'm fine. Gotta go. Be safe."

Maggie wondered which mess she should step into, the one here or the one in Tallahassee. Tough choice, but a clean bed in an air-conditioned condo sounded good right now. Plus, she needed to tell Cheryl about the necklace.

Maggie hadn't wanted to take I-10. It was a pretty boring route, but the back roads would have taken hours longer. Plus, she worried the car would break down. She'd have a better chance of getting assistance on an interstate. Knowing Rhoda and Lute's attention to maintenance and detail, she checked under the hood before she left Starke. The dip stick revealed a tarry ball of oil on the tip. The good thing about the antiquity of the car was that she knew how to add oil to it. Cars made since the new millennium hid parts like oil caps and dipsticks, so you had to pay someone with a computer system to fix them.

Though she had resented it at the time, she was glad their dad made them take turns checking and adding oil, radiator fluid, changing tires and hooking up jumper cables correctly. (Red from the dead, to red on the good. Black from the good, to under the hood). She purchased a few quarts of oil and added them, let the engine cool and then idle a while before taking off again. She also looked at the tires which were balding with some separation between the retreads and the actual tire. Without enough money or time for new ones, she took a chance and headed to Cheryl's.

The delay worked in her favor. By the time she arrived at Cheryl's condo, it was four o'clock. Her sister would be home soon. Maggie parked the rust-mobile down the road, walked to the building, took the elevator up to Cheryl's floor, and sat in front of her condo.

A few minutes later, Cheryl walked off the elevator and stopped short when she saw Maggie. "What are you doing here?"

"You wouldn't answer my calls or texts so I decided to come on over. I don't know if you're mad or just avoiding me, but I'm not leaving till I find out why. Plus, I really do have news."

Cheryl avoided Maggie's glare as she unlocked the door. "I guess you'd better come in, then."

Maggie stepped through the door and stopped. Chief Osceola's canopy bed sat in front of the couch, the little stairway still led to the windowsill so he could look out, toys were strewn across the floor, and the Royal Albert dishes were crusted with old food.

Cheryl stepped over the toys, zombie-like, and threw her purse on the couch. "Now, what is so fucking important that you had to drive all the way over here?"

Yowch. Cheryl hadn't dropped the F-bomb since her divorce. "Do you want the good news or the bad news?" Maggie asked, trying to break the tension.

"Isn't it all bad?" Cheryl's eyes shimmered with either rage or heartbreak; Maggie couldn't tell which, since her usually animated sister spoke in a monotone.

"Well then, the bad news is, Lute tried to kill Rhoda and her old boss, Ben, and demolished her little scooter."

This got Cheryl's attention. "Oh, dear Lord. Is she okay? What happened?"

"I guess he saw them together on the side of the road and tried to run them down, but stopped at the last second. Then he shoved Rhoda to the ground, stomped on her cast and punched out Ben. She says she's okay, just a little sore and scraped up."

"Why isn't she here with you? Surely she's ready to leave that maniac?"

"She's up to something. Suddenly, she went from drugged-out space cadet to super-focused woman of action. She told me she had a plan and for us to both stay out of it."

"What is she up to?" Cheryl's zombie face had turned to genuine concern.

"I don't know. All she keeps saying is, 'No questions. Trust me.' I hope she doesn't do anything too stupid." Maggie, though worried about Rhoda, was glad to see Cheryl come back to life. "In fact, she encouraged me to come over here."

"Very troubling. Between the two of them, it's hard to say what will happen, but I can't think of a good outcome, no matter what," said Cheryl.

"So, are you ready for the good news?"

"I forgot. What good news could possibly come out of that hell hole?" Cheryl refused to give rise to the thought that Chief might still be alive.

"I found your necklace," Maggie said.

"Mom's diamond? Really? Oh my God. I knew I left it there somewhere." Cheryl hugged her.

"Oh no, dear sister. You did not lose it. I found it at the pawn shop where Lute hangs out."

"I don't understand. How would it end up there?"

"How do you think? He stole it and pawned it. He probably would have gotten away with it, but I had to go get another knee walker for Rhoda, and there it was. The pawn guy looked all nervous when I noticed it. Gave me some bullshit about some old man who lost his wife, blah, blah, blah."

"You're sure it was mine?"

"I would know Mother's necklace anywhere. I'll never forget how surprised she was when Dad actually broke down and bought her a nice anniversary gift."

"Oh, Lute really is a scumbag. How do I get it back without having to pay for it?" Cheryl asked.

"Please tell me you still have Mom's will when she divided up all her jewelry for us girls. I think she even had everything appraised." Maggie had Googled this after she saw the necklace.

"I do. It's in my jewelry box. Do you think that'll work?" Cheryl started to emerge from her zombie shell.

"It better. It's all we have," said Maggie. "I thought we could go back to Eugenia with the papers and get it back. Could you get off early and drive over there?"

"I will not go and stay anywhere near that crazy son of a bitch. In fact, I don't even want Rhoda to know I'm in town," Cheryl said. "We don't have to tell her that Lute stole it and pawned it. I mean, maybe I did drop it and someone else found it."

Maggie leveled a you're-an-idiot look at her. "I'm not going to dignify that with a response. You're right. We won't even tell her you're coming."

"I'll see if I can take off after lunch tomorrow. I'll just dash over there, go to the pawn shop and come back."

"That'd be perfect. We can stop at the pawn shop first. Then you can head home, and I'll get Rhoda's car back to her."

"I guess," Cheryl sighed. "I'll let you know."

While Cheryl went in the bedroom to change, Maggie found some Lean Cuisines in the freezer. They were the only actual food in the refrigerator. Otherwise, there was nothing but Smart Water and Skinny Girl Protein drinks. Yuck. If that's what it took to look like Cheryl, Maggie wanted no part of it. She checked the freezer again and spotted a frozen margarita pouch behind another box dinner. Score. She put it in the fridge to thaw and then nuked the meals.

The sisters sat in relative silence, eating out of their little plastic trays and watching *America's Got Talent.* At the end of the show, Cheryl tossed out her dinner tray and put her fork in the dishwasher.

Maggie did the same. "We have to get you on one of those shows, Cheryl. You really are so talented," she said, trying to buoy Cheryl's spirits.

"Stop. I can't even go there. Please," Cheryl said. "In fact, I think I'm just going to bed. I'm whipped."

Maggie pursed her lips. "Really? That's it? I come all the way over here to try and cheer you up, and you're going to bed?"

Cheryl stopped. "I'm sorry. I really am glad to see you, and I'm so thrilled you found the necklace. Just give me a little time, okay?"

"Sure," Maggie sighed.

"And Mags?"

"Yeah?"

Cheryl pulled her into a hug. "Thanks. For everything." She held on for a long time, tears soaking Maggie's shoulder. Finally, she headed for the bedroom, calling back, "Make yourself at home. Sleep tight."

"You, too, Sis. Love you." Maggie, taking full advantage of the nice digs, ran a deep bubble bath (clear, odorless water!) and soaked, scrubbed and shampooed until there was no hint of sulfur water left in her hair. Then she put on one of Cheryl's nightshirts, grabbed the drink pouch out of the fridge, and propped herself up in the lilac scented, zillion thread-count sheeted guest bed. With no TV in the room, Maggie fiddled with her phone. She checked her email, messages, and Facebook. Nothing. That was depressing. She took a gulp of the Margarita and started to scroll through her pictures. Oh my god. She had completely forgotten about the "Amazing Grace" practice video.

She watched it again while she finished her drink. Cheryl's talent was undeniable. Maybe she could edit this down to just Cheryl's solo and go back to Plan A - *Florida's Hidden Treasures*. Cheryl would be so excited. This video was much better than the Underwear Alto audition.

She couldn't wait to tell her in the morning.

Chapter 40

Tuesday, June 18, late afternoon

Lute, at Rhoda's command, used the outside shower. He stepped under the tepid water fully clothed. The soap and water sluicing over him didn't do much to relieve his headache or his nausea, so he stripped down, left the clothes in a pile on the floor, and returned to the house. He was still so dizzy from his bender, he collapsed, wet and naked, on one of the beds in the sleeping porch.

He woke after dark. The throbbing in his head had dulled. He sat up and replayed the last twenty-four hours. The scenes at the church and on the sidewalk with Rhoda forced up bile. Shame overwhelmed him. Wrapping himself in the damp bed sheet, he walked into the kitchen.

Rhoda sat at the table under the glaring light, arms crossed tight across her chest. "It's about time you got up, you worthless piece of shit."

He dropped into the chair across from her. "I'm sorry, honey. I went crazy. I don't know what got into me. It was all just too much, the stress of starting a new business, then getting not just fired, but banned from the church. When I saw you with that damned Dr. Stout on the sidewalk…" Suddenly his remorse turned to anger. "Are you screwing that quack? You are, aren't you? You've been screwing him all along, haven't you?" He lunged out of his chair toward her.

Unfazed, Rhoda grabbed the cane from her lap, poked him in the chest with it, and shoved him back into the chair. "Shut up, you prick. I went to see him about my back, which was killing me, thank you very much, from sitting at that stupid piano with my broken leg propped up on a folding chair. And how did I break my leg again? Oh, that's right. You tripped me. And you have the goddamned gall to accuse me of screwing the doctor? You asshole. I'm outta here. Tonight. I've put up with your crap long enough." She stood and limped over to a suitcase she had set in the doorway to the living room.

"Rhoda, wait!"

Rhoda picked up the suitcase and turned toward the front door.

"Wait. I'm sorry. You're right. I am an asshole. I, I just love you so much it hurts. We haven't been able to spend any time together since you tripped and broke your leg and your stupid sisters showed up. That damned Maggie hasn't left us alone for a minute."

Rhoda's head snapped around at his revision of events. "I tripped?" She turned back to the door and opened it.

"Stop, please. You're right. It was my fault. All of it. And your sisters are okay. I just miss us, just the two of us. Please, give me another chance," he cried.

Rhoda stopped but didn't turn. She had to erase the smile from her face before he saw it. This was all playing out better than she dreamed. She had him right where she wanted him.

"Please," Lute said, as he blew his nose on the edge of the bed sheet.

After composing herself, she turned around. "Give me one good reason to stay."

Wednesday, June 19, morning

Rhoda woke to Lute whistling in the kitchen.

Minutes later, he came in the bedroom with the top of a TV tray laden with coffee, eggs, bacon and toast. He had even pulled some weeds from the back yard and put them in a jelly glass. "Good morning, darling."

Rhoda batted her lashes and flashed a saccharine smile. "Oh, Lute. How sweet. You didn't need to go to all this trouble."

Lute set down the tray and fluffed her pillow. "You just eat your breakfast right here; rest that leg a while."

"It does hurt a little after last night, you wild dog, you," she winked at him. The bedroom romp had been unbearable. She hated pumping up that stupid Cobra, but it was an essential part of her plan to regain his trust. "But I'm okay. Are you going crabbing today?"

"I thought I would," he said, "unless you need me to stay here and take care of you."

"No, no. You go. It'll be good for you. Plus, who knows? Today might be your lucky day."

"I could use a lucky day," he said.

"Well, you go on. Oh, I almost forgot. I fixed up a big mess of chicken Vindaloo yesterday. It's in those containers in the fridge. Take them so you'll have a good hardy lunch on the boat." Again, she fluttered her lashes and gave him the most adoring look she could muster.

"My favorite. You did that for me? Even when you were so mad? Aww, Rhoda. I thank Jesus every day for you." With that, he raised his arms crucifix-style, closed his eyes and commenced praying at the ceiling. "Dear Sweet Jesus, our one and only Savior, thank you for the light of my life, Rhoda, and," he lowered one hand to her cast, "use your Almighty Power through my hands to heal my beloved."

Rhoda bowed her head so he couldn't see her grimace. When he called her Beloved, she knew he was one step from the edge. The pattern never varied - cloying sweetness, extreme piety, and manic elation followed by paranoia, depression and rage. Hopefully, her plan would reach fruition before he bottomed out.

Chapter 41

Wednesday, June 19, morning, Tallahassee

Maggie forced herself out of bed the minute she heard Cheryl stirring. "Morning, Cher. Did you sleep okay?"

"Not bad. How about you?" Cheryl still sounded like Eeyore on a bad day.

"I slept great. That's a fantastic bed, and those sheets and pillows! Beats the hell out of the sleeping porch."

Cheryl fixed her coffee. "Good. I'm glad you were comfortable. What are you doing today?"

"Well, I thought I'd hang around here a while, until you're ready to go to Eugenia. What time do you think you'll be able to get off?"

Cheryl expelled a long breath. "I don't even know if I can. I'll have to call you after I check my schedule at work."

Maggie grabbed her phone. "Look what I ran across last night after you went to bed." She started the "Amazing Grace" video and set in on the counter in front of Cheryl.

Cheryl shoved the phone away. "Turn that thing off. I don't think I can stand to watch anything from that whole horrible ordeal."

Maggie grabbed the phone. "Come on, Sis. I just want you to view this clip objectively. It is incredible. I turned it on while I was waiting in line at McDonald's on my way over here yesterday, and the man and woman behind me asked, 'Who is that singing? She's amazing. Would you mind playing it again?' Then the girl at the counter wanted to watch. They all had tears in their eyes when you finished." Maggie paused to watch Cheryl's reaction. A little white lie never hurt anything, especially if it got Cheryl out of her funk.

"Really? You're just saying that," Cheryl turned around and then stopped. "Let me see it one more time."

Hook, line and sinker. Did Maggie know her sister's buttons or what? "This is so much better and more professional looking than the one you did in your bathroom. In fact, I'm all ready to submit it to *Florida's Hidden Treasures*. I pulled up the video audition page on their website last night, and I think this video fits the criteria. We just need to add you introducing yourself; they want to see your personality."

"Can we do that? Add it to the video, I mean?"

"I think I have it all figured out. I mean, I edited this down to just you last night. Surely I can figure out how to add two together."

Cheryl was afraid to hope. "Let me think about it. I'm certainly not in the mood right now to be all chipper and bubbly for an introduction. Plus, I have to get to work if I'm going to take off later."

"Okay. But we'd better do it soon. The deadline for this next season is August first."

Cheryl looked relieved. "Maybe later. I'll text you when I decide and to let you know if I can take time off."

"No problem." Maggie tried not to show her disappointment. She had so wanted to lift Cheryl's spirits. "That gives me more time to work on the mechanics of the whole thing. Have a good day."

"You too. By the way, here's an extra key, in case you decide to go for a run or something."

Maggie clenched her teeth. Very subtle, Cher. Let me know you think I need more exercise. "Bye."

As soon as Cheryl left, Maggie called Rhoda.

"Maggie?" Rhoda sounded awake and alert. "Is everything okay?"

"I might ask you the same thing. Did Lute ever show back up?"

"No questions."

"Right. Sorry. We're fine here. Cheryl's doing better. Still clinging to hope that Chief is alive. But she hasn't said 'my whole life is ruined' in the last hour or so."

"Poor thing. I wish I could go back and change everything," Rhoda said.

"How far back would we have to go, I wonder?" sighed Maggie.

"Good point. What's up?"

"I'm going to head back in a little while. Do you want me to pick up anything on my way? I never did get your pizzas."

"Actually, why don't you stay a few more days and wait till the weekend? I don't really need the car, and if I run out of food, there's always pork and beans," Rhoda chuckled.

"Are you sure? I can help you, plus I hate to keep your car." Maggie was a little hurt that Rhoda didn't want her around. She was also worried. Lute could do anything, given his mental state.

"Yes. Absolutely. In fact, I'm resting and just trying to heal from the whole thing. The head of the quilting club came by to say I wasn't banned from the church, and they would help me anyway they could. In fact, one of them already brought a casserole and that god-awful carrot and raisin salad they serve at socials. I'm fine, really. I think Cheryl needs you more than I do." Rhoda knew that last remark would keep Maggie in Tallahassee for a while.

"Okay. If you're sure. But call me if anything changes. And stay in touch. I'll worry if I don't hear from you."

"Okay, Mother Hen. I promise," Rhoda laughed.

"See you in a few days, I guess," Maggie sulked.

"Whatever. Love you. Give Cheryl a kiss for me."

With Cheryl gone to work, Maggie didn't know what to do with herself. She started to panic. She had to help Rhoda and Cheryl, but she didn't know how. After pacing the entire condo and checking her phone every three seconds, she fixed a cup of coffee, found an oldies station on the radio, and cleaned up the guest room and bath. Cleaning always helped clear her head. When Leslie Gore belted out "You Don't Own Me", Maggie recalled her school psych's advice - "You don't own other people's problems. You can be sympathetic, but they're not your problems to solve."

While she wasn't sure that was entirely true, she realized that right now, there was nothing she could do to help either sister. Maybe some retail therapy might be in order. She hadn't brought anything with her since she came unexpectedly. Yeah. She could shop until she heard from Cheryl. There were lots of stores and restaurants in walking distance. Buoyed by the idea, Maggie put on the same clothes she wore last night, grabbed her purse and headed out.

At work, Cheryl watched Maggie's video again and again. It was pretty darned good, if she did say so herself. Plus, she looked fantastic. With all the trauma and sadness the last few days, she had forgotten how perfectly her outfit, her hair and make-up, and the UberBoob came together. Imagine complete strangers at McDonalds asking to see it again and again.

Maggie texted that she'd been in touch with her tech director from school who told her how to add an introduction, and they could record it when Cheryl got off work.

The whole idea circled in Cheryl's head for about an hour. If she could just muster up some enthusiasm, she might give this audition a try. What else did she have to lose? Still, she wasn't sure. Depression hung just a millimeter over her head. It was so close, she sometimes had to gasp for air.

Maybe this was a bad idea. Maggie tended to take over every bad situation and try to fix it. Unfortunately, her fixes weren't always in sync with what Cheryl or Rhoda wanted to do. They had talked about it many times. Maggie would swoop in to save the day, then if something went wrong, or things didn't go exactly her way, she turned into a martyr; "How come I'm the one doing everything around here - nobody appreciates me..." blah, blah, blah. She knew Maggie meant well, but she just went too far and ended up making it all about herself.

Cheryl decided she wasn't quite ready to audition. Thanks for checking into everything. I really appreciate all the work you've done to make this audition video, but I just don't think I'm ready to tackle it yet. I will, eventually, just not right now. In fact, I don't think I'm up for a trip to Eugenia today either. Maybe Friday night or this weekend. Sorry. LU

Cheryl knew she faced one of two things - an evening with a sulking, pouting Maggie, or an evening without her at all.

Chapter 42

Wednesday, June 19, morning

Buddy and Del pulled their bikes up to the *Eula Mae*, shocked to see Lute there with the trailer already hooked to the truck.

Lute shouted to them as he finished hosing out the boat. "Hey, guys. Sorry about yesterday. I had a bad night Monday night. Took me a while to recover. But I'm ready now."

"You owe us money for yesterday. We were here, like we agreed," Buddy glared at him, arms folded across his chest.

"You know what? You're right," Lute pulled his wallet out of his pocket. "Here's twenty dollars each for yesterday, and then you'll get your normal cut today. Conditions are perfect, so we ought to make a killing out there."

"What happened on the boat? We checked it out yesterday. It was a mess," Buddy glared at Lute.

"Oh, I got in a fight with the wife and tied one on. Passed out up here on the deck," he laughed.

Buddy and Del did not.

"Oh, come on; give a guy a break," Lute said. "We're all set to go. I worked on the engine, so it doesn't miss and sputter like it did last time. The coolers are loaded with ice, the baskets are stacked, and the lines are coiled and ready. Let's go crabbin'."

Buddy climbed in the back of the truck, so Del could ride in the front. Del wouldn't mind listening to Lute's bullshit all the way to the St. Johns.

♦♦♦

I'm sorry about the other night. Are you all right? I know you're mad that I stuck up for Lute, but you have to trust me. I know how to handle him, especially when he goes off the deep end. I'm used to him knocking me around, but I'm really sorry he coldcocked you. I only intervened so you wouldn't kill him. I know you were ready to. But then you'd go to jail and we'd never get to be together. Please try and understand. I'll make it up to you, I promise.

Rhoda reread the text to Ben before sending it. She hadn't heard from him since Monday. Not that she blamed him. He'd be smart to run fast and far away from her. But she'd miss him. He and her sisters were the only sane people in her life.

In the meantime, she had work to do. The vindaloo was almost gone, and she had to keep a steady stream of toxins in Lute's system if her plan was going to work. She dug through the freezer until she found the answer. In large *I Can't Believe It's Not Butter* tubs were shucked oysters Lute had bought on the side of the road. She remembered the day. They were on their way home from church and Lute suddenly slammed on the brakes and backed up.

She hadn't even seen the rusted Impala tucked in the trees just off the shoulder. "Fresh Osters - Cheap" was scrawled on a piece of cardboard, propped against the back bumper.

"How cheap is cheap?" asked Lute. He loved oysters, but he loved a bargain more.

Chhht-thew. The greasy man spat out an egg-sized wad of tobacco. "Well, sir. They are damned cheap. And fresh. Just got 'em and shucked 'em myself." He opened the trunk to reveal baggies full of shucked oysters heaped over what had been a ten-pound bag of ice. He pointed at them like a magician's assistant. "Ain't they beauties?"

Rhoda only noticed the slime of tobacco drool that stuck to his beard.

"They sure are," said Lute as he leaned in closer. "How much for a gallon?"

"Let's see, they're twenty-five for two quarts. But I'll give you a deal, since it's gettin' late. I'll give you a gallon for, say, forty bucks."

"Your ice is about gone," said Lute. "Forty for everything you got in there."

The man dug another plug out of his tobacco pouch and thought about it. This was the first car he'd seen all morning. "You drive a hard bargain, son. Forty-five and we got a deal. Final offer."

Lute pulled a five out of his pocket. He looked back at Rhoda. "Honey? You got any money?"

Rhoda clenched her teeth and handed him her last two twenties. Lute snatched them through the open window.

"Here ya go, partner. Nice doin' business with you," Lute said. He grabbed the rest of the oysters, sans ice, and threw them in the trunk.

"Don't you want the ice?" Rhoda asked.

"Naw, just get the trunk all wet. We'll be home soon. What a find."

Idiot. She hadn't tried the oysters but was glad she'd kept them. She carried the tubs out to the yard and set them under a laundry basket. He'd never look there.

Chapter 43

Wednesday, June 19, St. Johns River

"We're kinda' getting a late start, but it's not as hot today. Let's go." Lute dashed from one end of the boat to the other, moving coolers and baskets, checking and rechecking lines. "This is great. I got a real good feeling."

Buddy had seen guys like this in jail. The wild eyes, excess enthusiasm and energy. He had learned to tread carefully. The last thing he wanted to do was set this nut-bag off out in the middle of the river. "Got it, boss," he called as he unhooked the winch line and reeled it back in. He parked the truck and trailer and walked back to the dock. "Del, you hop on. I'll untie us and shove off."

Lute, revving the engine until it smoked, threw it in reverse and piloted into the channel. Passing out of the no wake zone, Lute throttled up until the boat planed out. "It's a little rough today, but I think we have enough weight on those lines to drag the bottom," he shouted into the wind.

When Lute finally found his "spot," he idled the engine and told Del to check the snoods and set the lines. "Hey, Bud," Lute called, "make sure that numbskull brother of yours attaches the line to the anchor this time."

Buddy clenched his fists and walked toward Del. One more word about his brother and Buddy was going to flatten that guy.

With the trot lines baited and set, they moved down river to drop some traps. After that was accomplished they headed back to run the lines. Lute was right. They couldn't haul in the crabs fast enough. It was going to be their best day so far. They worked together in relative silence, Lute adjusting the tow board as they worked down the line, Del using the gaff to hoist it on the prop stick so Buddy could net the catch.

"We're gonna need longer lines next time," laughed Lute, exhilarated by their success. "Those babies are fightin' to get on these."

After re-setting the lines, they moved to go check the traps. Lute wanted in on the action, so he stopped the engine and joined his crew. While the traps weren't as full as the lines had been, they were still worth the effort. "Okay, guys. Let's head back and haul in some more gold." Lute said as he returned to the helm to start the engine. At first, the only sound was the click of the key turning. After jimmying the throttle, the engine finally choked and sputtered, but when he put it in gear, it died. "Del, go back and check the fuel lines; in fact, pull the cover and check the whole thing out."

While Del bent over the back, Lute tried again to get it going. Buddy walked up behind him. "I don't think you need to slam the throttle back and forth like that. Let me try." He moved to edge Lute out of the way.

"So now you're the captain? What the fuck do you know about boats?" Lute turned and grabbed Buddy by the front of his shirt.

Not sure which lines were which, Del wiggled and pulled them all, then fiddled with the connection to the gas

216

tanks. Hearing shouting from the helm, Del whipped around to check it out, still grasping the fuel lines. He saw Buddy shove Lute which forced the throttle and the boat forward. Lute then turned and tackled Buddy sending them both to the floor.

Engine roaring, Del scrambled to gain his footing when an explosion rocked the *Eula Mae.* Flames chased leaking fuel across the deck.

Buddy and Lute disengaged at the sound, turning in time to see Del fly over the side, his head thudding against the prop stick before he hit the water.

Chapter 44
Wednesday, June 19, Gainesville

Weldon was elated. His attorney, after listening to the doctored recording, reading affidavits from some of the nursing home employees, and watching the videos of Lute going in and out of Burt's house, agreed to file for emergency guardianship of Burt for Weldon and an injunction against Lute for stalking. Finally, that shyster minister was going to get what he deserved, and Weldon would be in control of his father's estate.

Ready to celebrate this first step to victory, he stopped at his favorite Cuban café, Bonito y Barato, on the edge of town. Technically, it was a dive, a small cubby-hole located in a mostly abandoned strip mall. A testament to the quality of the food, the parking lot was full. Weldon parked on the far end and walked past a bail bondsman and a pawn shop sandwiched between boarded storefronts. Though the restaurant was packed, he managed to snag a stool at the counter and ordered picadillo and a beer. He reviewed the paperwork from the attorney. Finally, he felt like a winner.

His appetite and ego sated, he strolled back to his car, scanning the pawn shop window. As he pulled his keys out of his pocket, he stopped. What was that? He doubled back and took a closer look. Seeing some familiar items, he thought for a minute, then went inside.

Sure enough. There in the display case. True, there were probably lots of charm bracelets around, but he knew this one. Twenty-four carat gold (his dad had brought it

218

from Europe for his mother after the war), it was loaded with charms. There was his first-place medal from the third-grade spelling bee. And her wedding band, after it had become too loose when she got sick. Dad's Army Soldier and Commendation Medals, and, of course, the Distinguished Service Cross and Purple Heart. In addition to the bracelet, he spotted his mother's silver tea service, her diamond and pearl earring and necklace set, and his father's perfectly polished Army saber. Blood pounded in his ears.

"Can I help you, sir?"

Weldon continued to stare at his family heirlooms.

"Sir?"

Slowly, a voice echoed through the tunnel of his wrath. He looked up.

"Can I help you, sir?" A white-haired gentleman stood behind the counter. "Are you okay?"

Thoughts swirled through his mind. Pull yourself together. Don't let on. He took a deep breath, looked around the room and out the front window before speaking. "Good afternoon," he said, tamping down the tremor in his voice. "I, um, I'm supposed to meet someone here. A friend of mine recommended your shop and even offered to join me here. Maybe you've seen him? I hope I didn't miss him."

"Nobody's been in for a while," said the gentleman. "Who's your friend?"

"I don't know if you'd remember. He's not from around here, but his name's Lute Mason." Weldon watched the man's face.

"Sure, I know Lute. Nice guy. He's in here every couple of months. But he hasn't been in today."

Exactly the frequency that Lute had paid visits to Burt's house, according to the security camera footage.

"Oh, shoot. I thought we were supposed to meet today, but maybe I got it wrong. I have trouble keeping my schedule straight these days," Weldon chuckled and pointed to his head. "Old-timers, you know?"

"I hear ya," said the man. "Maybe, I can help you."

"No, he was going to show me something but didn't mention what it was. I'll check with him, and we'll reschedule."

"You sure?"

"Yeah. No problem. I was in town on another errand anyway. I'll give him a call. I'm sure we'll be back soon." Weldon shook the man's hand and turned to leave the shop.

The owner, afraid to lose a sale, spoke up. "I noticed you staring at this beautiful charm bracelet here. Surely a handsome guy like you has a pretty little lady who needs something unique like this?"

Weldon stopped and turned. "Yeah, that's a beauty. Is it real gold?"

"Sure is. In fact, it's twenty-four carat."

"Huh. I noticed it has some military charms. Are they real, too? I have a buddy who collects military stuff."

"Those are genuine World War II Army medals. They're getting more and more rare as those vets die off."

Weldon decided to fish a little. "Who would give up something like this? It looks like some family's whole history right here."

The owner looked around to make sure no one was in ear shot. "Actually, funny coincidence. Your pal Lute Mason brought that in just last week. He's a minister and said one of his parishioners died and left all of his belongings to the church to help keep it afloat."

Weldon could feel his blood pressure rise. "Mind if I take a picture to show my girl and my buddy? If they're interested, I'll come back and get it." He tried to sound excited rather than enraged.

"Sure, why not," said the owner. "Anything to make a sale."

Weldon snapped the picture, backing up enough to capture the tea service and the pearl jewelry as well. He hoped the pictures his dad had taken for insurance purposes were still in the safe deposit box. Pocketing his phone, he extended his hand. "Thanks, man. I'll get back to you soon."

Feeling his neck and face flush, he raced out and through the parking lot. He sat in his car a full ten minutes trying to calm down enough to drive.

Chapter 45

Wednesday, June 19, St. Johns River

"DEL," Buddy screamed as he watched his brother sink in the river. He shoved Lute out of his way and dove off the burning boat.

Lute landed on his ass, legs akimbo. Stupefied, he noticed the hole in the stern where the tanks had blown and watched the water seep in carrying flames toward him. Only the sound of Buddy screaming, "Throw me a life jacket or something," disturbed Lute's inertia. He jumped up and threw a cooler overboard; life jackets and other safety gear had seemed like a waste of good money. Seeing the extent of the damage anew, Lute stripped off his shirt and pants and tried to smother the flames. As he gained some control over the blaze, he watched as the stern became submerged. Backing toward the bow, he stood in nothing but his underwear, listening to the glug of water filling the hull. When the boat finally heaved its last sigh of surrender and slipped beneath the surface, Lute swam toward the bobbing cooler that Buddy clung to while holding Del's head above water.

Buddy, ready to pull the Glock from his pants and finish Lute off for good, realized he could not let go of either the cooler or Del. He tried pushing Lute away with his feet, but gave up when the bulky cooler began to pitch wildly. "I'll kill you for this, you son of a bitch," he screamed.

222

♦♦♦

Please. I'm sorry. I'm sorry. I'm sorry. If you'll just give me a chance to explain, I promise it will all make sense. I miss you. I think I'll be rid of Lute forever in just a few more days, and then it's smooth sailing for us. Please call or text. Or I can meet you somewhere. Please.

Rhoda reread the text before hitting send. Ben had gone completely silent this time. Before, when they'd had an argument about Lute, he forgave her pretty quickly. He really must be hurt. She couldn't blame him. He didn't know that when she defended Lute the other night, it was all part of her plan to get away from him. And she was so close. Thank God Maggie had stayed in Tallahassee for a few more days. Rhoda didn't have to worry about her interfering or about her accidentally eating some of the spoiled food she was feeding Lute.

The oysters stunk worse than the septic tank and the swamp combined. Pulling the neck of her tee shirt up over her nose, Rhoda began mincing three heads of garlic, two yellow onions and enough celery to disguise the green scum that had formed while the oysters sat in the sun. Browning the vegetables in butter, she added a handful of dried chili peppers to further mask the smell. Mixing everything together in the slow cooker, she covered it with milk and set it on low. She wasn't sure when he'd be home, but she intended to be gone. She wrote a note and propped it up where he would see it. "Sweetheart - made your favorite oyster stew. It's ready to eat. Help yourself. Love, Rhoda"

Just the thought of cozying up to that bastard made her gag. Or maybe it was the stew. She couldn't really say which was more putrid.

◆◆◆

Though it seemed like hours, a boat full of beer-drinking college boys came by within minutes and offered assistance. Pulling Del from the water first and realizing the seriousness of his injuries, one of the rescuers administered CPR, as Del had not regained consciousness. Buddy hoisted himself aboard, leaving Lute clinging to the cooler.

"Grab the rope," one of the boys called to Lute.

"Naw, you go on and get that man tended to. I'll catch the next boat that comes by," said Lute. He knew something about the consequences related to a sunken vessel and did not want to face any authorities just yet.

Reassured that Lute would be okay, the boys in the boat sped toward the docks. As soon as they were out of view, Lute swam to the river's edge. It took a great deal of time and effort, but he had to get away. Lute felt certain the college kids wouldn't call any cops because of their drinking. He figured Buddy would be so concerned about Delmont that he wouldn't bother with the police either. Lute doubted that Buddy and Del combined had enough sense to understand marine law. Lute didn't know much about it either, but he hoped he could just walk away from the whole mess.

Finally, Lute reached the shore and hoisted himself onto the banks. He had to think. The best thing would be to leave the boat and pray no one would discover it. River and lake bottoms around here were littered with abandoned vessels. If he had bothered to insure the boat, he might try to salvage it, but he'd never paid for insurance in his life and wasn't about to start now. Unfortunately, he'd been forced to register the damn thing when Shivey sold it to him. The old salt had insisted they go down to the DMV to transfer the title. Maybe he'd dive down and scrape off the registration.

He looked out at the expanding oil slick. The fire had died down, but the boat continued to leak fuel. The hell with it. He'd just take his chances; that had always worked before. Oblivious to the fact that he only wore boxers, Lute made his way up Rt. 17 to the marina. He unhitched the trailer, removed its license plate, got in the truck and headed home. Thankful he always kept a bottle of rum under the seat, he drank the whole way. He had to lay low for a few days. Del, he was certain, wouldn't remember anything. He just hoped the asshole, Buddy, wouldn't talk. Lute had a feeling Buddy was hiding something, so maybe he'd stay quiet. That was the good thing about hiring stupid or shady people. They didn't follow rules and didn't want to get involved with the law.

Chapter 46

Wednesday, June 19

Rhoda's phone pinged.

What lame excuse do you have this time?

She knew Ben would come around; he just needed a little space and time to cool off. Rhoda had to play this just right, so she wouldn't spook him.

Hey. I'm so glad to hear from you. Can we please meet? This is not something I can put in writing or even discuss on the phone.

She sat and stared at the blank phone screen for a full ten minutes. He was not going to give in that easy. The radio silence would probably last another day. But, she reassured herself, he had made contact. There was hope.

Rather than wait for his response, she tied a garbage bag around her cast and went to the outside shower to clean up. She would have preferred the indoor bath because of the air conditioning. She always joked that she didn't sweat much for a fat woman, but it was true; she could work up some massive armpit stains just sitting still. But, thanks to Lute the handyman, that shower was out of commission.

Feeling refreshed, with just a hint of eau de sulfur, she hobbled back inside to cool off. Not sure when Lute would get home, she planned to be as far away as possible.

Donning her nicest rummage-sale sundress, she added to the note she had written earlier.

Lute - Had to go to Shands Medical Center to get my leg x-rayed. Hopefully I'll get a walking cast so we can go out and have some fun. See you later. The girls are gone, thank God, so help yourself to the oyster stew. I had some for lunch - it's my best batch ever. Try and get some rest. Love you, Rho. She did a little one-footed happy dance when she found Lute's car keys in the bowl in the kitchen. Thank heavens he'd driven that old truck to work; otherwise, she'd be stuck here.

The parking lot at Ben's office was packed, so she went to his house. Sometimes he went home for lunch. Using the garage door code she had memorized, she pulled in to hide her car and entered through the kitchen. Even if he didn't come home until later, she would wait. Here she was well hidden, safe and comfortable.

For the first time since she broke her leg, her shoulders relaxed. Though her life always ran toward the crazy side, this last month had been beyond the pale. The leg, Maggie and the Great Bean Explosion, then Cheryl, the Hollywood producer, Lute's firing, and the dog-turned-gator-chow. Insane.

Dusk passed and night fell, unbeknownst to Rhoda. She had dissolved into a deep sleep in Ben's massaging recliner. His entrance through the kitchen startled her. "Ben?" she tried to climb back to consciousness. "Hey. Sorry to sneak in here, but I have to talk to you."

Ben looked down at her. Those eyes melted his heart every time; behind the spark of mirth, he saw years of self-doubt, recrimination and guilt. He knew she often lied, but he also knew she had to so she could do things normal people took for granted - like enjoy her sisters and friends, or go to a real restaurant or shop occasionally. No wonder she snuck drugs from his office. He would too if he somehow landed in her life. It pained him more to see she had tried to dress up. She even had a nice sandal on her good foot.

"Oh, Ben," she cried, "I'm so sorry."

He pulled her into a hug and whispered into her hair. "Me too. I'm more sorry than you. I know what a powder keg that bastard can be. I was just so frightened and mad that he almost killed you. To watch you defend him - well, I just lost it."

Rhoda sobbed into his shoulder for a few minutes, then pulled herself together. "I have it all planned out, and I've already started working on him. He'll be long gone soon."

"I don't even want to hear about it. I trust you," he said. "Just don't do anything to get yourself hurt or in trouble."

She laughed. "Me? Have you ever met a better liar? By the time I'm done with him, he'll think getting away from me was all his idea."

"Just be careful," said Ben, "and let me know if you need my help."

"Actually, you can help tonight. Can I stay here? He has no idea where I am, and I'm hoping he'll pass out before he realizes I never came home."

"You know you can always stay here. Anytime and all the time."

"Trust me," Rhoda said, "I'm working on it."

Chapter 47

Wednesday, June 19, afternoon, Eugenia

The house looked empty when he got home. Though Lute was pretty fog-brained from the booze, he realized that was either good news or bad. It was good that the place wasn't surrounded by police, but bad if Rhoda wasn't there. He knew she'd protect him and make him feel better.

Opening the door, the strong scent of garlic, onion and the sting of hot peppers drew him toward the kitchen. His stomach growled; he hadn't had any food since mid-morning when he ate the last of Rhoda's curry. He turned on the light, looked down at himself and realized he wore only his stiff-with-river-mud boxers. Food first, he decided. Maybe sober him up a little. Then a shower and bed.

Affectionately drunk, he teared up when he read Rhoda's note. She called him sweetheart. She hadn't done that since before that brood of sisters arrived. He knew once he got her away from everybody, they would be happy. The hot, creamy, spicy stew tasted so good, he had two big bowls. How did she know soup would be the perfect balm for the day he had? His stomach had been upset all afternoon, but he chalked that up to the sunken boat, the possible legal ramifications, and consuming entirely too much oily river water before walking to the truck in the heat of the day.

Once again, he showered outside and never made it past the sleeping porch before passing out.

Chapter 48

Wednesday, June 19, midday, Tallahassee

Maggie had stumbled on a great sale at Nic's Toggery and bought a pair of comfort-waist capris and a shirt that camouflaged her lumpy parts. She also grabbed a bagel sandwich and some chips, since Cheryl's cupboard was beyond bare.

Just as she opened the door to the condo, her phone pinged. She put down her bags and read Cheryl's text. Maggie almost understood Cheryl's reluctance about jumping back into a singing competition, but not wanting to try and recover her necklace? After all the trouble Maggie had gone to for her?

Bunch of damned ingrates. Maggie fumed as she gathered up her stuff. They don't want my help? The hell with them. Let 'em wallow around in their own little miserable worlds. Rhoda didn't want her back yet, and Cheryl chickened out on what used to be her lifelong dream. Well, those were their problems. Every time she tried to help them get their lives straightened out, they did this.

She'd show them. She'd just disappear off the radar for a few days. Then they'd start begging her to come back. Well, tough. Let them figure it out. It wasn't like she didn't have a life of her own. It may not be much of one, but it was hers, and she could do with it what she wanted.

She was determined to get that necklace back, though, before it got sold at that pawn shop. That was one of the few things their parents left them – Cheryl got the diamond necklace, Rhoda the sapphire ring, and Maggie got both of their wedding bands and her mother's engagement ring. Sure, it was a tiny diamond, but she loved it anyway. To Lute, those things were nothing but easy money, but to the girls, they were all they had left - something their parents had worn every day of their lives together. She grabbed the will and appraisal out of Cheryl's jewelry box, so when she did go back to Rhoda's, she could claim the necklace.

But she wasn't headed back today. She could use a day or two on her own. Maybe stop somewhere along the way. Surely Starke had decent hotel. She didn't have too much money, but she could afford some little place for a few nights. Her standards for lodging ran somewhere between Cheryl's luxury digs and Rhoda's dung heap. She knew neither Rhoda nor Lute came all the way into Starke very often, so it might be a safe haven.

The drive across I-10 calmed her down. Boring as it was, the monotonous landscape and peace and quiet were comforting after the last few weeks. About an hour into the trip, her stomach started growling, the bagel sandwich a distant memory. Surely, there was a place to eat along here, a real place where you could sit down. Maggie had pretty low standards when it came to food, but she could not stomach a gas-station roller dog. She started paying attention to road signs. Just after crossing the Suwannee River, "Suwannee, how I love you, how I love you…" she spotted a possibility – White Springs and the Stephen Foster Folk Culture Center State Park. The three girls always used to sing Stephen Foster songs. Her favorite, in fact, was the "Lemon Sister's" version of "I Dream of *Maggie* with the

Light Brown Hair." It was fate. She didn't care how far off the interstate it was. She was going; she had plenty of time.

Surely, the town of White Springs would have a decent place to eat. While waiting at a four-way stop, she rolled down her window and asked a mailman if there was a good restaurant in town. He recommended Fat Belly's. "They serve fresh, home cooked food there, and everybody treats you like family." Perfect. After stuffing herself with barbeque, Maggie managed to kill a few hours wandering through the Stephen Foster museum, the Craft Square, the grounds, and the gift shop. Maggie loved a good gift shop. It was one of her secret pleasures, buying tacky souvenirs wherever she went. Before she left town, she decided to find a grocery to pick up a cooler, ice, and some food and beer for her mini-vacation.

She was back on the road by five and headed for Starke. Stopping at a few of the chain hotels, such as they were, she decided on a low-budget, but clean mom and pop place called "Motel 12 – We're twice as good!" It was kind of quaint – individual little cottages painted pink with peeling white shutters. She checked the beds for bedbugs (clear) and was relieved to see terrazzo floors (a bit cracked and stained, but clean and cool). This would work. Just a little respite. Amber, the "mom" of the mom and pop, told her there was a block nearby with art shops, bookstores and cafes. That's just what she needed. A little shopping and some good escape fiction to take her mind off things. She even turned off her phone. Let them all be frantic for a while.

She popped a beer, flipped on the TV (the motel sign touted "Cable TV, Beauty Rest Mattresses, and Air

Conditioning"). Perfect timing. NCIS, her favorite crime show, was on. The storyline, that used to seem fraught with tension, action and angst, was so tame compared to her life recently, she fell asleep before it ended.

Wednesday, June 19 evening, Shands Medical Center, Starke

Buddy paced between the ER waiting room and the smoking area outside. Most hospitals forbade conceal/carry; plus, as a convicted felon, he was carrying illegally. He had wiped the gun down while they loaded Delmont on the ambulance at the dock and stuffed it in a plastic bag one of the EMT's dropped opening oxygen tubing. When they got to the hospital, he stashed the Glock in the bushes by the door. Convinced the gun was safely hidden, Buddy went back inside hoping for news on Del.

Staring at a TV where a saccharine evangelist begged for money and forgiveness, Buddy could feel the blood pulsing in his neck and his brain. His jaw and fists were clenched in rage. If anything, any little thing happened to his brother, Lute was going to pay dearly for it - hurting a poor innocent kid like Del. Buddy hadn't liked Lute from the start, but he and Del were both eager to get some cash. Then, he kept working for the bastard so he could find out where all his stash was hidden. But the money and guns didn't matter now.

"Mr. Crapps? Mr. Buddy Crapps, please report to the registration desk."

Buddy jumped up and raced to the window. "How is he? Can I go see him? What's going on?"

"First things first, sir. We need your brother's medical insurance card and some kind of I.D. Also, complete these forms, both front and back, and then return them to me."

"I don't know if he has a goddamned medical card, or an ID card, for that matter."

"Sir, I'm going to have to ask you to calm down, or you will be escorted out by security," said the prissy bitch behind the counter. "You are his brother, correct? That's what you said when they brought him in."

Buddy took a deep breath. He did not need security involved. "Sorry, ma'am. I'm just upset about my brother."

"Right." She rolled her eyes while her fingers tapped across a keyboard. "What do you have?"

"Well, I just got in town. We haven't seen each other in a few years. I think I have his address."

"Social Security number? Birthdate? Employer? Any other next of kin?" She continued tapping, though he had no idea what she could possibly be writing down.

"I don't have those on me. We were in a boating accident, and we weren't carrying our wallets or anything. I can bring them in later, once I make sure he's okay and can get back to the house." Buddy tried to sound conciliatory.

She finally looked up, her disgust for "his kind" evident in her entire being. "Try to complete these forms to the best of your ability. Then, when you bring back in the documentation, we can add that to his file."

"Thank you, ma'am. I will. Oh, you know, he might be on disability. He had a pretty bad head injury as a kid."

"Then, hopefully, you'll be able to find those documents when you go home as well," she said, shoving the clipboard through the slot in the bulletproof service window. "Next."

Somewhere between furious and despondent, Buddy sat down with the forms and began writing what information he could remember and making up whatever he couldn't.

Chapter 49

Thursday, June 20, morning

Lute woke to the sound of pounding on the front door. He opened his eyes and tried to break through the haze of disorientation. How the hell did he get here? Was this his house?

The pounding continued. Sitting on the edge of the bed, he saw stacks of brand new pork and beans in the closet. Ah yes. It was coming back. Sleeping porch.

His stomach lurched. The boat. The fire. The injured kid. Shit.

His stomach rolled again. Interesting. Guilt wasn't an emotion he was used to, but this must be it. Or fear. Yeah, that was it – fear of getting caught.

"Lute Mason? You in there? Never mind, I know you are; I see that truck you been driving out here. Open up."

Lute wrapped the bed sheet around himself and went to the door. It was the sheriff. Should be safe to answer. They were brothers in the fight. Lute opened the door and gave the sign of solidarity, "Mark of the Beast."

The sheriff did the same.

"Jesus, Joe. What's so all important that you have to practically break my door down?" Lute asked.

"Sorry, brother, but I wanted to give you a heads up. You might be in big trouble. Seems some group called the St. Johns River Waterkeepers spotted a big oil slick and suspected a sunken vessel. So those tree-huggers called in the local patrol who brought their marine equipment. They sent a diver down who did, indeed, find a boat. Now, they've traced the registration to you. The sheriff over in Clay County called and said they want you to pay for the clean-up and to get that thing out of the water. There's a pretty hefty fine for every day it stays down there."

"Damn communists. There they go trying to take over our lives and our money. Fine my ass," Lute said. "They'll have to catch me first."

"Now, Lute, be careful. Remember, I am sworn to uphold the law. But what I don't know, I can't report, so don't say anything to me you don't want repeated."

Lute nodded. "Thanks for the heads up. I'll check into it; see what I can do."

"No problem," said Joe as he stepped outside. "Just don't tell anybody I came by."

Lute said a quick prayer thanking God for the Brotherhood. They watched out for each other. Good old Joe would take care of him.

His prayer was interrupted by another knock. "Lute, buddy? You still there?" asked Joe.

Lute opened the door. "Of course. I was just thanking the Lord for good folks like you, Joe. What'd you forget?"

Joe pulled an official looking envelope out of his pocket and handed it to him. "Sorry, pal, but I got to serve this. I don't think it's any big deal though. Looks like something from the circuit court. Probably just some picky-ass little thing, but I gotta do my job. Play it safe, brother," he said as he turned and walked back to his patrol car.

Lute closed the door and locked it. What the hell was this all about? He ripped open the envelope and skimmed over the legal bullshit until he found a name he recognized. "…prohibiting Respondent Luther Mason from going to or within five hundred feet of any place Petitioner Burt Cosgrove lives, or to any specified place owned or frequented by Petitioner BC … and any named family members or individuals closely associated with Petitioner BC … filed by Weldon Cosgrove, duly authorized agent acting on behalf of Burt Cosgrove …."

That rat-bastard, Weldon. Lute didn't understand how Burt would allow a son he hated and had disowned to act on his behalf. That greedy son of a bitch must have forced Burt to sign a bunch of papers without explaining anything. Burt would never turn his back on Lute intentionally.

Lute needed to talk to Rhoda about this – about everything. She had a way of sorting through legal jargon and making sense of it for him. He checked the house, but no Rhoda. Her stuff was still here, though, so she couldn't have gone far. He checked outside. His old car was gone. She probably went out to buy more cancer sticks, damn her. Always sneaking around either buying the things or smoking them. He tried calling her cell, but of course, it went to voice mail. She always forgot to charge it.

Pouring the day-old dregs of coffee in a cup, he warmed it up and drank it, hoping it would clear his head. He knew one thing. It was time to get out of this place. They had nothing to stay for – no job, no boat, nothing. He'd have to wait till nighttime to dig up the stuff in the yard. Then he'd find Rhoda, and they'd take off.

His gut suddenly seized and rumbled. From the john, he heard a truck stop out front, then the thunk of a package against the door. Dizzy and unsteady, he eventually made his way to the living room and peeked through the curtains. Satisfied no one was around, he opened the door and grabbed the cardboard mailer off the porch. The return address said United States Coast Guard.

Shit.

Chapter 50

Thursday, June 20, morning, Starke

Buddy waited to turn in the forms until the early morning shift change and, hopefully, a more compassionate receptionist took over the ER desk. He finally remembered Del's birthday. Their mom had tried to have a party for Del, with a pitiful little cake and some party hats made of newspaper, two days before "the night." She had scratched the number five on top of the cake in lieu of candles. Buddy counted back from there, figured out the date and wrote it down. He made up the social security number, figuring it might be one number greater than his. It was worth a shot.

The only address he knew was "white and blue single wide at the Gone Fishin' Mobile Home Resort, Eugenia, FL." Except for Del's first head injury and hearing loss, Buddy made up the rest of the medical history. He left employment, income and insurance blank, writing a note in the margin that he might be on disability. He did put his father's full name, in the event that the SOB might still be alive, and they could hunt him down for payment. Buddy listed himself as the emergency contact, though he had no phone number. Just as well. He didn't want to be found, especially by a bunch of medical billing agencies.

Before handing it in, he went in the bathroom, splashed water on his face and finger-combed his hair. He knew he looked like a derelict after treading water in that stinking river, but he wanted to make the most positive impression he could on the receptionist, so she'd let him back to see Del.

"Here are the papers they asked me to fill out for my brother," he said to the not-altogether homely girl. "His name's Delmont Crapps. They brought him in several hours ago, and nobody's told me anything yet." He tried to force some tears and a crack in his voice. "He was hurt pretty bad yesterday, but they said I had to fill these out before I could see him." He turned his head, sniffed, and wiped his eyes across his shirt sleeve.

"Oh, you poor thing. You must be worried sick. Let me go see what I can do. Just wait right here." She disappeared into the bowels of the ER. A minute later, the heavy automatic door opened. The receptionist stepped into sight and waved him back. "He's in the last cubicle on the left."

Buddy opened the curtain. Except for Del's size, it could have been "the night" all over again. Oxygen tubes, IVs in both arms, monitors beeping, dried crusted blood on his face. The only difference were the burns. Buddy went to grab his hand, but it was heavily bandaged. "Del? Del? Can you hear me?"

Nothing.

Buddy sat in the vinyl recliner next to the bed, kicked it back and fell asleep, his hand resting next to Del's.

Thursday, June 20, morning, Eugenia

"I'm afraid to ask, Rhoda, but what, exactly, are your plans for Lute?" Ben hoped asking this question while the bloom was still on the rose, so to speak, would elicit an honest answer.

Rhoda waited before she turned onto her back. "Good morning to you, too. How long have you been lying there waiting to pop that question?"

"Truth?" said Ben. "All night long. I'm worried about you. I'm afraid you'll do something out of desperation that you'll end up regretting."

"For god's sakes, Ben. Lute is not worth that much of your time," she sighed long enough to think. "My only plan, as you call it, is to let him think I'm going to run away to Panama with him."

"Panama?"

"Yes, he says it's so much cheaper to live there, and they speak English and use the American dollar. 'We'll live like royalty down there,' he promises me. Ha. Royal pain-in-the-ass." She fumed for a minute. "I'm just going to encourage him and try to get him to leave before me. I thought I could tell him I need to stay until the cast comes off, but that he should go ahead and get us a place to live."

"Then you'll never show up. Is that it?" Ben was skeptical.

"Bingo. Then I thought I, um, we, could disappear," Rhoda flashed him the most beguiling smile she could muster.

"I have serious doubts about the viability of that plan, but it's better than what I thought you were up to," said Ben. "If you can shake that monster, I, too, will begin to believe in miracles."

Satisfied that her ruse was feasible, she sat up on the edge of the bed. "I should get home. I thought I'd even start packing some stuff. But I'd better get back. I'm sure he's been wondering where I was last night."

"What are you going to tell him?"

"He hasn't stopped drinking since the church fired him; I'm hoping he'll be too hung over to notice. Oh, that reminds me. Can you change my cast? I told him that's where I was going."

Chapter 51

Thursday, June 20, morning, Starke

The freezing air from the window unit forced Maggie from under the sheet. She made it a general rule not to use the slick, god-knew-what-kind-of-synthetic bedspreads in motels, since she'd never seen a maid throw one in the laundry. Gick.

She had to admit, though, she slept hard. Somehow, being away from all the craziness must have relaxed her. Sitting on the edge of the bed (the Beauty Rest had been surprisingly firm), she realized there was no coffee maker in the room. She got dressed and headed to the office.

"Good mornin', darlin'," said Amber. "How'd you sleep last night?"

"Good morning to you. I slept great, thank you. Is there a place to get coffee nearby?"

"I'm glad you were comfortable. We have some coffee in the back here. You want some?"

Maggie could smell the burned sludge. "Thanks, but I want to get a bite to eat, too. Can you recommend any breakfast spots?"

"Well, sure. Everybody seems to like the Over Easy Café. It's two blocks west of here. When you get to the stop light, look for the HOSPITAL sign and head in that direction. You'll see it right across the street from the main entrance to Shands Medical Center. In fact, the medical center's cafeteria is pretty good and cheap."

Maggie thanked her and set out. She didn't equate hospital cafeterias with great coffee, so she headed for the café. The sun blared so hot, she was in a full sweat by the time she found it. It looked dark inside. Then she spotted an official looking document taped behind clear plastic. "Restaurant Closed Until Further Notice – Florida Department of Business and Professional Regulation/Hotel and Restaurant Division, Bradford County". Not good. Medical center cafeteria it was then.

She expected more of an urgent care/doctor's office, but this was a hospital, albeit a small one. Plus, it was air conditioned. And clean. And the health department probably hadn't shut down their food service, a win-win in Maggie's book.

The cafeteria bustled with activity. Obviously, a shift had just changed, because most of the diners wore scrubs. Maggie looked down at herself. She still had on the "new" outfit she bought in Tallahassee. She really should be more careful with her things. All the crispness had sweat out of it; wrinkles from the car and seatbelt etched it, and she noticed she had dribbled iced tea down the front. Thankfully, she didn't know anyone here, so she could look like a bum anonymously. She grabbed a large coffee and asked for a doughnut.

"I'm sorry, ma'am," said the man behind the food bar. "We only serve nutritious foods here."

Sheesh. "Right – hospital. Well, I guess I'll take the turkey bacon, egg white and cheese wrap." Might as well eat Styrofoam. She took her tray to the checkout line. The hair-netted clerk looked her up and down and said, "Your EBT card, please?"

Jesus. Did she really look like she was on food stamps? She had to get home and get back to her normal life. This whole trip had obviously taken a tremendous toll on her. "I have money," Maggie spat. "How much is it?" She settled up and walked to a table by the window, her back to the rest of the room. Her phone dinged.

Cheryl. Of course. Where are you? flashed on the screen. Let her worry. Maggie turned it off and stared out the window, then down at her plate. She should have grabbed a newspaper or something.

She felt a presence looming behind her. Probably someone wanting to share a table. Maggie looked up and saw the reflection of a very grungy man.

The man caught her eye in the reflection.

Shit. Leave it to her to be in a random cafeteria and run into someone she knew. She turned.

"Warren?" Maggie took a guess.

The man looked at her blankly. "Huh?"

"Aren't you Warren who works on the oil rig?"

"Um, yeah, Warren," Buddy said. Unbelievable that he would run into Lute's sister-in-law. "Maggie, right? What are you doing here? You sick?"

Maggie took in his disheveled appearance. "I think I should be asking you the same thing. What happened to you?"

Buddy paused for a moment. "Mind if I sit down?"

"Sure. Have a seat. And no, I'm not sick. I just stopped in for a cup of coffee and some breakfast on my way back to my sister's."

Buddy half smiled. "You always eat at hospital cafeterias?"

"Not when I can avoid it, but the only other place nearby was shuttered by the health department. This was close, and I was desperate for caffeine. What about you? Why are you here?"

He had to remember what all he had told her before. "I told you about my brother, right?"

Maggie nodded.

Whew. Lucky guess. "We got in a boating accident the other day, and he got hurt pretty bad."

"Oh, that's terrible. Is he going to be okay?"

"I don't know. He hit his head, and he's been unconscious ever since. But the doctors said everything else seems normal."

"I'm so sorry," Maggie said, touching his hand. She felt that little zing and remembered their drunken kiss at the bar. "Are you staying here in town?"

"I'm just staying in his room with him. They have a recliner in there."

Maggie looked him over again. "How long have you been here? If you want, I can sit with him while you run home and get cleaned up."

Buddy looked down at himself. He still wore the mud-caked, petroleum-soaked clothes he had on when they were rescued. "Yeah, I should, but I came here in the ambulance, and I don't have a way to get home. I've been so worried, I hadn't even thought about what I looked like."

"Understandable. And you look fine, just worn out. I'd offer to take you, but I'm not quite ready to get back to Eugenia yet," said Maggie.

Buddy did not want to get in a car with Lute's sister-in-law. "Naw. I'll be okay. I can stand being filthy a few more days."

"Oh, wait," said Maggie. "I have an idea. My hotel is just about two blocks from here, and they have a coin-op washer and dryer right next to my room. Why don't you go there, get cleaned up and your clothes washed, and I'll stay here with your brother?"

"That's real nice of you, but I couldn't do that." Buddy was tempted, though there were several ways this could go wrong. "Are you here by yourself?"

"Yeah. I was headed back from one sister's to the other's and decided I wasn't ready for more chaos, so I stopped. I have to say, it's the most relaxed I've been since I got to Florida. Really. Go on over to the Motel 12 – here's my key, room 4, oh, and here's some change." She handed him the change the judgmental cashier had given her. "What room is your brother in?"

"He's on the second floor by the main desk. His name's Delmont Crapps."

"Crapps?" Maggie tried to suppress a smile. "I guess I never heard your last name."

He had not meant to do that. Too late now. "Would you tell people if your name was Crapps?"

"Good point," Maggie laughed. "Here's the key. The place is just a few blocks to the right and then look down the road. You'll see the sign. I'll call the motel if anything happens while you're gone."

Buddy decided to go for it. He hadn't stunk like this since he was in prison.

Chapter 52

Thursday, June 20, midday

After several intestinal explosions, Lute decided a hair of the dog was the only solution. Unfortunately, there was no booze in the house. Rhoda must have finished it off. Despite the dizziness, he got in the truck and headed for the Broken Cleat, but got worried Fish and Wildlife might be looking for him. He turned around and drove west toward Waldo. He knew a little joint over there.

The parking lot was practically empty. He opened the heavy door and smells of stale beer and cigarettes hit him like a wall. He gagged, but headed into the dark room. A few old men slumped on stools, but other than that, the place was empty.

"What can I get you, honey?" rasped the bleached blonde behind the bar. Heavy makeup filled the creases in her skin, pendulous breasts stretched her tank top and a nonfiltered cigarette hung from her bottom lip.

"I'll take a bottle of Ron Rico and a glass. No ice," he said.

"Oooh, baby. My kind of guy – likes it strong and cheap." Her purr sounded more like a growl. She leaned across the counter, getting as close to Lute as she could when her laughter broke into a phlegmy bark.

When her coughing slowed, she handed him the bottle and glass. "Here ya go, baby doll."

"Thanks. Run a tab," said Lute, moving to the darkest booth in the place.

Halfway through the bottle, his stomach started to calm. Able to focus, he reviewed the last few days. His boat sunk, the government and the local law after him. And that stupid kid he hired; Lute didn't know if he was dead or alive. The kicker, though, was being rejected by his church – his own flock. He couldn't even go to Burt for help, thanks to that dumbass son, Weldon.

The longer he drank, the madder he got. It all started with the board of trustees and that damn choir director. He never did like that weaselly little milk-toast. Acting all pious and prissy like he owned the church. Then the prick didn't even have the balls to fire him to his face – wrote a letter, for chrissakes – didn't even sign his name, but Lute knew it was from him. None of the other trustees would have gone along with that.

By the end of the bottle, Lute knew what he had to do.

Thursday, June 20, afternoon

"What's up, Cheryl?" Rhoda turned her phone back on once she was ready to face Lute.

"Where have you been?" Cheryl said, shrill with panic. "Is Maggie with you?"

"Maggie? No. I thought she was still with you."

"I hurt her feelings and she took off. I haven't been able to reach her since. I'm worried something happened to her," said Cheryl.

Rhoda considered the situation. "Think about it, Cheryl. You hurt her feelings, and so did I when I told her to go to your house. This is typical Maggie – she goes overboard trying to help and then turns all martyr on us. She probably disappeared on purpose, so we'll worry and feel bad. I'm sure she's fine. Plus, she's in my car. If she'd been in an accident or something, I would have heard about it."

Cheryl took a breath. "You're probably right. But, if we don't hear anything by tomorrow, I'm calling the police."

"We'll hear. Her curiosity will get to her. She won't want to miss out on anything. Just keep texting and calling. She'll pick up eventually. Let me know as soon as you hear from her."

"I hope you're right," sighed Cheryl. "If you hear from her first, let me know immediately."

"Okay, worrywart. She's fine. Trust me." Rhoda truly believed that, plus, she had bigger things to deal with than Maggie's little temper tantrum.

It was time to face the music with Lute, if he was home. If he wasn't, she was going to cook up some other god-awful concoction for him. She remembered there was some hamburger that had been in the fridge for a couple of weeks. A few hours in the sun, and it ought to be good and ripe. Chili would be perfect.

She practiced her loving-and-caring face in the rearview mirror as she drove down their road. When she arrived home, the truck was still gone and the lights were off. Praise Jesus.

Chapter 53

Thursday, June 20, afternoon, Shands Medical Center, Starke

Three hours. Surely Warren would have finished his laundry by now. What had she done? One touch of the hand and she'd invited a total stranger (practically) to her motel room. Idiot. Fortunately, she had locked her things in the trunk of the car – more to avoid bedbugs than robbers. But still.

Bored to distraction, she turned on her phone. The incoming texts pinged like a slot machine - Cheryl, Cheryl, Cheryl, Cheryl, Cheryl, Rhoda, Cheryl, Cheryl. She didn't open them. There were also fifteen missed calls and three voicemails. She listened to those.

"Where the hell are you, Maggie? Are you okay? Please, just let me or Rhoda know you're okay. I'm sorry if I hurt your feelings, but I just wasn't ready. Call or text me."

"Come on, Maggie. I'm ready to call the police."

The last one was the clincher. "You're being a spoiled brat. I'm the one who's had all the problems. Quit making this about yourself. Call me."

Maggie burst out laughing. Typical Cheryl. She had a great job, plenty of money, a beautiful home, an active social life, good health and incredible talent, but a Hollywood producer dumped her, and she acted like she was sitting on a dung heap with boils. First world problems for sure.

If only they could think more like Rhoda, the one who truly had major problems. She rarely complained and never asked for help, while Cheryl and Maggie volleyed woe and worry over any minor issue. Then again, neither Maggie nor Cheryl depended on pharmaceuticals to get through the day.

The messages made her stop and think. She didn't feel badly about taking time to herself, but she should reach out to them. I'm fine. Just ran into an old friend (small world! Lol). Decided to take a few days off to rest and give you two some time without me hovering around. Will be back at Rhoda's soon. Don't worry. She hit send and turned off the phone, knowing Cheryl would call right back.

◆◆◆

Buddy stood under the steaming shower until it turned cold. After the run-off changed from brown to clear, he assessed his situation. Fresh out of jail, his only brother badly hurt, no place to live, no car to drive and no job. The only money he had was whatever he had unearthed at Lute's house or earned on the boat.

He should just hitch a ride back to Del's, grab his stash and head for parts unknown. But Del was such a sweet kid. Buddy had basically raised him until he was old enough to fend for himself. Del had been the only one who understood when Buddy went after their father and almost bludgeoned him to death with a tire iron. Del testified on his behalf at the trial, but he came across as an ignorant redneck to the jury. Del wrote Buddy every week while he was in prison. No. Buddy couldn't leave him now.

Soooo, here he was in Lute's sister-in-law's motel room – a woman he had only met once. The old Buddy would have ransacked her room or stolen a car from the lot, but she had been so nice. Plus she'd laid a pretty fine kiss on him at the Cleat that night. His opinion of her also went up when she described Lute as crazy. From the way he saw it, she probably wouldn't mind if Lute disappeared.

Chapter 54

Thursday, June 20, afternoon

Rhoda checked the fridge when she got home. No curry, no oyster stew. Perfect. One more strong dose of e coli or botulism ought to do it. She hummed show tunes as she waved flies off the rancid hamburger and stirred up a spicy pot of chili.

The whole house seemed brighter and nicer when Lute wasn't in it. She wasn't sure where he was, but seeing the papers from the Coast Guard, Fish and Wildlife, a county sheriff and the Circuit Court, she figured he was in hiding somewhere. Maybe this was how his revolution started. She laughed - looked like THEY really were coming to get him.

Rhoda was still laughing as she packed a bag, and wrote Lute a note. *Sweetheart, made you some chili. Help yourself. Cheryl called about some crisis with Maggie, so I'm headed to Tallahassee for a few days. LU.* She threw her bag in Lute's car and headed back to the safety of Ben's.

Thursday, June 20, late afternoon

Lute closed one eye to focus as he careened toward Eugenia. That bitch at the bar had cut him off after the second bottle. She must be one of THEM. He'd show her. He'd show them all. But first things first. He had to start with the worst offender and then work down the list, starting with that pussy choir director.

Lute had lost all sense of time in that darkened bar. In fact, he had no idea what day it was, how long ago he'd been fired, or when his boat had sunk. But it was still daylight, so he had a chance of catching Arnold at home. He gripped the wheel attempting to keep the truck on the road until he skidded up to Arnold's house. Staggering up the steps, Lute pounded on the door. "Arnold, you son of a bitch, open up. Quit being such a coward and come face the music." No one answered. "Fuck 'em," he said as he turned the knob and stumbled into the living room.

It took a few seconds for his open eye to adjust to the dark room, but there on the couch sat a wide-eyed young woman. Arnold's daughter.

"Where's your stinkin' father?"

Ramona pressed herself back against the couch. She had been hoping Delmont would stop by. "Mr. Mason?" she squeaked. She'd never seen a drunk person before, and he terrified her.

"PARSON Mason, bitch! Now where's your father?"

She gasped. A tear rolled down her cheek as Lute staggered toward her. "He might be at work or at church." She gripped the armrest. She felt trapped as Lute propped an arm on either side of her and put his face inches from hers.

"Church, huh? You mean the one I'm not allowed in anymore, thanks to your old man?"

She nodded and cried harder.

"And he'd leave a pretty little thing like you here, all alone?"

She tried to push him away, but he kneeled on the couch straddling her and caught her wrists in one hand. "Bet you never seen a real man before, have you sweet thing? Is that what your daddy calls you? Sweet thing?" As he spoke, he reached down with his other hand, unzipped his fly and pulled out his flaccid penis.

Ramona screamed. "STOP! PLEASE, STOP! WHAT DO YOU WANT FROM ME? Stop, stop, please..." she sobbed as he grabbed one of her hands and forced it to his scrotum.

"That's right, baby, beg for it," he panted. "Now just start squeezing that pump right there nice and easy. Then I'm going to make a real woman out of you. Meet the King Cobra, sweet thing."

Ramona yanked at the limp mess in her hand and thrust her knee as hard as she could, knocking Lute off balance. He fell back while she ran out the front door screaming and sobbing.

Stunned, Lute sat on the floor. What just happened? As the scene came into focus, his stomach lurched and he discharged the two bottles of rum on the floor. Staggering to his feet, penis dangling, he made his way outside, climbed in the truck and sped off. After a few blocks, the guilt passed and pride took over. "I showed that bastard. Teach him to fire me."

Ramona was still collapsed, sobbing on the sidewalk when Arnold got home. After helping her inside, he dialed 911.

Chapter 55

Thursday, June 20, afternoon Starke

"Sorry that took so long," said Buddy when he found Maggie in the waiting room. "Any news on Del?"

"Warren, I worried you'd taken off," said Maggie. "But you definitely look a thousand percent better than when you left. I haven't really heard anything. They won't let me in since I'm not family, but the nurses have been real nice. All they've told me is he's holding steady."

"Damn. I was hoping he'd wake up." Buddy looked toward Del's room.

"You go on in," said Maggie. "I ought to get back to whatever I was doing."

"Listen, Maggie. I can't thank you enough. I think you may have saved my life. I didn't realize how much I needed a break."

"That's okay. It gave me some time to chill, too. Hey, before I leave, do you need to call anybody? Your boss or maybe somebody else who should know about your brother?"

Buddy just stared. He sure as hell didn't want her calling his boss – not the made-up oil rig one and definitely not Lute. But Ramona. She should probably know about this. "I'm all good, but my brother has this girlfriend, Ramona, in Eugenia. I don't even know her last name. All I know is that her dad is the choir director at one of those churches in town."

"Does the name Arnold sound familiar?" asked Maggie.

"That might be it. I can't really remember," said Buddy.

"Let me at least look up the church. Maybe they have a directory or something." She tapped on the screen searching for the Eugenia Healing and Helping in the Name of Jesus Tabernacle. Amazed they had a website, she clicked on the link. "Luther Mason - Parson, Arnold Chance – Music Director, Rhoda Mason – Accompanist."

She found an A. Chance in Eugenia in the White Pages. "I think I found it," Maggie said. "You can use my phone, if you'd like."

Buddy hadn't seen a cell phone like this. Before jail, he'd had the old kind you bought at convenience stores, but this looked completely different.

"Here, you want me to dial? You can take it over to the waiting room for some privacy," Maggie said.

"Uh, thanks," he said, grabbing the phone and walking down the hall.

A few minutes later, he returned.

"Did you find her?" Maggie asked.

"Yeah, I think so. I mean the man who answered knew Delmont. But her dad, or whoever it was, sounded pretty distracted. So I told him Delmont was hurt and over here at Shands. He thanked me and hung up."

"Well, at least they know," said Maggie, taking back her phone. "Anybody else before I leave?"

"No. Thanks. Really, I mean that, Maggie. I don't know why you've been so nice to me, but I appreciate it." He leaned toward her and gave her an awkward hug.

"You would have done the same for me."

Not likely. "Anyway, thanks again. Maybe I'll see you around sometime."

"Maybe, though I'll be headed back north soon," said Maggie. "You take care. I hope your brother makes a full recovery."

Chapter 56

Thursday, June 20, dusk Eugenia

Lute, spraying gravel as he swerved to miss an oncoming panel truck, pressed the accelerator even harder as he looked back. So what if he ran the bastard off the road? He had to get the hell out of there. He'd park Burt's truck behind the house, so THEY couldn't tell he was home. He'd go in, grab his Bug-Out Bag, and wait until dark. Then, he'd dig up his fortune and take off. He'd send word to Rhoda later when things calmed down.

There was no one around when he arrived at the house, thank the Lord. He pulled through the carport and parked in back. He felt the ground give a little near the septic tank. He'd have to be careful pulling out. He flat-backed his way along the wall and into the sleeping porch, where he dropped to the floor and crawled to the main house.

The smell of chili triggered a pounding headache and rolling gut. Probably just starving, since he'd left the contents of his stomach on Arnold's living room floor. Seeing no one outside, he grabbed the crockpot and Rhoda's note off the stove. Propped against the cabinets, he devoured the chili while he read the note. It was just as well she wasn't here. THEY would rape and torture her when THEY came.

♦♦♦

Weldon instantly recognized the truck that ran him off the road – his father's. And he knew damned well who was driving it. A theft and injunction violation would surely be enough to get Lute thrown in jail. He called his attorney's office.

"What do you mean 'you'll try to work it out'?" Weldon shouted into the phone. "I thought violating an injunction was cause for immediate arrest." He listened to the secretary's detached response, then screamed, "No, I don't know if he has a goddamned attorney you can contact, and no, I do not want to handle this myself. That's what I hired you for. No wonder people take the law into their own hands. You fucking billboard attorneys are nothing but a bunch of bottom-feeders shitting out red tape to delay everything, so you can get more money." He hung up and threw the phone down.

Fuck 'em. He'd take care of this once and for all. With the safe deposit box key now in his possession, thanks to his guardianship, he raced to the bank before it closed to retrieve everything, most particularly his mother's pearl handled pistol. That son-of-bitch, Luther Mason, would not get away with this.

Thursday, June 20, afternoon, Starke

Maggie decided she should head back to Eugenia. Regardless of Cheryl's refusal to go near Lute, Maggie wanted to see if that necklace was still in the display case. She paid her bill at the Motel 12, promised Amber she'd come back sometime, and hit the road. She'd have to hurry to get to Eugenia before the pawn shop closed.

Main Street was deserted, but the shop still had the OPEN sign in the window. She parked and walked in. Vern was counting out the register. "Hello, again. Can I help you?"

"I hope so," Maggie said, as she glanced at the display case.

"Still thinking about some jewelry?" Vern followed her eyes.

"Oh no. It's just all so pretty. I think I am going to need that nice handicap toilet seat you had here the other day, though." Maggie couldn't believe the words came out of her mouth. How the hell was she going to get that foul thing out of here?

Vern stared at her for a minute too long. "Rhoda still havin' trouble, is she?"

"She's doing okay, I'm just trying to make life a little easier for her. I'll be heading home soon, so I want to make sure she has what she needs."

"That's right nice of you." He worked his way around the counter, unearthed the despicable item, and handed it to Maggie. "That'll be twenty dollars."

Never in her life had Maggie pictured herself buying a handicapped toilet seat, much less one well-used and never cleaned. "What a bargain," she said, handing him the twenty. "By the way, how late are you open tonight?"

"We usually stay open till seven on Thursdays, but it's been kind of slow. I may shut down early. Why? You comin' back?" Vern almost sneered at her.

"Ha. No, I don't think so, but the way things have been going lately, you never know," Maggie tried to laugh, but it came out more like a bark.

She wrestled the thing out to the car and shoved it by the handles into the backseat. She couldn't find her hand sanitizer fast enough. She was tempted to drink it.

Vern waited for her to drive off before flipping the sign to CLOSED and dialing Lute's "brotherhood" number. He was surprised when no one answered.

Thursday, June 20, late afternoon

The 911 dispatcher for Eugenia was actually located in an adjacent county. The operator processing Arnold's call about a disturbance and possible sexual attack relayed the message to the Florida State Highway Patrol. Arnold, knowing of Lute and the Bradford County Sheriff's close relationship, was relieved someone else showed up to investigate. The responding officer inspected the scene, noting the vomit on the floor and a nasty looking gauze pad on the edge of the couch. He picked it up with his gloved hand. "Is this yours, ma'am?" he asked Ramona.

Shrieks and sobs ensued until she was able to speak. "It come out of Parson Mason's pants when he pulled his man thing …" Ramona collapsed into her mother's arms before finishing the sentence.

The officer bagged the evidence and completed the report, despite Ramona's sobbing in her squeaky, broken voice, and Arnold's incessant raging against the perpetrator. The officer accepted the church bulletin picture of Lute Arnold gave him and offered to drive Ramona to the nearest emergency room.

It was only then that Arnold remembered the call from some man about Delmont being hurt. "Thank you officer, but we can take her." He liked Delmont and hoped seeing him would distract Ramona enough to help her get past this horrible trauma.

"All right, sir, but please have the medical personnel complete this form and return it to us, so we can add it to the case file. And don't worry, miss," he turned to Ramona. "We're going to find this man and make sure he is prosecuted to the full extent of the law." He handed a duplicate copy of the report to Arnold. "You hang on to this, and if you think of anything else, or need any more assistance, just call the number at the top of the page. My name is at the bottom. You can ask for me."

Arnold thanked the patrolman and turned to his family. His wife sat holding his hysterical, abused daughter. It had been a bad week for the Chance family, all thanks to Lute Mason. First, the maniac had screamed profanities at the choir, flattened Arnold, caused the Hollywood producer to abandon their big project, and now this unforgiveable act of violence and evil.

His wife, mirroring his thoughts said, "Lute Mason is the devil incarnate. God will smite him dead."

Chapter 57

Thursday, afternoon, Eugenia

"Where the hell have you been?" screeched Cheryl when she answered Maggie's call.

"Jesus, Cher, calm down. Hello, to you, too." This was exactly why Maggie hadn't called. "I just took a break. Don't worry yourself with the details. Listen, the reason I'm calling now is the necklace. It's still at that pawn shop, but I think the owner is suspicious of me for some reason. I took your documents thinking I could go to the cops myself…"

"You stole my documents out of my jewelry box?" Cheryl yelled so loud, Maggie had to put the phone on the seat next to her. "Who died and made you God?"

Deep yoga breath. Maggie tried again. "You said you were never coming here again, and I thought you might want Mom's necklace back; but you know what? Just forget it. I'm scared of that pawn guy anyway. So, never mind. I'll mail you the documents, and you can wear those around your neck." Maggie hung up.

The phone rang instantly, as she expected.

"I'm sorry, Maggie. Of course I want the necklace back. You just had me scared to death, disappearing like that. Plus, I've hardly heard from Rhoda, which worries me."

"Well, I was going to take the papers to the sheriff's office, but since everything's in your name, I was afraid they'd accuse me of stealing them."

"You're probably right," Cheryl said. "We do not need that right now."

"Anyway, I worry that guy at the shop will sell it or take it home, just to get rid of me."

"Okay, okay. You've convinced me. I'll leave work now and try to get there before that pawn shop closes."

"Well, you'd better hurry. The guy said he's usually open till seven, but he might close early."

"Damn," said Cheryl. "I hope I make it. But if I have to wait till tomorrow morning, I will. I guess we could stay at their house, as long as Lute's not around. Have you been by? Is Rhoda even there?"

"I drove by once and didn't see any lights or activity, so I'm not sure. There were no cars or trucks outside. I really don't want to go in unless Rhoda's there. If we miss the pawn shop, we'll figure something out."

Cheryl sighed. "Okay, I'll see you later. It'll be easier to travel without, without Chief…" the words turned into sobs.

"Awww. Hang in there, sis," Maggie said. "Just let me know when you get to Starke, and we can arrange to meet up."

♦♦♦

The sound of the ringing phone finally penetrated Rhoda's consciousness. She opened her eyes and took a second to remember where she was. Certainly not in Kansas anymore.

Ben's bedroom was clean, decorated with new furniture, and soft, fluffy linens as opposed to the church rummage sale cast-offs she was used to. "All right, all right, already," she said grabbing the phone. Maggie. Okay, she was ready for this. "Hey, Mags. What's up?"

Maggie gratefully noted no interrogation or accusations. That was one good thing about Rhoda's furtive ways. She took everybody and everything at face value. Usually. "Hey. Good to hear your voice. Are you home? I still have your car, which I'm sure you need."

"Glad to hear from you, too. Cheryl's been driving me nuts, calling and worrying. You'll have to fill me in on what you've been up to," dodged Rhoda.

"So are you home?"

"No, not yet. I've been staying at a friend's."

"Is everything okay? Did Lute hurt you again?" A constant worry.

"No, not really. But, well, it's a long story. Really long story. Where are you?" Rhoda asked.

"I'm here in town, but wanted to make sure you were home before I went over there. I have a few things to fill you in on as well."

271

"I don't think Lute's home, but I'm not sure. He's been AWOL." Rhoda hoped he was passed out somewhere, near comatose with food poisoning. "I heard a rumor that a crab boat sunk the other day; it could have been his."

"The boat sunk?" Maggie gasped and then started laughing. "Wow. Who saw that coming? It looked like a pile of crap when I saw it and that was after he 'fixed it up like new.' That's a riot." Getting no response from Rhoda, she stopped laughing. "What happened?"

"I don't know the details. I heard it through the grapevine," said Rhoda. She stalled. She wasn't at all sure she wanted Maggie any more involved in her business. "I don't think I can meet you today. I have to get my new cast checked. It's rubbing me funny."

"Oh, no. I didn't realize you had a new one. I can take you," Maggie jumped back into rescue mode.

"It was time for a smaller one. But I can drive myself; I have Lute's car. No need for both of us to waste a day in a waiting room. You go on by the house. I'm ninety-nine percent sure Lute's not home. But he's trying so hard to make up to me, he wouldn't bother you if he was. I'll call you when I get back, and if you haven't been by already, I'll meet you then. Okay?" Rhoda knew it sounded lame, but she couldn't face Maggie or that house right now.

"Isn't it a little late for a doctor's appointment?"

Rhoda's voice went up half an octave. "Oh, this doctor is a friend of mine. I told him it was bothering me, so he said he'd take care of it."

272

Maggie recognized the dodge. There was no prying the truth out of Rhoda until she was good and ready. "Okay. I'm just glad to know you're safe. I do want to see you before I leave though."

"You're leaving? To go home? When?"

"Don't sound so excited, Sister. I know I've done enough damage here to last a lifetime. You'll all be better off without me," Maggie pouted.

"Oh, no, Mags. You've been a big help. Things have just been insane lately. I mean, our life is crazy, as a rule, but this last few weeks has really been off the charts. It's not your fault that Lute's supposed Armageddon seems to be bubbling up around us. You're just a victim of bad timing. Anyway, my leg is much better. This smaller cast really helps." Sometimes Rhoda amazed herself at how easily the lies rolled out of her mouth.

"Whatever," sighed Maggie. "Talk to you later."

Rhoda shook her head as the line went dead. Poor Maggie. But she'd survive, and they'd all forgive each other. They had to. They were family – the only family they had left. She had bigger problems than Maggie's hurt feelings right now.

Chapter 58
Thursday, June 20, evening

Arnold glanced in the rearview mirror and saw his wife rocking his precious daughter, both women broken and afraid. "Don't you worry anymore, Pumpkin," he said as calmly as he could. "We're just going to the hospital to make sure you're okay. They'll sign some papers that will help the police put that monster in jail." The quiet weeping from the backseat both broke his heart and filled him with rage.

Ramona looked at her dad through swollen eyes. "Will they hurt me?" Her normally shrieking voice was barely a whisper.

"No, baby. They definitely will not hurt you. They'll do everything they can to make you feel better," Arnold white-knuckled the steering wheel. "Oh, I know something else that might make you feel better. I got a phone call from a guy claiming to be Delmont's brother."

"Buddy?" Ramona sniffled.

"That was it, Buddy. He said Delmont was also at the hospital, so after we're done we'll go see him."

"Is he sick or hurt? Did Parson Mason hurt him, too?"

"Oh, I don't know, but he must be good enough to tell his brother to call you." It dawned on Arnold perhaps news of Delmont being in the hospital wasn't as cheerful as he hoped. "I'm sure he's fine."

"Okay," Ramona sighed. The muffled sobs continued.

Thursday, June 20, early evening

Maggie, unsure what to do with herself until Cheryl got there, decided to go to the Broken Cleat for a bite, a beer and possibly some dirt on the sunken crab boat. Hopefully, Lute wouldn't be there.

Still in her car in the parking lot, she texted Cheryl. I'm at the Broken Cleat Bar and Bait Shop by the river. Text me when you get close to town and I'll meet you at the shop if it's open.

Maggie started to mention that Rhoda was at a friend's, and no one seemed to know where Lute was, but decided too much information might scare Cheryl off. Maggie would feel a lot better if they went to the pawn shop and Rhoda's house together. She sent the text and walked up to the window to order.

"Hey, Pops. I'll take a light beer if you have any."

"You're Rhoda's sister, right?" Pops said, wiping bait residue off his hands onto his apron. "Haven't seen you around for a few days."

"Well, it's not like I'm a regular. I've only been here once. But you're right. I've been out of town visiting my other sister," Maggie said. "Have you seen Lute?" She tried to sound nonchalant. "I thought he kept his crab boat here."

"I guess you didn't hear," said Pops.

Maggie waited for him to continue. He didn't.

"Hear what?"

"Lute's boat blew up on the St. Johns the other day. Sunk straight to the bottom. Ever' law enforcement agency in the state's been here lookin' for him. Have you seen him?" Pops handed her the beer.

Maggie grabbed it by the top to avoid the blob of chum sliding down the side of the can. "What? It sunk? Was anybody hurt?"

Pops narrowed his eyes and stared at her. "You been gone, you say? Didn't Rhoda tell you about it?"

Maggie felt her heart skip. She couldn't tell the truth, since she was sure Rhoda didn't want anyone to know she was staying with a friend. "Actually, um," she had not inherited her sister's gift for lying, "you see, um, well, Rhoda's been with me and my other sister. We've tried calling the house and Lute's cell, but no one's answered for days. She said his phone probably got turned off or something. That happens every once in a while. Anyway, I had to come back to get some of my things from the house." She looked at Pops. "You don't think he got hurt on the boat, do you?"

Pops shrugged. "I heard a young guy he had working for him was taken by ambulance to the hospital. The kids who rescued him said an older man stayed in the water. I'm figuring that was Lute."

"What does law enforcement want with him? It was just an accident, right?"

"Well, a boat accident ain't no different from a car accident. Somebody's gotta be held accountable. Plus, the owner has to get all the oil and gas cleaned up and get that boat out of the water."

"Wow," Maggie said. "I had no idea. What a mess. How in the world would an average guy like Lute get all that done?"

Pops shook his head. "I don't know, but it'll cost him a chunk of change just to clean up the oil spill. Then there's usually a mess of fines from every agency you can think of. If he can't get the boat up himself, he'll have to pay a salvager to do it. Lute may have had some luck with crabbing, but not enough to pull in that kind of dough."

"But nobody's seen him? I haven't been by the house yet, but I hate to just barge in over there," Maggie said. She really was afraid to go now. If Lute was hiding out, he'd most likely shoot first and ask questions later. It sounded like all his paranoid fears were crashing in on him.

"I know what you mean. But if he's there, he probably wouldn't mind. He is family, after all," said Pops. "Did you want anything to eat with that?"

Maggie looked at the chum now drying on her flip flop. "Naw. Not yet. I think I'll just pick a shady spot and keep trying to reach Lute. How much do I owe you for the beer?"

"Two bucks," said Pops. "You sure you don't want some catfish? Just gettin' ready to pull a fresh basket out of the fryer."

Maggie shivered, wondering how much of the chum made it into the batter. He had been forthcoming with information about Lute, though. "Sure, Pops. That sounds tasty."

He disappeared for a minute and came back with a greasy basket of fish. "Here you go. That'll be $4.95. If I see Lute, I'll tell him you're lookin' for him."

"Thanks," she said as she handed him the money and stuffed a dollar in the tip jar. "I'd appreciate that. I'm getting kind of worried now."

Pops put the money in the cash register and turned back to the bait cooler, obviously finished with the conversation.

◆◆◆

Lute scrambled around, stuffing a few clothes and toiletries in his Bug-Out Bag before he army-crawled through the house toward the carport. He sweat and shivered. His head pounded, and his stomach lurched and rolled. "Lord, I promise to be a better man. Just stop this cramping. I'll never drink again, Lord; just make it stop," he whispered toward the ceiling.

He lay on the concrete floor of the sleeping porch waiting for total darkness before going outside to retrieve his buried treasure. If Rhoda didn't make it home before he left, he would send a note to her P.O. Box (the one she didn't know he knew about) and ask her to join him wherever he ended up.

Chapter 59

Thursday, June 20, evening, Starke

Mary Chance held her daughter's hand while the ER doctor had Ramona relate the grisly details of Lute's assault.

"I'll have to examine you for any genital or extra-genital injuries sustained during the attack," said the hospitalist.

Ramona looked at her. "Huh?"

Mary leaned in and whispered, "This nice woman doctor wants to look at your lady parts to see if that monster injured you."

Tears flew out of Ramona's eyes. "Ain't nobody touchin' my lady parts," the shriek in her voice returned.

"I'm sorry, miss," said the doctor. "It's standard procedure. The more medical evidence we can collect, the stronger the case will be against the man who assaulted you."

"But he didn't never touch my lady parts. I tole you, he just unzipped his pants and waggled his man thing at me an' then he grabbed my hand and made me touch it." By now she was screeching like barn owl.

The doctor patted Ramona on the shoulder and handed her a little cup with two pills. "Take these, sweetheart. They'll help you not feel so scared."

Ramona looked at her mom. Mary nodded yes, that she should take the pills.

"The only thing I have to do right now is to clean under your fingernails. You've done that before, right? I notice you have this pretty polish on, so you know what it's like to have your nails cleaned." The doctor spoke in her most soothing tone.

"I reckon that'd be okay," croaked Ramona.

After collecting samples from under the victim's nails, the doctor left the room long enough for the pills to take effect. "Okay, dear. I've read the police reports, and I think we can get by with just a regular exam." She noticed the look of terror in Ramona's eyes. "Don't worry. It'll just be like an exam you have when you go to the doctor for a sore throat or for a medical record for school. This nice nurse, Sally, will be helping me." Sally served to block Ramona's view of the doctor and tried to distract her from the exam.

While the doctor checked Ramona's vital signs and visually inspected her arms, back, chest, and stomach, Sally noticed Ramona's small diamond ring. "Oh what a pretty ring you have. Where did you get a lovely thing like that?"

Ramona looked at the ring and then at the nurse. "My boyfriend got it for me. It's called a promise ring."

The distraction helped. "A promise ring? I don't think I've ever heard of that. What's that mean?" Although Sally had seen plenty of such rings in her day, she wanted to keep Ramona talking.

Ramona smiled for the first time since her arrival. "It means he and I are promisin' to get engaged someday."

"What a lovely idea," Sally said. "Who's the lucky man?"

Ramona blushed. "His name's Delmont. We went to high school together. He's real nice."

"He must be, to buy you something that pretty. He must love you very much."

The doctor asked if she could look at Ramona's legs and thighs. After a quick visual inspection, the doctor felt certain there had been no genital penetration or injury. Finally, she swabbed and sampled as many places as she could and whispered to Mrs. Chance to place Ramona's undergarments in a bag.

"I must say, Ramona, you are one brave young woman. I want you to know that you did nothing wrong. That man did everything wrong. What happened was not your fault, so don't you feel bad about yourself. Like I said, you are a very brave woman coming in here and helping us catch a criminal. You must be very proud of your daughter, Mrs. Chance," the doctor looked at the mother. Sometimes she had seen parents judge their daughters in sexual assault cases, but she didn't see anything like that reflected in Mrs. Chance's eyes.

◆◆◆

"Hey, Bud. Do I smoke?"

Buddy jerked awake in the vinyl recliner. He shook his head to clear the dream he was having that Del was awake.

"Bud? D'ya hear me? Do I smoke?"

Buddy looked over to see Del, upright and alert.

"My god, you're awake." Tears actually formed in Buddy's eyes.

"Where are we?" Del asked.

"We're in a hospital, Del. You've been unconscious for days. Do you remember anything?"

"Do I smoke?" Del looked hopefully at Buddy.

"What?"

"I can't remember - do I smoke or not? If I do, I'd like me a cigarette," Del said, his goofy grin returning.

Buddy laughed and punched him in the arm. "You asshole. You scared the shit out of me."

Del looked at him blankly.

"No, Del. You don't smoke."

"Huh. Well, never mind then."

Just as Buddy pushed the nurse call button, he heard a screeching voice sob, "Oh Delmont!"

"Ramona!" Del gasped as he tried to sit up.

So this is the girlfriend, Buddy thought as he looked her over. She, and the two people with her, probably parents, looked frazzled.

Delmont held out his hand. "Whatcha' doin' in a wheelchair?"

Ramona jumped up and ran to Del's side. "I can't even tell you about it. What happened to you?"

Del looked to Buddy for help on that one.

"Hi, Ramona," said Buddy. "I'm Del's brother. He was in a boating accident, and he got knocked out. He's been out for a long time, but he just woke up before you walked in. I got to say, you all made tracks getting over here since I called."

Ramona gave him the same blank look Del had. No wonder they liked each other.

"Did someone call for a nurse?" squawked the call box.

Buddy related that Del had come out of his coma.

"We'll send someone right in."

Buddy stepped into the hall to give Ramona and Del a chance to catch up. He introduced himself to her parents. "I'm the one who called you earlier. Sorry if I interrupted something, but I thought Ramona would want to know."

Mary sniffled into a tissue while Arnold shuffled uncomfortably. "You did the right thing, son." Arnold decided there was no reason for anyone to know what happened to Ramona. Not now anyway.

A nurse entered the room and sent Ramona to the hall while she examined Delmont.

"Daddy, can I stay here tonight with Del?" Ramona's tears had dried up, but her voice still sounded like fingernails on a blackboard.

"No, baby. Not tonight. I'll bring you back in the morning. He needs his rest, and so do you."

Buddy perked up. "You all going back to Eugenia?"

"I think we'd better. We just wanted to check on Del," said Arnold.

Buddy looked back and forth from the room to Mr. Chance. "Um, if Del checks out okay, do you think you could give me a ride? I've been here since yesterday. I don't have clothes or money or anything. I came here with Del in the ambulance."

Arnold looked at his wife, who nodded her consent. "I guess that'd be okay. Where do you live?"

"Oh just drop me off in town. I can walk. After I talk to the nurse, I'll just wait for you outside," said Buddy. He needed to retrieve his gun from the bushes before heading back to Eugenia.

Chapter 60

Thursday, June 20, evening

Cheryl drove to Eugenia almost as fast as she'd left it. She wanted to get this whole damned business with Lute and the necklace over with. That son of a bitch. She had tried. God knows she had tried to get along with him, but when that selfish lunatic not only stole her mother's diamond but left her poor little defenseless Chief outside to be devoured by the swamp thing – well, that was it. Even Cheryl, God-fearing, Pollyanna Cheryl, had her limits, and that prick had pushed her past all of them. She actually thought she might kill him if she got the chance.

As she neared Starke, she read the text about meeting Maggie at the pawn shop, but it was already past seven. Screw it. She was going straight to that hell-hole Lute had stuck Rhoda in for all these years. Bastard. She picked up her phone and pushed the voice-to-text button. She shouted over one of her favorite gospel songs, "Swing Low, Sweet Chariot," blaring on the radio. Sure the pawn shop is closed. Headed straight to the trailer. You can meet me there if you want. If Lute's not there, we can stay the night and get the necklace in the morning. If he is there maybe we can run him off. I should be there in about a half hour.

Maggie felt her butt vibrate. "Wow," she shouted. She was a little buzzed from the beer (man she couldn't hold her liquor any more), but then remembered her phone was in her back pocket. She tapped the screen to read Cheryl's message.

Sure pawn swing low straight to the trailer carry me if you swing flutes we can stay the night and get the breakfast in Jordan and what did I run him off I should carry me home.

Maggie reread the text. What? Goddamn Cheryl and her voice texts. They never came out right. She tried calling, but Cheryl didn't answer. Jesus. The cell-phone queen not answering her phone? She must really be in a state.

The best Maggie could make out was that Cheryl was going to the trailer. Breakfast? Swings? Who knew? But Maggie decided she'd better head over to Rhoda and Lute's just in case. She finished her beer and catfish, threw away her garbage, then got in the car and headed out.

Thursday, June 20, Eugenia, evening

Finally arriving home after dropping Buddy off in town, Mary and Arnold Chance were barely able to drag Ramona into the house. Whatever pills the doctor had given her, plus the trauma from the assault and the joy of seeing Delmont had done her in. One parent on each side, they took her to her bedroom, removed her shoes, loosened her clothes and put her to bed. She slept instantly.

They tiptoed into the living room, carefully avoiding the floorboards that creaked, and collapsed in their easy chairs.

"I try not to question God's ways," Arnold finally spoke, "but this travesty makes me doubt my belief in a benevolent God." A tear rolled down his cheek.

Mary folded her hands in her lap. "Arnold, you know that now is the time to strengthen our resolve and have faith that Jesus will see us through this and show us the way forward. Why don't we pray?"

Arnold would rather go beat the shit out of Lute Mason, but decided to humor his poor, distraught wife. She was so helpless and frail; if prayer helped her cope, they would pray.

Mary grabbed his hand. "Dear Lord Jesus, we beseech you to give us strength to help our precious Ramona through this crisis. We pray, most especially, for you to guide us in righteousness to be good Christians and make the world a better place for our daughter and for all of God's children. Make us your tools in Healing and Helping for Jesus. Amen." Mary raised her eyes toward heaven before looking at her husband. "Now doesn't that feel better?"

Arnold squeezed her hand. "You are a saint, Mary Chance. I am humbled by your devout faith."

"I just trust in Jesus to guide me," she said. "Now, in the spirit of true Christian fellowship, I think I need to go see that poor Rhoda Mason. She is Lute's victim as well, I'm sure of it. Do you mind driving me over there?"

"Over to Lute and Rhoda's house? Are you crazy, woman?" Arnold gasped.

"Now, now. Just hear me out. I bet Lute's not even there, and I would really like to talk to her, as sisters in Christ. In fact, let me get my quilting bag. Rhoda and I always talk better when we're quilting for the Lord. If you don't take me, I'll drive myself, even though I can't see at night." Mary's voice sounded more resolute than he'd ever heard.

"I think you're asking for trouble, but since you're so determined, I'll drive you over, but I'm going in with you," Arnold puffed up his chest like the great protector.

"Absolutely not, Arnold. You and Lute would just get in a fight. Like I said, he may not be home. Plus, I want you back here in case Ramona wakes up. You just drop me off, and I'll spend a little quality stitching time with Rhoda. I'll call you when I'm ready to come home or if there's any sign of trouble. I promise."

He knew when he was beat. "All right. Let's lock Ramona in here tight, so that maniac can't come back."

"He's not ever coming back, Arnold. Why that would be suicide," Mary said as she grabbed her big bag of supplies and headed for the car.

Chapter 61

Thursday, June 20, evening

Lute woke on the floor.

The darkness intensified his vertigo and disorientation. He felt the space around him. The sleeping porch; okay. Searching further, he felt his Bug-Out Bag. Good. Now that it was dark, he could safely go outside, retrieve his gold and guns and escape before THEY came and got him.

Protected by the cloak of night, he grabbed the bag and staggered into the carport. He started to overturn the dinghy when a tsunami of nausea overtook him. He fell to his knees as shit and vomit blasted from both ends.

◆◆◆

Cheryl didn't see Rhoda's old car when she approached the trailer, but figured Maggie would be along any minute. It didn't matter if Maggie did show up. Cheryl was not afraid to confront Lute about the necklace and her precious Chief. In fact, she relished the idea of standing up to that worthless bastard. It was about time somebody did.

She parked the car on the side of the road and got out. It was darker than a cave out here by the swamp. Obviously, no one was home yet. Not a problem; she would wait. Turning on her flashlight app, she made her way up the sidewalk when she heard a gagging, retching sound in the carport. She turned her light that direction and spotted Lute on his hands and knees erupting from every orifice in his body. Perfect.

"Stand up, you bastard," she screamed as she made her way toward him. "I know what you did, and you're going pay me back for everything you took from me, if I have to take it out in a pound of flesh."

Lute, despite his weakened state, dug with one hand under the dinghy until he found Burt's gun. With all the strength he had left, he grabbed the gun and bolted up, howling like a beast.

Cheryl, seeing his crazed eyes and the gun, dropped her phone and grabbed the closest thing – the shovel. As he lunged toward her, she gripped the handle like a baseball bat and swung with all her adrenaline-fueled might. The shovel blade connecting with his head rang like a church bell. Stunned that she had actually made contact, she dropped the shovel and retrieved her phone.

The flashlight beam found him as he dropped to his knees then fell back against a carport pillar. "Lute? Lute?" She took a tentative step toward him. "Lute? Wake up."

Panicked, she slid through the fetid mess he made and reached down to check for a pulse. "Lute?" She took a deep breath and concentrated. Finally, she felt his heart beat. Not pounding, but strong enough to indicate he was alive. Gagging from the smell, she backed into the yard onto a patch of weeds and grass. She looked down and swiped her feet to clean the foul matter off her shoes.

When she looked back at Lute, the enormity of what she had done hit her. She ran in the house, turned on every

light she could find, and looked for Rhoda or Maggie. No one was home. What if he regained consciousness and shot her with that gun?

Hysterical now, she got in the car, made a U-turn and headed for town. Where the hell was Maggie? A few cars passed, but none of them were Rhoda's old jalopy. Suddenly, the adrenaline drained from her body, and she felt faint. She pulled to the side of the road and stopped. Looking back, she could just barely see the lights from Rhoda's trailer. Surely Lute couldn't make it this far after being knocked out. She swung her feet out the door and planted them on the ground. Gasping for air, she bent over and put her head between her knees until the dizziness passed.

♦♦♦

Arnold did not want to drop his wife here alone in the swamp with a mad man.

"Oh stop your worrying, silly," said Mary. "Look. All the lights are blaring. I'm sure Rhoda's in there. Now quit being ridiculous and let me out." She noticed Arnold's white knuckles on the steering wheel. "How about this? If Lute's here, I'll turn right around and come back out. If he's not, I'll flash the porch light for you to let you know I'm safe."

"I don't like it one bit," Arnold grumbled.

"Well, I'm going. I'll call you when I'm done. Remember, honey, I am here doing God's work. He will protect me." She patted her quilting bag for reassurance before she opened the car door and walked up the steps. The screen door was askew, so she waved to Arnold, and walked in, saying loud enough for anyone to hear, "Well howdy-do, Rhoda. How are you this fine evening?"

Arnold saw the porch light flash and reluctantly pulled away.

♦♦♦

Buddy hated to leave Del, but he hated that fuck-up Lute Mason more. If he had to serve time for killing him, it would be worth it. But Buddy didn't intend to get caught. His old daddy had been right. Hang out in grungy old trailer parks and nobody questions nothin'. Plus, Lute's dump was out in the middle of nowhere, so Buddy thought he had a pretty good chance of getting away unnoticed.

He worried Maggie or her sisters might be there, but he could wait until they went to sleep. He'd been out there before, and no one noticed. He could do it again.

Buddy slipped on a pair of latex gloves he'd lifted from the hospital. Stuffing his few belongings in a bag, including the gold he'd unearthed and the wiped-down Glock, Buddy stopped to look around Del's trailer one last time. It, too, was a dump. Del deserved better, especially if he ended up marrying that screeching-mimi girlfriend of his. Buddy opened his bag, took out most of the gold, and put it in the cooler/coffee table. On top of the table, he left a note.

Bro - sorry to leave before you get home from the hospital, but something came up. It was great spending time with you. We'll do it again soon, I promise. In the meantime, I left you some goodies in the cooler. Enjoy. Take care of yourself and that pretty girlfriend of yours. – Bud.

Outside, he tied the bag to the handlebars, jumped on the bike and headed for the swamp.

♦♦♦

Weldon was smarter than most people believed. He knew exactly how to get to and from Lute's house without being seen. That asshole had screwed him for the last time. He pulled his panel truck into an abandoned county park on the other side of the swamp from Lute's house. He made sure the truck was camouflaged by weeds and brush but still on terra firma.

Weldon tugged on his boot-foot waders, a black long-sleeved tee shirt and a black stocking cap. Armed with his mother's loaded pearl-handled pistol and a mini-Maglite, he headed out across the swamp. Truth be told, he was a little afraid of the gun. He'd never even held one before, but if his dear sweet mother used it, surely he could, too.

♦♦♦

After ensuring her husband was well out of sight, Mary checked the rest of the house. Empty. Perfect. She didn't want to go out the front or side doors in case someone did show up, so she went in the bedroom, pushed out the window screen, threw out the quilting bag and jumped to the ground. Fortunately, the trailer had settled quite a bit, so she didn't have to jump far.

She peered across the dark yard, seeing only a pick-up truck in the back and a rusty shed by the clothesline. It was only a matter of time before someone came home, so she grabbed her bag and ran for shelter. She slipped soundlessly into the shed and searched through her quilting supplies

Relatively inSane

until she found the revolver she had inherited from her granddaddy. Before closing the shed door, she spotted a figure in the carport propped against a post. Ha. Lucifer in the flesh. The faithless sinner had no doubt passed out from drinking. Steeled by the power of the Almighty, she positioned herself by a rusted-out hole with good sightlines, propped up the gun and prayed her aim would be true.

♦♦♦

Listening to the Chance family on the ride back from the hospital, Buddy realized that Lute was a wanted man. Lute didn't seem like the type to let the judicial system decide whether he was guilty or innocent. Buddy had to act before that SOB could get away.

Pedaling as fast as the single-speed Huffy would let him, Buddy was determined to get this over and on the road himself. Unfortunately, the grocery bag with his possessions hanging from the handlebar kept catching in the spokes. He stopped, put the gun in his waistband and slung the bag over his shoulder. If he could do this right, he'd never have to worry about Lute hurting his kid brother again.

The lights were on in the trailer when he pulled up behind the jasmine bush. He squatted and held his breath, listening for voices. He couldn't see anyone through the windows, but that didn't mean much.

The hell with it. He didn't even care if someone was home. Buddy knew Lute would show up eventually to either take or check on his buried treasure. He turned his head away from the lighted trailer and stared into the dark swamp to readjust his eyes. Finally able to make out shapes, he

294

looked toward the areas of the yard where he knew things were buried.

Out of the corner of his eye, he caught some movement. There, something leaning against the pillar in the carport. He strained forward, squinting to make it out. Gold mine. Lute, probably coming to after a hangover, raised his head and leaned it back against the post. Buddy grabbed the Glock.

♦♦♦

The swamp was a lot deeper and darker than Weldon expected. He stumbled through the muck and over roots and rotten stumps. Branches and moss slapped across his face, while mosquitoes sang like sirens. Finally, he saw house lights twinkling. He'd made it. Standing just on the edge of Lute's yard, Weldon spotted his arch enemy slumped against a post in the carport. Easy pickins.

He cocked the gun as he'd seen his dad do many times and stepped forward through the brush into the yard. As he brought his back foot up, it caught on a root, causing his arms to flail and the gun to fire.

♦♦♦

At the sound of gunfire, Mary Chance, safety unlatched, barrel pointed directly at Lute's heart, pulled the trigger.

♦♦♦

The firecracker-like pop from the edge of the woods caught Buddy off guard, and the Glock fired, sending a spray of sparks toward his target. He didn't wait for the smoke to clear. Buddy hopped on the bike and headed down the road, winging the Glock as far into the swamp as he could.

♦♦♦

Weldon, recovering his senses from the trip and the misfire, realized his pants were wet. He took out the MagLite and looked. Jesus. There was a bullet hole in his pants, right near his testicle. He thought he'd pissed himself, but realized he'd been shot. He must not have hit Lute, if the single bullet had gone in his own leg.

Wait. He'd heard more than one shot. Was Lute firing back? Panicked, Weldon turned into the swamp, slogging his way toward the van.

♦♦♦

Lowering her gun, Mary heard thrashing, a scream and then quiet. Satisfied with her success, she put the revolver back in her quilting bag, peered through the hole and scanned the surroundings. Nothing moved. Lute lay motionless on the carport floor. After a good thirty minutes of silent Bible verse recitation and prayer, Mary was satisfied she was alone. She opened the door to the shed, grabbed her bag and walked to the old truck behind the house.

Who said prayer didn't work? The keys were still in the ignition and the engine fired right up. Mary adjusted the seat, drove around the carport and out onto the road, humming "Onward Christian Soldiers" all the way home.

Chapter 62

Thursday, June 20, late evening

Maggie swerved wide to get past a car on the side of the road. Squinting into the lights, she realized it was Cheryl. She slowed to a stop and cranked down the window. "What are you doing? Did you go to Rhoda's by yourself?" As her eyes adjusted to the dark, she noticed Cheryl was translucent she was so pale. "Are you okay?"

"Oh my God, Maggie," Cheryl cried, "pull over. We have to talk."

Maggie pulled to the side of the road and got out. "What's going on, Cheryl? What's the matter?" Maggie didn't like it one bit that Cheryl had gone to Rhoda's alone. As well she knew, anything could happen at that place.

Cheryl grabbed Maggie in a fierce hug and sobbed. Before she could start to explain, they both heard a volley of pops, the deafening roar of a gator, thrashing, splashing and finally, a piercing scream.

"Jesus Christ," said Maggie. "What was that? What in the hell happened back there?"

Cheryl looked in the direction of Rhoda's house. "I have no idea. It was quiet when I left." She continued to cling to Maggie.

"So you were there. By yourself. I thought you were smarter than that. Was Rhoda home?"

"No, but Lute was," Cheryl whimpered onto Maggie's shoulder. "He came at me. With a gun."

Maggie held Cheryl out at arms' length. "Are you hurt?"

Cheryl shook her head.

"Okay. Take a deep breath, and tell me what happened."

"I missed the pawn shop. I texted you. Didn't you see it?"

"I got it, but it didn't make any sense. All I could figure out was straight to trailer something. I thought we were supposed to meet up."

"Sorry. It was a voice text. I was going to wait for you, but I was so worked up by the time I got to town, I just wanted to confront that bastard myself. So I pulled up and didn't see any cars. The house and yard were dark. I started up the steps and heard a noise in the carport. It was Lute. He was on all fours puking and god knows what else. It smelled like shit."

"That place always smells like shit," said Maggie, remembering the ersatz septic system.

"Whatever it was, it reeked," Cheryl took another breath. "So I walked over to tell him off, when all of a sudden he lunged toward me with a gun in his hand. He looked like a crazed derelict."

"What did you do? Did he shoot at you?" Maggie realized she was gripping Cheryl's arms so hard it would leave a bruise.

"Not before I grabbed that shovel that's always out there. I teed off on his head and he sunk to his knees, then passed out against the post."

Maggie could barely speak. "Did you kill him?"

"At first I thought I had, so I stepped toward him, sliding in something disgusting, and checked his carotid in his neck. He had a pulse."

"Even though I hate that man, I'm glad you didn't kill him."

"I guess. I was scared he would come to, so I ran in the house and turned on all the lights looking for Rhoda. She wasn't there," Cheryl finally started to speak in a normal tone.

"What did you do then?"

"I got the hell out of there. I went out the front door, down the steps, got in the car and took off."

"Smartest thing you've done all night," said Maggie.

Panic crept back into Cheryl's voice. "Should I call 911?"

Maggie considered it. They probably didn't want a bunch of police around who might arrest Cheryl. "Let's wait on that. I mean, you said he was okay, right?"

"He had a pulse."

"Good enough. Let's call Rhoda." Maggie got her phone and dialed. "No answer." She looked at Cheryl. "You try."

Cheryl dialed. "Voicemail," she mouthed. "Rhoda. Call immediately. This is an emergency."

Maggie tried one more time, with no success. "What now?"

Cheryl thought for a moment. "Let's text her the old code. Remember back when we started staying over at friends' houses? Mom made us come up with a phrase we would never use in a normal conversation. If we called her with that phrase, it meant 'extreme danger – get me out of here now'."

Maggie nodded and texted the phrase. Projectile Stinky. A smile tugged at her mouth. "Where did we come up with that one?"

"I think Mom and Dad were drunk," Cheryl half-smiled. "Seemed as good as anything else."

Maggie's phone rang one second after she sent the text. She answered on speaker.

"Where are you?" Rhoda shouted. "Are you safe? What's wrong?"

"You would have known earlier if you'd answered your damned phone," Maggie scolded. "Yes, we're safe for now. We're out on the road about a quarter-mile from your house. Cheryl went by to ask Lute for her necklace back and…"

"Lute has Cheryl's necklace?" Rhoda asked.

"Well, he pawned it. Anyway, Cheryl went by to confront him. She found him on his hands and knees puking his guts up."

Rhoda smirked. Slow and steady wins the race. Her plan was working. "Oh my. So what's the emergency?"

"He pulled a gun and lunged at me," Cheryl shouted into Maggie's phone.

"A gun? Cheryl, are you all right?" Rhoda gasped.

"Yes, but I whacked him in the head with a shovel and knocked him out. He was still breathing when I left, but I'm afraid I've killed him," Cheryl sobbed again.

"Oh honey," said Rhoda, "that man has the hardest head in the world. I've hit him with a shovel before. I'm sure he'll be fine."

"We're afraid to call the police," said Maggie.

"God no, don't do that. Don't worry. I'll take care of it. So are you safe now? Do you have a place to go?" Rhoda really didn't want them coming to Ben's. She wasn't ready to get into that yet.

"Yes, we're safe. We'll go stay in Starke for the night. I found a nice little place there. Can you meet us at your house in the morning? Things won't be as scary in the daylight," Maggie said.

"Sure. Call me when you get up, and I'll head over there. I'm so sorry about this," Rhoda said. "I promise you.

Lute will never bother either of you again. He's pushed me too far this time. I'm done."

"If you really mean that," Maggie said, "then this may all have been worth it. We'll call in the morning."

"Rhoda?" Cheryl asked.

"Yeah?"

"Don't go over there tonight. He could still be dangerous. He really looked like he'd gone completely crazy."

"Don't worry. I'm not as stupid as I act," Rhoda said. "Now get out of there. I'll see you in the morning."

Chapter 63

Thursday, June 20, late evening

"Did I hear you talking to somebody?" Ben asked, as he came in from the kitchen.

Rhoda tried to think of a good cover story, but Ben knew her too well. "It was my sisters. They went to my house looking for me."

"I thought they were in Tallahassee or something. Did you know they were coming back?"

"No. I've had my phone off a lot. But I turned it on a few minutes ago and had all these emergency messages from them."

"Uh, oh. Lute?" Ben asked.

"Apparently, Lute stole Cheryl's necklace and pawned it, and, I already told you about him letting her precious little dog get devoured by a gator. I guess Cheryl came to confront him and found him sick or drunk, and he pointed a gun at her." The horror Cheryl must have felt began to dawn on Rhoda.

"Did he shoot? Is she okay?" Ben jumped up and looked for his keys and his bag.

"She's pretty shook, but she's okay. I guess she whacked him in the head and knocked him out."

"Go, Cheryl," fist-pumped Ben. "But you said it was both of your sisters. Where was Maggie all this time?"

"I guess they met up on the road. They wanted to call the police, but I told them not to. He can survive a bump on the head." Rhoda looked at Ben for reassurance. "Can't he?"

"Probably. I mean, Cheryl isn't a very big woman, but why don't I go check things out just in case?"

"But he has a gun," Rhoda teared up.

"So do I, my dear. And I'm not drunk or sick. Don't worry about me. I won't be long. He probably took off by now."

"I'll go with you," said Rhoda.

"Like hell you will. If he sees us together, he will shoot. You stay here in case your sisters need you. Don't worry." Ben kissed her on the cheek and grabbed his medical bag, his keys and hers off the counter, just in case she decided to follow him. He didn't know what he'd find there, but he knew one thing. One way or another, Lute would be out of their lives before the night was over.

◆◆◆

Mary Chance drove past the road to her house and pulled the truck into an abandoned gas station/junk yard two blocks away. She took a piece of quilting cloth out of her bag, wiped down the inside of the truck and the driver's side door. Then she grabbed the bag and walked back to her house. Arnold was asleep in the recliner.

"Come on to bed, Arnie," she shook him gently.

He looked at her through sleep-glazed eyes. "What? How'd you get home? You were supposed to call me."

"Oh, that sweet Mrs. Mason gave me a ride."

"Was Lute there? Did you call the police?" Arnold jumped out the chair.

"Calm down. No, he never showed up," Mary said as she stashed her quilting bag in the coat closet. "I didn't tell her what happened, because I was afraid she might tip Lute off somehow. Although after we prayed on all our troubles and woes, I think that woman would be relieved to see Lute behind bars for a long time. But no, I never saw any sign of that godless heathen."

Arnold stared at her a long time. Finally, he put his arm around her shoulders, and they headed for bed.

Mary lay awake for some time trying to figure out how to get Rhoda to confirm her story, if need be. She'd just have to pray extra hard on that one.

Chapter 64

Thursday, June 20, late evening

Maggie hated driving at night, especially on these dark country roads. She didn't even have the lights from Cheryl's car to help. Cheryl got the address to the motel and flew off before Maggie got in her car. She leaned forward over the wheel to get a better view. You never knew what kind of critter might come slithering out of the brush. After a few miles, she dropped her shoulders from around her ears and started to relax. Once again, she was glad to be retreating to the relative sanity of Motel 12.

Music might be a nice distraction. She reached down to turn on the radio. Of course all the buttons were missing. Typical Rhoda vehicle. Never mind. She looked back at the road and saw a man on a bicycle just ahead. Alarm bells rang. She had seen that man and bike before. Where the hell was it?

The intruder in the yard. The one behind the jasmine bush. She couldn't help it; she had to find out who it was. She sped up, pulled around the bicycle and stopped in front of it. Dust from the dirt road enveloped both the bicyclist and Maggie's car as they stopped. When it settled, she looked through the window.

Warren. He'd been the intruder. Now it all made sense. He rode a bike, and he helped her find Rhoda's house after that night at the bar. Oh my God, she had kissed that man. And let him use her hotel room. She didn't know if she was mad or scared.

Mad prevailed as she threw open the door and marched around the car. "Warren. It was you all along?"

Buddy was glad he'd tossed the Glock. Had she seen him shoot at Lute?

"Say something. Was that you about a week ago I saw digging stuff up in Lute's yard? I distinctly remember seeing a man just your size riding away on a bike." Maggie crossed her arms like a teacher meting out punishment in the classroom. "Was it?"

Buddy sucked in a deep breath. Okay. She obviously saw him one night, but she didn't mention tonight. Plus, he hadn't seen this car at the house when the shots were fired.

Maggie tapped her foot, waiting for his reply. "Well? Was that you the other night? Never mind. I know it was you. And what are you doing out here now? Back for more goodies in the yard?"

Buddy dared to breathe. She hadn't seen him. "Yes. Yes. It was me last week. But let me explain."

"Oh, I'm counting on it," said Maggie.

"Del and me worked for Lute for a few days and he hadn't paid us anything. Then I heard him bragging about having gold buried in his yard. I just went to get our share."

"Really." Maggie's left eyebrow touched her hairline.

"Really. But that was the only time, I swear." Buddy couldn't quite figure out why this woman got to him. Normally, he would have knocked her flat and taken the car, but she had some power over him.

"Why didn't you tell me you worked for my brother-in-law when we first met?"

"I didn't think it mattered," Buddy stared her down. "But he's the reason Del got hurt so bad, him and that piece-of-shit boat."

Maggie shook her head in sympathy for poor Del. She and Warren were on the same wavelength when it came to Lute. Her eyebrow dropped an inch. "So what are you doing out here tonight?"

"I got a ride back from the hospital with Del's girlfriend's family. They'd come to visit Del in the ... oh yeah," he brightened, "Del woke up, and he seems to be okay. Doesn't remember much, but he's gonna be okay."

Maggie's face softened. "Oh, Warren, that's great," she said, throwing her arms around him. She felt his strong embrace and clung to him for a millisecond. Her mood change was momentary. "So what are you doing here now?" she said as she stepped back.

"I came to tell Lute I was going to press charges for what he did to Del unless he paid all the medical bills." Buddy puffed up, impressed with himself for coming up with such a plausible explanation on the fly.

"Did he?" Maggie resumed the cocked eyebrow.

"I couldn't find him. All the lights were on, but nobody answered when I went to the door."

"So where are you going now?" Maggie was relieved Warren hadn't seen a body in the carport. Maybe Lute had woken up and run off.

"Back to the hospital. I thought I'd stay with Del until they release him, and then I think I'll hit the road. I'm sure as hell not working for that crazy bastard again. And Del has a nice girlfriend to take care of him."

Maggie searched his face and decided he was telling the truth. What was it about this guy? Okay, obviously, there was his magnificent body. And the chiseled face with those soft lips. She felt that internal *schwing* remembering their drunken make-out session at The Cleat. She had even seen his steely eyes soften when he talked of his brother. For some reason, she wanted to believe he was one of the good guys. "Okay," she sighed. "Just so happens I'm headed to Starke myself. Throw your bike in the trunk, and I'll drop you off at Shands."

He stashed the bike and got in the car. "And, um, while I'm at it, Maggie, full disclosure? My family calls me Buddy."

◆◆◆

As he coasted to a stop, engine and lights off, Ben got mad just looking at the dilapidated trailer where Lute made Rhoda live.

The house lights were on, but Rhoda said Cheryl clubbed Lute in the carport. Ben grabbed his bag which, ironically, had all the things one might need to save or kill a person. He slipped on a pair of latex gloves as he treaded softly toward house.

From the shelter of a big bush on the edge of the yard, Ben surveyed the property to see if anyone was there. Sure enough, Lute lay on his side next to a pillar in the carport. He seemed to be the only person around though. Nothing moved in the house. The yard was empty. Ben crept toward Lute. It looked like he had, indeed, been sick from the dark puddles of vomit and excrement and who knew what else on the concrete around him. Looking in all directions before squatting down, Ben checked Lute's pulse and respiration.

Nothing. In fact, Lute's skin was already turning cold despite the hot, humid night air.

Ben's physician brain told him to call the coroner. But that would involve legal authorities, and legal authorities would bring Cheryl in for questioning, at the very least. Then he thought of Rhoda's assurances that Lute would be out of their lives soon. "What have you done, Rhoda?" he whispered as he inspected Lute's head for significant blunt force trauma. Though the night was dark, he was able to make out a smudge of dirt and a small cut on one side of Lute's head. Ben didn't see much of a lump or bruise where the shovel must have connected, so he doubted Cheryl's blow had been fatal. He tried to examine the rest of the body, but it was so dark and the immediate area so befouled, he gave up.

Ben sat back on his haunches, studied the scene and ran through possible scenarios. There was a slim chance Cheryl's blow could have caused a life-threatening subdural hematoma. Rhoda could have drugged or poisoned him. In fact, any number of people probably wanted Lute dead, himself included.

The carport was a hoarder's mess - towers of cans, plastic pots and crates covered in dirt and spider webs, tools and debris strewn across the floor as if Lute had started a project and then abandoned it. It would be so easy to dispose of the body and walk away. All Ben had to do was kick some of the trash around and no one would ever notice.

Yep. That would be the easiest course of action for everyone. Ben stood, grabbed the shovel and walked to the weed-infested, hole-pocked yard. He found a place where leaves would most likely fall that was not clearly visible from the road and began to dig. The first plunge of the shovel clanged against metal. Moving a few inches to the side, Ben was able to dig a trench just big enough to accept the carcass; Lute didn't deserve more effort than that.

Ben found a ragged tarp, rolled Lute's body on it, and dragged it across the yard. Grunting with effort, he flipped the corpse into the hole. The body settled, face up. Lute's rigid gaze didn't bother him, really. The bastard earned this fate, whoever caused it. Ben quickly covered everything with soil and pushed leaves and debris over top. He straightened up and looked around. The entire yard was such a mess, no one would notice this particular mound of dirt.

Back in the carport, Ben saw the gun Cheryl had mentioned and a large duffle bag near where Lute had fallen. Inside were Lute's passport, cash, some ammo and clothes. The old bastard was planning to run.

Ben pocketed the gun, stuffed the tarp in the bag and picked it up. He kicked more leaves and rubble over the mess Lute had made, and went to his car. It would be best if Rhoda never knew about this. He would tell her Lute was gone when he got there. All the way home, Ben wondered about his lack of guilt or shame, but decided Lute wasn't worth either one.

♦♦♦

Well before dawn, a family of raccoons came to scavenge the carport and yard. This particular yard usually had tasty treats moldering somewhere. They pulled down cans and cartons and then gravitated toward the organic mess on the floor by the pillar. Had there been a dinner bell, they would have rung it. The gaze of raccoons descended on the puddles and lapped them clean.

Sated but always hunting for more, the largest raccoon climbed on the washer to search the refuse there. Stretching to his limit, he grabbed a can of used motor oil which spilled all over him, the washer and the floor. Bolting away from the scene, Papa Raccoon's last jump knocked over a plastic jug, which rolled and slammed against the pillar with a crack. Bleach seeped in every direction.

Chapter 65

Thursday, June 20, late evening

"Thank heavens Rhoda's a/c works in this junker," said Maggie. Buddy had been quiet for most of the ride so far, which made her chatter nervously. "It's hotter than blazes here tonight. I don't know how people stand to live in this day after day with no relief."

"It doesn't always last," Buddy finally mumbled.

"What?" Maggie asked, turning down the air conditioner so she could hear.

"A lot of times, when it's really still like this, it means there's a bad cloud comin'."

"A bad cloud? What the hell is that?"

"Big, fast, windy storm. Lots of lightning, sometimes tornadoes," Buddy said. He remembered them blowing up out of nowhere in the prison yard.

Just as the words left his mouth, a huge raindrop flattened on the windshield. "Huh," said Maggie, "d'you learn your weather forecasting skills out on the oil rig?"

Damn her memory. He had to get away from this woman before she found him out. "Naw. I lived in these parts as a kid. The storms used to scare Del to death."

Less than a minute later, the sky darkened even more as the wind kicked up, blowing sticks and gravel against the car. Pelting, horizontal rain followed.

Maggie slowed until the gravel road dead-ended at Highway 18. At least the county road was paved so she could try to outrun the weather. A few more turns would put them on a lighted highway toward Starke.

Behind them, the spectral storm raced toward the swamp.

Friday, June 21, morning, Starke

"Oh, What a Beautiful Morning" woke Maggie from a deep sleep. Cheryl was already up, in the shower, and obviously, in a much-improved mood.

"You're right, Mags," Cheryl said as she stepped through a cloud of steam from the bathroom. "This place isn't so bad. Kind of cute in a kitschy way."

"Feeling better?" Maggie asked.

"Much. What took you so long to get here last night? I thought you were right behind me."

"I wasn't that far behind." That electric charge raced from Maggie's gut to her heart just thinking about her evening. She had pulled in the Shands parking lot to drop off Buddy. Rain pounded the car, so they sat, awkwardly, as the storm continued. Maggie turned toward him to say something. Buddy stared at her, not with the steel eyes, but the blue ones. He reached out and grabbed her hand. Maggie gasped as he slid across the seat, unbuckled her seatbelt and pulled her toward him. She didn't even try to resist. That man, petty criminal or not, could kiss like nobody's business. At first, the kiss was urgent, almost forceful, but his lips softened as they moved from her mouth to her neck. She heard herself moan. No one had touched her like this in, well, forever.

Before she could take a breath, they were both shirtless. His rough hands played her like a piano. She did not resist when he pulled off her capris and continued his overture, burying his face far below her navel. As she rose toward a crescendo, he stopped to pull off his jeans. She begged for more. With renewed urgency, he braced himself above her. Maggie, her legs wrapped around his waist, literally sang as he thrust into her. They rode in perfect rhythm until, finally spent, he collapsed on top of her. Tingling in post-coital bliss, Maggie thanked God for that big, old car with the bench front seat.

Her muscle memory was about to reenact the whole scene when she looked up and saw Cheryl. She could feel her face turn crimson. "A-hem. Yeah. Well, you know that old clunker of Rhoda's. It only goes about forty miles an hour. I got caught in a terrible storm and had to pull over for a while. You must not have been too worried about me. You were sound asleep when I got my key and came in the room."

"I know. I threw myself in bed and tossed and turned fretting about Lute. Then I thought, 'I am not going to let him steal one more minute of my life.' I mean, I didn't kill him, and it was self-defense."

"You're right. And, after that stunt he pulled at the church, I'm surprised half the choir wasn't lined up behind you waiting to take a swing at him," Maggie said, wishing she were alone so she could relive her tryst from last night.

"Enough about Lute. I'm ready to get back over there, meet Rhoda at the house, get your stuff, and then head to the pawn shop and claim that necklace," ordered Cheryl. "So move it already."

On that note, Maggie, realized it was time to head back to South Carolina. Buddy had said he was leaving town, so there was no sense waiting around for him. He did ask for her number, though, which she had wanted to tattoo on his bulging pecs. Otherwise, she was way more than ready to get away from all things swamp and madness. What sometimes seemed like her sad little life at home was looking pretty damned normal about now. She was ready for normal.

Friday, June 21, morning, Gainesville

Attorney Darrell Handy sat behind the big desk in a tiny, strip mall office on the edge of Gainesville. He bought the oversized, ornate, wooden monstrosity so he would look distinguished and successful in the billboard ads he had scattered throughout Northern Florida. "Have You Been Screwed Out of Your Money? Call The Handyman. He Can Fix Anything - Darrell Handy, Attorney at Law." The signs weren't helping much; he'd only added one new client since they went up. Plus, his secretary quit yesterday.

He started going through the messages she'd thrown on his desk. *Weldon Cosgrove called re: violation of an injunction and theft by one Luther Mason. Wants him arrested. Told him he we would contact the other party's attorney and try to work things out.*

Not a bad answer. Amazingly, she had remembered to write down the phone number. She'd also made a note on the bottom of the slip - *FYI – he was pissed.*

Great. Darrell put the phone on speaker and dialed. After several rings, voicemail picked up. "You've reached Weldon Cosgrove. Please leave a message."

"Weldon, this is attorney Darrel Handy regarding your claim of an injunction violation. I'll call you again later, if I don't hear from you."

♦♦♦

On the seat of the panel truck parked on the edge of the Oolehatchee Swamp, a cell phone rang throughout the day and into the night.

Chapter 66

Friday, June 21, morning, Rhoda's house

Cheryl and Maggie pulled up at the same time to the scene of terror from last night. They both parked on the edge of the road, got out, and holding hands, crept toward the carport.

"Wow," said Cheryl. "What in the world happened here? I mean besides what we know happened here."

They surveyed the scene. Junk cans, bottles, leaves, branches, even garbage can lids were scattered throughout the carport and yard. The rusted shed lay sideways in the grass, its roof upended a few feet away.

"Man," said Maggie. "That must have been some storm. I bet it's that monster I drove through."

"This looks like tornado damage, except the trailer's still intact."

They gawked at the mess for a few seconds and then braved a peek at the carport.

"Oh thank you, Jesus," Cheryl raised her eyes toward heaven. "Lute's gone. He must have come to and left. Oh, thank God."

A horn blasted behind them. "Hey girls," Rhoda said from Lute's old car. She opened the door and slowly lifted her bad leg out before standing on her good one. "Look," she said, "walking cast."

Maggie and Cheryl ran to help her. They grabbed one another in a hug and checked to make sure they were each okay.

"Is Lute here?" Rhoda asked. Ben had told her he was gone last night, but she wanted to make sure before they all went inside. It was only then that she noticed the destruction in the yard. "Good Lord. What happened?" Rhoda asked Cheryl. "Did Lute make all this mess when he was trying to shoot you?"

"I don't think so," said Cheryl. "I mean, I didn't really get a good look at the place, it was so dark, but he was just on his hands and knees when I walked up and started yelling at him. I didn't notice anything else except the gun in his hand."

"What a mess," Rhoda said. "Worse than usual. So, is Lute here?"

"We don't know," Maggie answered. "We just pulled up. We were waiting for you to go inside."

"Chickens," teased Rhoda.

Maggie noticed Rhoda seemed exceptionally detached and unfazed by the whole situation which usually meant she was either high or hiding something.

With Rhoda in the lead, the three made their way to the front door. After last night, none of them was anxious to go in the carport. The screen door had come loose at the top, and the front door was slightly ajar. Their eyes were wide with fear as they stepped inside.

"Lute? You home?" yelled Rhoda, shoving Cheryl and Maggie behind her in protective big-sister fashion. They didn't argue.

They looked in the kitchen as they walked toward the bedroom. No Lute.

Trailing one another like ghost hunters, they made their way back to the kitchen, down to the sleeping porch and finally to the carport.

"He's not here. That old truck he's been driving is gone," Rhoda said. Concurrently, they expelled their held breath.

"I gotta sit down," said Maggie. "I think I'm going to pass out."

"Let's go in the kitchen. I'll start some coffee," said Cheryl.

"So you haven't heard from him at all, Rhoda?" asked Maggie.

"Not a word, since early yesterday. Which is odd. He's usually such a pest."

It wasn't until they were all seated at the table that they noticed the stacks of envelopes. Maggie picked up the top one. "This looks official," she said, noticing the Priority Mail and "IMPORTANT" stamped on the outside. "United States Coast Guard."

With that, they all dove into the pile of mail.

"State of Florida Department of Fish and Wildlife."

"Florida Department of Environmental Protection."

"St. Johns River Waterkeepers Association."

"This one's already been opened," said Rhoda. "It's from the Eighth Judicial Circuit of Florida."

Maggie whistled. "What has he gotten himself into?"

"According to this, somebody filed a restraining order against him," she paused while she read further. "Oh, this is that old friend of his Lute's dad's. That guy's in a nursing home. Lute goes to see him every week. I wonder what brought that about?" Rhoda sighed.

Maggie stacked up all the others. "I bet these are all about that boat sinking."

"Lute's boat sunk?" asked Cheryl. "How did I miss that?"

Before Maggie could launch into what she knew about it, the house phone rang. Maggie grabbed it and handed it to Rhoda.

"Hello? Yes, this is Rhoda Mason. Yes, Luther Mason is my husband, but no, he's not home." Rhoda's detachment gave way to shock. "He what? Can you say that again?" Her brow furrowed. "Oh my God. Are you sure?" She listened, slack-jawed. "Well, no. I haven't been home. I've been away with my sisters." She looked up, her eyes pleading with Cheryl and Maggie. "In fact, I haven't seen or heard from Lute in a few days. That's why I came home, to see if I could find him. I thought maybe something had happened... Yes, officer. I can verify where I've been...

Yes. Yes, I'm here at the residence now… Okay… Goodbye."

Rhoda put her head in her hands. "Wow. Lute's been busy."

"Who was that?" asked Cheryl.

"It was the Highway Patrol. Seems Lute's been accused of aggravated sexual battery against the choir director's daughter." Rhoda never looked up.

Maggie patted Rhoda's arm. "Sounds like he's really come unhinged this time. I bet he took off, with all these injunctions and warnings and then an arrest warrant to boot."

"Let me go check something." Rhoda eased away from the table and clonked into the bedroom. "Yep," she called. "His Bug-Out Bag is gone."

"Bug-Out Bag?" Maggie shook her head. What alternate universe had she landed in? "So what did the police say?"

"They're sending the sheriff over to ask some questions. Will you guys cover for me? Say I've been with you?"

Cheryl looked doubtful. "I hate to start lying to the police. Where have you been, anyway?"

A tear rolled down Rhoda's cheek. "I've been at my boyfriend's." She saw the shocked look on both their faces. "Don't judge. He's been protecting me since Lute tried to run us both down. But I don't want him all caught up in this. He was just trying to help me out."

Maggie gave Cheryl a stern look before slamming her hands on the table. "Don't worry, Rhoda. The 'Lemon Sisters' to the rescue. Let's get our story straight." They filled her in on the last few days.

"Okay, so we've been at the Motel 12 in Starke and your place in Tallahassee, right?" Rhoda said, looking at Cheryl.

"Right. Don't volunteer any information. Just answer questions with yes and no if you can." Cheryl had testified in many hearings at work regarding some of the people enrolled in her studies. "Besides, this is about Lute. Keep the focus on him."

Chapter 67

Friday, June 21

Joe grabbed his brotherhood phone out of the desk drawer. Sometimes Lute Mason, though he was a loyal soldier in the fight, could be a pain in the ass. The boat mess was bad enough. As the county sheriff, Joe could have helped him out there. But an arrest warrant originating from the Highway Patrol for aggravated sexual battery against one of the town's best families? This was not going to be an easy fix.

Joe walked out into the parking lot and pushed a number on speed dial.

"Talk to me," said a gruff voice on the other end.

"Sam. It's Joe. We got trouble." Joe told the local judge about Lute's latest activities.

"Damn," said Sam, Eighth Circuit judge in Bradford County. "I saw an injunction come through the other day, but that didn't seem too bad. I hadn't heard about the boat or this. What the hell did he do to that girl? Did he actually rape her?"

"No. I mean the labs haven't come back yet, but I'm pretty sure he just waggled his junk in her face and took off," said Joe, shaking his head.

"Were there any witnesses?"

"No. Just her word against his."

"Good." Sam thought for a minute. "The best thing for all of us would be if he just took off. If we can't find him, we can't serve the warrant. I'll do what I can to muddy up the waters here, and you do the same. Let's try to keep this thing on a real slow track. Lots of red tape."

"I can do that. I just hope he doesn't pop up somewhere," said Joe. "He causes any more trouble, he's gonna bring the revolution right down on top of us."

"I don't think it'll come to that. He's a pretty small player in a very big game. Like I said. Let's keep it tied up as long as we can."

"Got it. Thanks, Sam. I'll go over to his place and check things out. Surely to God he was smart enough to skip town. I'll keep you posted."

"Keep the faith, brother." Both men jabbed a finger to their foreheads.

◆◆◆

The three sisters huddled over the kitchen table working out their story for the police. Maggie wasn't surprised that Rhoda effortlessly wove a plausible story out of the few details they'd given her. Rhoda had always walked a fine line between fact and fiction and often came to believe the fiction as gospel.

Cheryl, with her fact-based science background, was so uncomfortable with this plan, she broke out in hives. "I don't think I can do this. What if I slip up? What if…"

Rhoda grabbed a Xanax from her bra and shoved it at Cheryl. "Take this. Don't give me that look. It's just for nerves. If you get too tongue tied, just fake a coughing fit or something, and I'll take over."

Cheryl popped it in her mouth.

A rap on the door made all three gasp. Rhoda, leveling a screw-this-up-and-I'll-kill-you look at Maggie and Cheryl, calmly yelled, "Just a minute." She dramatically thudded to the front door and opened it. She winced in pain while rubbing the cast. "Well, hey, there, Joe. What can I do for you?" Her innocence brightened the room.

"Hey, Rhoda. Sorry to make you get up," Joe looked on sympathetically as Rhoda grunted from the effort of standing upright. "How's that leg doin'?"

"Oh, it's coming along. Good days and bad, you know," Rhoda gnashed her teeth.

"Well, I was hopin' to catch Lute this morning. Is he home?"

"You know, he's not. I've checked everywhere," Rhoda said, opening the door and letting the sheriff inside.

"Do you know when he left or where he went?" Joe asked, looking around the room.

"I don't. In fact, I haven't heard from him in a few days, which is odd," Rhoda started in on the script. "Can I get you some coffee?"

"Sure," Joe said, as he followed her into the kitchen.

"Joe, these are my sisters, Maggie and Cheryl. We've been off having a cluck-fest, as Lute would call it."

"A cluck-fest, huh?" Joe raised his eyebrows.

"Lute says we sound like a brood of hens when we all get together. He can't stand all the gabbing and singing, so we took off for a few days. We just came back this morning because, like I said, I hadn't heard from him. Have you seen him?"

"No, ma'am. I haven't. I don't know if you're aware, but Lute's had a little trouble lately," Joe fished for information.

Maggie wondered if he knew she was at the pawn shop and Broken Cleat last night. Probably. Could she get her story straight? "You mean about the boat?" she volunteered.

Joe looked at her. "What do you know about that?"

"Well, we were staying over in Starke last night, and I realized I'd left my credit card here. It was my turn to pay for the room, so I zipped on down and got the card and stopped at the Broken Cleat to get a bite before I headed back. Pops was telling me about it. What a shame."

"Did you go anywhere else?"

The sheriff took out his notepad and paper. Cheryl's eyebrows shot to her hairline, but Rhoda nodded at Maggie to proceed as planned.

"Besides Starke? Oh yeah, Rhoda wanted me to pick up some handicap equipment for her at the pawn shop."

"Did you see Lute in any of the places you went?" Joe stared at her.

"No. I thought maybe he'd be at the Cleat, but Pops said he hadn't seen him in a while."

"Did you go anywhere else?"

"No. I wanted to get back to the girls, and it looked like a bad storm was forming to the west, so I headed for the hotel."

"And you never saw Lute."

"No."

Joe folded up the notebook and put it in his pocket. "Rhoda, you mind if I look around? See if I can find any hint of where he might have gone?"

"Well, sure Joe. I've kind of done that already, but all we found were these letters from the government," Rhoda stabbed herself in the forehead. She knew Joe was one of the conspiracists and hoped the gesture showed solidarity.

Joe stepped forward and picked up the stack of notices. "Woo-boy," he whistled as he thumbed through them. "That's a mess of fines and citations." He tossed them on the table like they stung him. "I'll just mosey around a bit, if you don't mind. You girls get back to your cluckin'," he winked at Rhoda.

He headed straight for the bedroom closet, where all the brethren were to keep their Bug-Out Bags ready to go. He sighed with relief at the absence of the kit. He scanned the dresser tops for a wallet, money, ID, anything that might indicate Lute was still around. Nothing.

Cheryl had burst into song to cover her nervousness, so the three sisters were butchering a round of "Oh Shenandoah" when Joe returned to the kitchen.

"I don't see any sign of him, Rhoda. Mind if I check around the yard?"

"Not at all, Joe. Let me show you the way," Rhoda began the exaggerated struggle to stand.

"No, no, you stay put. I think I can find it," he winked again, then turned and walked out through the sleeping porch.

"Oh sweet Jesus," Cheryl whispered. "Not the carport. He'll…" she stopped short when Rhoda reached across the table and smacked her.

The three were silent until Joe poked his head in the door. "Looks like you got a lot of storm damage out here."

"Yeah," Rhoda called back. "I just saw that this morning. Haven't really checked it out yet, though. Any sign of my husband?"

"Nope. Not a trace," Joe made his way back to the kitchen. "You want to issue a missing person's report?" He didn't mention the warrant he had in his pocket. He could probably delay an APB for a good while yet.

"Missing persons?" Rhoda had to suppress a laugh. "Wow. I hadn't thought about that. I mean, you know Lute.

Sometimes he goes off on a tangent, and I don't hear from him for a while. I don't think that's necessary, do you?"

"Between you and me? No, I don't. Just wanted to check. You know, Rhoda, I'm not sure it's real safe for you all to stay here. I mean, there could be a lot of structural damage to this place, and that septic tank stinks to high heaven. Plus, with all these government notices, somebody might try and come after you."

"Oh no. Really?" Rhoda thought leaving here was the best idea she'd ever heard. "Oh my. That never would have occurred to me, Joe. Aren't you sweet to think of our safety?"

"Well," Joe said. "I don't think it could hurt. That is if you have somewhere else to go."

Rhoda, Cheryl and Maggie nodded like bobble-heads.

"Okay then. I guess I'll be going. Just keep in touch. Let me know if you hear anything."

"You, too, Joe," said Rhoda, silently vowing to change her phone number before the day was out.

Joe, convinced Lute had gotten away, headed to his car. Glancing back at the trailer as he pulled out, he mumbled, "God speed, brother. God speed."

Chapter 68

Friday, June 21

Rhoda lit up a cigarette, and squinting through the smoke, watched the road for any more cars. Maggie concentrated on her coffee cup like a tea reader. Cheryl sent a silent stream of prayers toward the ceiling fan. Several minutes passed before anyone spoke.

"I kind of like that Xanax," Cheryl finally said. "Really takes the edge off."

Maggie and Rhoda looked up at their often-goody-two-shoes, sometimes prissy sister and burst out laughing.

"Do you think we got away with it?" Maggie asked.

"Hell yeah, we got away with it. He wasn't interested in us at all," said Rhoda. "I'm telling you girls, truth-telling is overrated. But Cheryl, you have to work on your poker face. When Joe headed for the carport you turned the color of a stop sign."

"I can't help it. Being honest and factual is part of my personality. Somebody in this family has to do it," Cheryl said.

"Well, at least you kept your mouth shut most of the time. The singing was a good idea. And, even by mother's standards, we were incredibly off key. I don't think Joe could stand to be around us much longer."

Maggie looked up from her cup. "So that's it? No big interrogation or investigation? What about all these fines and warrants?" She looked again at the pile on the table.

"Not my problem," said Rhoda. "Lute and I have always kept separate finances. He never wanted me to know how much money he had. It always pissed me off, but now, I'm glad for it. I don't see how they could hold me liable for any of this."

"Well, the sheriff said we should clear out of the place," said Maggie. "Anybody feel a burning need to stay here much longer?"

"Hell, no," said Rhoda as she rose, quite nimbly, from the chair. "In fact, I'm going to pack the few things I value in this dump and let the rest crumble to the ground. I wish I knew what happened to Grandma's sapphire ring. I hate to leave that behind."

"Sister, you are in luck," Maggie jumped up and grabbed her purse. "I found this out in the carport the first week I was here." She handed the ring to Rhoda.

"Why didn't you tell me?" Rhoda asked.

"I didn't want Lute to know I found it, and sorry, but I was afraid you'd blow it. Here. Enjoy."

"That reminds me," said Cheryl. "I'm going to stop by that pawn shop and get my diamond necklace on the way out of town."

"We'll go with you, Cheryl," Maggie said. "Strength in numbers. Maybe that Vern guy will be more cooperative if Rhoda's along. So, after we get that back, then what?"

"I don't know about you," Cheryl said, "but I'm headed back to my nice, boring life in Tallahassee. You two want to come with me?"

"Not me," said Rhoda. "I'm headed back to Ben's. He has such a nice place, and he's really a good guy. You two would like him."

"Maggie, you want to stay with me a while?" Cheryl asked again.

Maggie frantically tapped on her phone screen, grabbed her credit card from her purse and continued tapping. "Got it," she finally looked up. "Flight from Tally to Greenville at 7:00 p.m. today." She looked at Cheryl. "Can we make that?"

"Yeah, I think so. We can't waste much time, but it's still early. You sure you're ready to head back so soon?"

"I was ready last week," Maggie muttered. "Oh don't give me that hurt look. This has not been a pleasure trip and you both know it. I think we're all ready for a little normal and boring."

"You're right," said Cheryl. "Okay then. We have a plan. Rhoda? How fast can you pack?"

Rhoda sped off toward the bedroom, barely limping. By the time the girls had the kitchen straightened up, she was back with a small suitcase and some grocery bags crammed with her belongings. "Anybody want these pills before I pitch 'em?" she said as she held up the bag-o-drugs.

Cheryl eyed the little pink ones. "You're getting rid of them?"

"Don't need 'em anymore," said Rhoda, as the baggie landed with a thunk in the garbage. She looked at her few belongings. "Kind of pitiful, isn't it? All these years, and this is all I have to show for it. Everything else in this place is trash."

"You can always come back if you forgot anything," Maggie said, grabbing the rest of her stuff from the sleeping porch. "All right, then. Everybody ready?"

Rhoda turned a three-sixty to survey her home and spied one last thing. A faded Polaroid of the three of them, in their early teens at the time, singing their hearts out while Rhoda played the guitar. "To the return of happier times," she held it up for them to see.

"Here, here," said Maggie and Cheryl.

Rhoda threw her bags in the backseat of her car while Maggie waited for Cheryl to pop the trunk. "Come on, Cheryl. What are you doing up there? Open the trunk."

Cheryl stared out the car window, then opened the door and walked, transfixed, toward the far corner of the yard. She grabbed the shovel as she moved toward some quaking underbrush, in case it was Lute coming out of hiding.

"Grrrrrr-ruffff."

Cheryl stopped short.

"Grrrr-rufffff." A matted, mud-caked, rat-like creature tore out of the bushes and ran straight to her feet.

Cheryl collapsed to her knees. "Chief! Oh Chief, my God." She bundled her precious dog in her arms and wept.

♦♦♦

Vern called Joe the moment the girls left the shop. "I couldn't think of any way to stop them. The one sister had all the documentation she needed to claim the necklace. I never did tell 'em who brought it in though. So I gotta find Lute and get my money back."

He listened to Joe for a few minutes. "Gone, huh? For good you think? I'll be damned. No, you're right. We don't want all those feds snooping around here. I hope he makes it, wherever he went. Sure. Sure. Just between us. Mark of the Beast."

♦♦♦

Ramona called Shands first thing in the morning and talked to Del. He told her he was allowed to go home, but Buddy had left town the night before, so he didn't have a ride. Thus, the entire Chance family went to get Delmont from the hospital. Miraculously, he hadn't suffered any permanent damage, except for the few deep burns on his hands and arms.

"You can stay with us, if you want, Delmont," Mary said from the front seat. Ramona looked pleadingly at Del.

"Gee, thanks, Mrs. Chance, but I think I'd rather get on to home. I'm thinking maybe Buddy'll show back up. Plus, I don't want to be no trouble."

"Well, the invitation stands, if you change your mind," said Arnold.

"Thank you, sir," said Del.

Ramona helped Del into the trailer and got him set up on the couch. "You sure you'll be okay here by yourself?"

"Yeah. Don't worry about me. You'll come back and see me, though, right?"

"You betcha," Ramona said, giving him a hug. "I'll bring some dinner over tonight. Maybe we can watch TV or something."

Del kissed her goodbye and looked around the room. Buddy must have straightened up, as clothes had been folded and the dishes were clean in the sink. It took a few minutes for him to spot the note on the cooler. Inside, little gold bars and coins glowed like the sun.

Chapter 69

Friday, June 21, evening

The previous night's storm had ushered in a breeze and drier air. Rhoda sat in a lawn chair by the fire pit in Ben's backyard. "This is sure nice," she said, reaching for his hand.

"This is how it's going to be from here on out," Ben said.

"You think he's gone for good?"

"That coward? Hell, yes, he's gone. You said a bunch of his stuff was missing, right?"

"His ridiculous Bug-Out Bag?" Rhoda laughed. "Yeah. It was gone, along with his ID and clothes."

"Good riddance," said Ben, as he grabbed another log and a dark bag and threw them on the fire.

The flames roared to life.

"What's in the bag?" asked Rhoda.

"Oh, it's just a bunch of soiled, worn-out exam gowns from the office. I burn 'em once they're too far gone."

Rhoda leaned her head back against the chaise and stared the starry sky, surprised how clear the heavens looked after a day with no pills.

♦♦♦

The minute the plane touched down, Maggie turned on her phone. She knew several texts would start dinging as soon as she got a signal.

Cheryl did not disappoint.

Safe travels! LU; Txt when you land; Call immediately. Big news; Where are you?

After retrieving her luggage and catching an Uber, Maggie called Cheryl. "What's up? Sounds important. Is everybody okay? Chief okay?"

Cheryl machine-gunned her news. "Oh my God, yes. Everyone's fine. More than fine. I can't believe it; you're not going to believe this; I tried calling Rhoda but she's already changed her phone number. Do you have her phone number? Maybe we could all SKYPE. Her SKYPE username wouldn't have changed, would it?"

Maggie laughed. "Take a breath, Cher. What's going on?"

"I must not have committed any mortal sins, because God is raining glory on me today."

"Such as," Maggie prodded.

"Well, of course you know about Chief, and that sheriff not questioning us about Lute's disappearance, but then, you'll never guess who called."

"I don't even want to try. Who?"

"The Hollywood producer, Ed. Me. He called me. I forgot we had exchanged numbers, and then I saw his name pop up on my screen and about passed out."

"Really?" Maggie truly was surprised. "I figured he was gone for good. Is he going to try the *Choir Wars* thing again?"

"No. He said that deadline had passed. But I guess he has some connection to the local show, *Florida's Hidden Treasures*. You remember that one, right?"

Maggie certainly did. "You mean the Underwear Alto audition?" Oops. They had never told Cheryl their nickname for the video.

"What?" asked Cheryl. "I don't know what that means, but never mind. He said he can't stop thinking about me or looking at the tapes he made, and he wants to use part of the tape to submit to *Florida's Hidden Treasures*."

Maggie was duly impressed. "See? That's exactly what I told you to do. Those takes from the choir rehearsals were fantastic. That's great, Cheryl. Really. Plus, an audition promoted by a big shot in the industry will carry a lot more weight than if you had sent it in blind."

"I know," squealed Cheryl. "I am so excited, I could pop. Let's try Skyping with Rhoda. I can't wait to tell her."

"Hold on," Maggie said. "I'm still in the Uber. Let me get in the house and settled, and then we'll try to link up. I'm really happy for you, Sis. You deserve it. Gotta go. I'll call back in a few."

Maggie paid the driver, got her bags and went in the house. After checking to make sure everything was okay, she looked under beds and in closets for intruders. This practice used to seem childish but had taken on real meaning in the last few weeks. Reassured of her safety, Maggie popped a beer and sat down at her laptop. While she waited to connect with Rhoda and Cheryl, she unzipped her luggage.

"Hey," Cheryl's face appeared in the corner of the screen.

"What's up?" Rhoda asked as she, too, came into view.

Maggie started in. "Well, I got home in one piece, thanks for asking. And, Rhoda, Cheryl has some tremendous news to share." Maggie busied herself unpacking her bag while Cheryl bubbled on about her new chance at fame. At the bottom of the suitcase, Maggie spotted her pajama pants; there was dirt all over the pockets, so she grabbed them and shook them out. Her eyes widened as small gold bars thunked onto the floor, the ones she'd unearthed in Lute's yard a few weeks ago. She'd forgotten all about them until now. She picked one up - *10 oz fine gold*. Huh.

"Maggie, are you with us, here?" commanded Cheryl. "I haven't gotten to the best part. He asked me out – on a real date. He said he would be in Tallahassee in about a month. Did I say how excited I am?"

Maggie and Rhoda both nodded. Maggie noticed Rhoda seemed a bit distracted, though she was with her boyfriend. Hopefully, the call hadn't interrupted them.

Rhoda looked back at the camera. "Congrats, Sis. I'm not surprised, but very impressed. A little jealous even."

Cheryl grabbed her robe out of her overnight bag. It seemed heavy. What in the world had she left in the pocket? "Thanks, you guys. I guess maybe all this was almost worth it." She reached in the pocket and remembered all the gold ingots she'd unearthed.

"Let's not get carried away, Cheryl," Maggie said. "Despite all the chaos and terror though, I miss you guys already."

"I know," said Rhoda. "Me too. I wish we actually had gone on a cluck-fest. We haven't done that in a long time."

Cheryl piped up. "I'm in. Anytime, except, of course, when I'm dating or auditioning."

Maggie got an idea. "You have a while before he comes to town, right?"

"Yeah. Why?"

"What about you, Rhoda? You have any free time?" Maggie asked.

"I got nothin' but free time, as long as Lute doesn't show up. But even if he does, he'll have to find me first. Whatcha got in mind?"

"I thought of it when we were singing "Shenandoah" this morning. Why don't you two come up here, and we'll rent a cabin up in Virginia. A friend of mine has a vacation rental she said she'd let me use really cheap." Not that it needed to be too cheap. Maggie stroked the gold bars. "And

Rhoda, don't say you can't afford it. I'll pay your part if you're short."

Cheryl also fondled gold in her robe pocket. "Yeah, we'll cover it for you."

Rhoda cradled her own bundle of Lute's cache she'd unearthed while everyone else slept. "Awww, thanks girls. But I think I can handle it. With Lute gone, I don't think my money's going to disappear so fast. That sounds like a great idea to me."

"Me too," said Cheryl. "But soon. Before I hit the big time."

Maggie laughed. "I'll try to set it up right away, before school starts again. I'll let you know."

"Sounds great," said Rhoda. "Love you guys."

"Me to you," said Cheryl.

"Love you more," said Maggie. "Later."

EPILOGUE

Sunday night, June 23, Lute and Rhoda's yard

Not a branch clacked, nor leaf stirred. Spanish moss hung like stalactites. The trailer sat dark and deserted. Only piles of debris and a shovel against the outside wall spoke of previous occupation. The moon, suspended in the velvet air, burnished oak leaves on the ground.

A raccoon lurched across the carport scavenging for food. Under cover of the overturned dinghy, a feral cat watched. With a mangled-ear reminder of past entanglements, the feline stayed motionless.

Finally alone, the cat twitched its ears toward a sound. In the center of the yard, leaf mold rustled. Focused on the movement, he slunk forward and crouched before the motion, ready to pounce.

Slowly, "King Cobra" broke through loose soil. It rose, serpent-like, growing in length and girth.

The feline extended a claw and batted the curious object. It exploded on contact, which sent the cat scrambling over the fence, causing an avalanche of cans, crates and pavers.

The methane activated penile implant collapsed to the ground, but the small blast and crashing debris caused a tremor. The ground rumbled, quaked, and noiselessly collapsed into the oil can septic tank. The surrounding sand, soil and debris shifted and sifted to fill the void, rendering the scene indistinguishable from before.

Made in United States
Orlando, FL
15 May 2023

33137028R00211